A Gift
for Abigail

Clasped in his strong and loyal arms the burden of her earthly struggles slipped away, and the glorified portals of a new life were opened wide for her willing feet.

A Gift
for Abigail

D. Tilton

EDITED BY
Heather Harpham Kopp

Harvest House Publishers
Eugene, Oregon 97402

Cover by Koechel Peterson and Associates, Minneapolis, Minnesota.

Interior illustrations by Joneile Emery, derived from original illustrations from the Victorian period.

A GIFT FOR ABIGAIL

Copyright © 1998 by Harvest House Publishers
Eugene, Oregon 97402

Library of Congress Cataloging-in-Publication Data

Tilton, Dwight.
    A gift for Abigail / Dwight Tilton.
       p. cm. — (Victorian bookshelf series)
    Updated ed. of: Miss Petticoats. 1902.
    Edited by Heather Harpham Kopp.
    ISBN 1-56507-785-7
    I. Kopp, Heather Harpham, 1964– . II. Tilton, Dwight. Miss Petticoats.
    III. Title. IV. Series.
  PS3539.I56G54 1998
  813'.52—dc21   97-31385
                                                   CIP

Printed in the United States of America.

98   99   00   01   02   03   / DC /   10   9   8   7   6   5   4   3   2   1

SAVED BY LOVE

As he clasped both her hands passionately in his,
he was sure that no such queen of women had ever
come to Old Chetford before. And come to him!
He could have cried aloud for joy!

Sometimes love confuses us. Sometimes love even makes us blind. But when we least expect it, love can also open the door to our best self.

A Gift for Abigail was written almost a hundred years ago, but its captivating story and moving message still resonate with our experience today. Who of us has not wanted to take revenge into our own hands? And how many of us have resisted love even as we were falling into it?

A Gift for Abigail is part of the Victorian Bookshelf series— old books rescued from dusty shelves or attics, and rendered beautiful again. Not only will you be charmed by the stories— out of scores of lovely antique romances, we've selected only those books that especially entertain—you'll want to place these beautiful books where they can be admired.

A Gift for Abigail, originally titled, *Miss Petticoats*, was written in 1902 by Dwight Tilton and an unknown co-author, presumably a woman. We follow our heroine as she takes a "situation" as an accountant for a rich, elderly widow. Abigail's only guardian, her grandfather, hopes that in the esteemed widow's company, Abigail will become a true lady herself.

Enter Guy Hamilton, an unscrupulous cad, who is also nephew and only living heir to the rich widow. Desperately afraid of his aunt's growing fondness for Abigail, yet undeniably attracted to her himself, Hamilton sets out to ruin her good name. Eventually, Abigail is the subject of scandalous gossip and flees to Paris. There, she becomes a lady of refinement and wealth, but remains obsessed with taking revenge on Mr. Hamilton.

Watching from the wings is one of Abigail's dearest friends, a handsome, young minister. He has secretly fallen in love with Abigail, and he is increasingly concerned about how society life is affecting her noble character.

As we follow the journey of Abigail's heart, the authors entertain us with glimpses into both city-life and the life of a small New England coastal town, the social atmosphere of "men's clubs," and even the early inner-workings of the New York Stock Exchange.

Because these authors wrote about a period in which they lived—versus a modern author creating a historical romance— *A Gift for Abigail* richly rewards us with the unmistakable ring of authenticity. While the novel has been slightly condensed, details of period charm, especially in language, dress, and setting, have been preserved whenever possible.

Readers will also appreciate the occasional passages excerpted here from popular etiquette books of the day, such as *Etiquette for Ladies and Gentleman* (1877), *The Modern Hostess* (1904), and *The Book of Good Manners* (1923). Here we read such timeless tips as, "In private watch your thoughts; in your family watch your temper; in society watch your tongue."

So much—and yet so little—has changed! So find yourself a cozy corner and curl up with this wonderfully new—and delightfully old—book.

—*Heather Harpham Kopp*

❧ I ❧

Poor but Proud

he great bell in the granite tower of old Number One mill clanged out its noontide release. Presently a swarm of men and women, boys and girls poured out onto the well-kept lawn between iron gates, like angered bees from a hive. Like bees too, these mill people of Old Chetford were excitedly buzzing about some special thing that had aroused their ire. That was clear from the broken bits of conversation that now and again rose above the monotonous humming of the majority.

"Yes, blast 'em," cried a burly, red-faced weaver, as he stopped at the gate to wait for some of his particular cronies. "They cuts us down because the market ain't strong, they say. Bah! That's always their cry when they wants to grind us out of the little we gets already. We knows better. It's more dividends they're after, and we ain't goin' to stand it. We'll—"

"Oh, *you'll* stand it right enough, Peter Grimes," broke in a tall, buxom girl with the flaunting comeliness of an overblown peony. "You're too fond of your gin to want to throw up your

7

job. If you men had half the spirit we girls have got, you'd have long ago taught these people with their carriages and fine dresses how to behave themselves."

"Ah," growled the weaver, his dull eyes lighted by a glint of admiration in spite of himself, "What do you know about it, anyway? You think more of your Sunday night sparking down on Promontory Road than about the rights of labor."

"What do I know about it?" replied the girl angrily, "I'll tell you what I know about it. Didn't I see that white-faced old Mrs. Copeland drive up to the gate an hour ago? And didn't they shortly after that post up a notice in the main hall that they'd decided to make a ten-percent reduction in our wages all around? Now, who's the heaviest stockholder in the mill?"

The man's red face flushed to a deeper hue as the full significance of this revelation dawned upon him.

"You're a smart girl, Bess. It's Mrs. Copeland as has done it, sure enough. And here's her hosses and monkey coachman comin' back after her. We'll wait right here for her ladyship, and just tell her what a nice old woman she is, and how we all love her."

On the magical wings that rumor always wears, the news quickly went through the excited crowd that now surged around the gates. The author of their trouble was a woman; she was rich; here was her carriage with its prancing horses at the curb; she herself was coming out in a minute or two. All the accessories for hate were before their eyes, and they forgot their hunger and weariness. The murmurs of discontent grew to vindictive snarling and then to loud threats of violence.

If the tall and rather stately old lady who walked briskly down the steps and on toward the crowd realized that she was the object of all this turmoil, she gave no sign. Her face lost its customary severity as she bowed and smiled at one of her acquaintances among the mill people, moving straight at the mob as if she expected it to stand aside in recognition of her birth and station.

As the turbulent waves of human passion closed about Mrs. Sarah Copeland, she remembered how she had sometimes bewailed her own femininity as partially shutting her out from many of the larger affairs of life. Now she knew that it alone might save her from great bodily harm. As she struggled on toward her carriage, the yells of denunciation that were hurled at her in full cry by the women hurt her pride more than did the physical indignities. That she should be publicly reviled in her own city was worse than blows.

"Oh, yes," taunted the peony-faced girl, "that nephew of yours is quite expensive now, isn't he? You want to raise a little something from us to pay his bills with, of course. I know him, you see." And she laughed.

The gentlewoman had ceased trying to find her carriage now, and stood with folded arms looking scornfully at the nearest of her tormentors. Her calmness and her silence angered the crowd to desperation. Violence would surely be the next vent to its fury.

Suddenly the crowd in front parted a little as the sturdy figure of the coachman tore its way to the beleaguered lady. It was in just such emergencies as this that James found his former career as a prize fighter of practical value. He was eminently respectable now, and never referred to the decently buried past. Grasping his mistress unceremoniously around the waist, James dashed back toward the carriage, surprising the mob into nonresistance. He pushed the lady into the vehicle—

for which he apologized most respectfully afterward—and prepared to mount and be off.

A well-directed stone from someone in the crowd hit one of the horses squarely on the flank. Both animals sprang forward violently, throwing the coachman to the ground. With frantic unreasoning they swerved from the street and made directly for an open space ending in a precipitous bank, below which bristled the remains of an old pier now left uncovered by the outgoing tide.

As James picked himself up, his quick eye saw at once the possibilities of a terrible catastrophe. He could not reach the horses himself, he knew. He could only pray for a miracle to happen.

Then he saw a young girl, whose flashing red skirts he never afterward forgot, dash out from the crowd, plunge across the path of the animals, and jump for their heads. He closed his eyes, imagining that she was dead. Then he looked again. She had caught the bit-rings of one of the horses and was clinging desperately to them, swaying in the air like a scarlet vine.

And then—victory! The girl's sheer weight brought the animals to a standstill, although they were still panting and snorting with fear. A window of the carriage was lowered and a calm face looked out—the face of his mistress, who was unharmed.

The heroine of this adventure would have made her escape, but it was not to be so.

"Come here, my girl," said the occupant of the carriage so sternly that the former could do no less than obey.

"Closer yet, my dear. I am very short-sighted."

She raised a lorgnette of gold to her gray eyes, and through it she viewed a charming picture. "M'm, yes; a good face. Who are you?"

"My name is Abigail, ma'am."

"Abigail? Well, Abigail what?"

"Abigail Renier."

"Who's your father?"

"My father is dead."

"Your mother, then?"

The girl's bright face lost its sunny smile.

"She is dead, too."

"Well, who *is* there?"

"There is Grandfather and me."

"Yes, where does he live?"

"On board the old whaler *Harpoon* at Tuckerman's Wharf."

"Indeed? A sailor, I presume."

"Yes, ma'am."

"Come closer."

The girl, with a little blush, did as she was told.

"Yes, a really good face. But don't get vain over it." The shrewd old eyes took in with one swift glance the shabby scarlet skirt. "Poor, I see. Yet," as she noted the piece of fine ribbon that put a dash of color to the dark blonde hair, "yet proud."

Abigail raised her glance valiantly to this strange old lady's. "My grandfather is a captain," she said.

"Captain what?" asked the lady, curiously unmoved by the importance of the disclosure.

"Captain Stewart."

"M'm, yes. I've heard of him. I'll see him. You've done me a service today, my dear. You must be repaid."

The girl flushed rosily now, and her pretty lips were set firm. "Poor and proud. Poor and proud," was the refrain that kept ringing through her very soul.

"I don't want any reward," she said brusquely. "It was nothing that I did—nothing that anyone couldn't have done. But," she continued, "you may pay for the tear in my dress, if you like. That will do for me."

The aristocrat gazed at the daughter of the people with keen curiosity for a moment. This type of working girl was new to her. They had generally been groveling, even deceitful. A trace of emotion stirred a heart not often given to sentiment, at least of this personal sort.

"Tut, tut, child," she retorted, "you scarcely know what you have done, and you certainly do not know what you are saying. You are in a bit of a huff, my dear, that's all. But lest you forget it, I am going to tell you again that you are poor and proud, as proud as—well, never mind. Home, James."

Furious with anger as she was, Abigail watched the beautiful carriage roll up the street until it turned a faraway corner and was gone. Then she slowly turned her steps back to the mill.

～II～
The Reverend Intervenes

As Abigail Renier walked back to the scene of the tumult, she felt a great longing to be done with the never-ending tasks in the grim fortress of toil she had now known for several years. She had seen many a fair and blooming girl transformed by the process of work into a drab, tired woman. Only last night she had looked into her little round mirror at home with a sort of dread lest she herself were going the way of others.

"Tell me the truth, glass," she had said, "no flattery, mind you."

She had laughed, yet with a sigh of relief. Her finely molded oval face was as delicately tinted as ever; her brown eyes were still brilliant; her hair waved with its usual saucy abandon around her low, smooth forehead. All was eminently satisfactory in this regard, and, being a very human young woman, Abigail had rejoiced.

"I'll do for a while yet," she had told her mirror and herself.

Unlike so many young children in Chetford, she had not been put to work under compulsion. Her grandfather's bit of property realized enough for the two to live upon, and the old man's pride in the pretty child, with her alternating moods of storm and sunshine, had made him determined that she should grow up a "lady."

She went to the public schools, where she was the delight and terror of her teachers. She acquired knowledge easily, and with equal ease gathered to herself all the inherent mischief of the schoolroom. She invented the trick of dropping a pinch of soda into some enemy's inkwell, and laughed at the horrible black eruption that would flood the hated one's desk. Once, she was summoned before the awful presence of the "committee" for some specially heinous breach of discipline, and only the rugged eloquence of Captain Stewart saved her from expulsion.

That incident sobered her much. Blows upon the hand she could endure with a smile and count herself something of a heroine. But to be turned out of school—that would be a public disgrace and a bitter blow to her pride. With that fear hanging over her head she managed to preserve at least an appearance of good behavior.

When Abigail reached her thirteenth year the leaven of unrest began stirring within her. She was now old enough to realize the poverty of her grandfather. There were little girlish luxuries she craved, and she saw but one way to get them— work in the mills. She saw the visible benefits of such employment, without at all appreciating the dull grind demanded as the price of obtaining them.

There had very nearly been a scene when Abigail ventured to inform her grandfather of her resolution—as near as the gentle old man's love for the girl would permit. In vain he had protested that they had enough, that Abigail would belittle herself in such surroundings, that she would grow up without education.

Abigail had ready answers for every objection and she triumphed. But her viewpoint had been gradually changing as she had grown older. She had caught glimpses of another life up on the "Hill," where Old Chetford's whale-oil magnates had established their noble mansions, and where their descendants still lived in the luxury of great estates. She began to hate the mill as the barrier that, in some indefinable way, kept her from the better life.

Now as she went toward the gloomy old building speculating as to what the strange old woman's last words might mean, Abigail felt that her days in the factory were at an end. She would find something else to do, something that would bring her into contact with men and women of another class. And as with her a thing thought of was as good as done, her spirits rose and she began to sing snatches of a gay little French song she had heard somewhere.

The mob that had been cheated of its fair game was still standing sullenly around the gates as Abigail approached. Grimes, the weaver, was mounted upon a box haranguing his fellow workers, so that the girl joined the crowd practically unobserved.

"I tells yer," he was shouting, "if we don't do something now we're slaves for the rest of our lives. It's cut, cut, cut with these rich folks. Now they cuts off our meat; then they'll cut off our clo's, after that our roofs, and then—"

"Well, what then, Peter?"

The question was asked in a strong, rich voice. The questioner was a young man of middle height dressed in gray tweed and wearing a soft black hat with a rather jauntily curling brim.

A pair of clear blue eyes spoke of an honest heart. A small white necktie gave the newcomer a clerical appearance not at all in keeping with his general make-up.

"Well, what then?"

The oratorical Peter stopped short in his speech and nodded rather shamefacedly to the man in tweed. The others stood aside respectfully and allowed him to come close up to the improvised forum.

"The parson," went round through the gathering, and with that announcement all the turbulence of a few moments before was stilled completely.

The Reverend Ralph Kane looked about him for an instant, his keen eyes picking out the faces that were familiar. Then a peculiarly attractive smile lit up his face, a smile as of indulgence for bad children.

"Now, then, Peter, what's all this rumpus about?" he asked cheerily. "I'm surprised to find you mixing in any disturbance, and you, John Hanson, and you, Margaret Evans. Why, all three of you were at the reading room last night, and a better-behaved trio I never saw. What's started you into mischief again?"

"It ain't us as has started it," declared Grimes doggedly, "it's the owners, Parson. They've cut our wages down ten percent."

"Ah, that's bad."

"Bad? It's worse than bad, sir. They put the notice up half an hour ago."

"And what happened then?"

"Well, sir, we learned that old Mrs. Copeland is the one who's chiefly done it, and when she came out a little while ago we just told her what we thought of her, and then—"

"Then you stoned her horses and nearly killed her in the bargain. I saw the whole of it from across the street. Do you know who Mrs. Copeland is?"

"We does, indeed, Parson. She's rich and owns a big lot of stock in the mill."

"But perhaps you don't know that she started your reading room and coffee house and pays their expenses; or that she owns that little hospital down on Water Street, where you and your children can be treated without paying a cent. And you stoned her horses!"

The burly workman lowered his eyes before the clear gaze of the minister. For the first time in his life, shame and regret were struggling within him to find utterance. The others looked sheepishly about, apparently seeking some shelter from the indignation of Rev. Kane.

The clergyman's heart relented. He had a genuine regard for many of these people, and he well knew the bitterness of some of their lives.

"Now, men—and women," he added, with a courteous bow, "I am going to see what can be done about the matter. I can't promise you anything. I know that these mills did not pay one cent of dividend last year; your income from them was more than Mrs. Copeland's. I don't believe that the owners would willingly grind you down without reason. You must never forget that they are too dependent on you to make you their enemies foolishly. I'll do the best I can for you, you may rely on that."

"We do rely on it, sir, and thank you hearty," and then the weaver called for three cheers for the "parson," which roared out lustily by the same throats that had a little while before been reviling a woman. The trouble at old Number One was over, for the present at least.

As the minister turned toward the mill door, he caught sight of Abigail Renier behind one of the gateposts busily engaged in pinning up a long rent in her cherished red skirt. It was a very charming sight, and if the Rev. Ralph Kane's blood stirred somewhat at seeing it, who could blame him? He was young and he was a man—that he had always insisted upon, in the pulpit and out. It had gained him the reputation of being eccentric, about which he cared little. He conceived his mission to be the saving of souls and the helping of the body. And he believed that whether he did his work in solemn black or rough-and-ready tweed was a matter of small consequence to the Almighty.

"A brave girl, as I have always thought," he said to himself as he entered the mill. "She is a brilliant girl and a beautiful one. God help her to go the right way."

Abigail, having finished her impromptu tailoring to her own satisfaction, started down the street for a walk during the few remaining minutes of the noon hour. This time she was not unobserved, and the crowd seemed determined to make the pretty young girl the scapegoat for its own misdeeds.

"Goin' to get into company on the Hill?"

"Puttin' on such airs, the wharf rat! Did yer ever?"

Amid such jibes Abigail walked haughtily along, until someone more bold than the rest seized her by the shoulder and pinched the tender flesh viciously. Then she faced her tormentors like an animal at bay. There was warning enough in her compressed lips and her heightened color, but the nagging crowd was too intent upon its business to see it.

"*She* put on airs," cried one of the girls. "Why, she doesn't even know her father!"

"And as for her mother—" sneered Bess, the peony-faced, "why—"

Before the sentence could be completed, Abigail, in a fury of passion, sprang upon the larger girl and scratched her face. It was like the darting of a panther upon a sluggish beast of burden, and the others retreated in terror. The luckless Bess fell on her knees and protected her face with her arms.

"Don't you ever dare speak ill of my mother again," said Abigail. And then she turned and walked slowly to the next corner.

Once out of sight of her routed enemy, her repressed passion again burst forth and angry tears filled her eyes. Then she was moved by a sudden determination, and turning her face toward her floating home, she hurried there as fast as her feet could carry her.

❧III❧

Laughter and Tears
on the *Harpoon*

he most picturesque and interesting feature of Old Chetford was that legacy from its glorious past, the wharves where the whale-oil industry once flourished. For years they had been slowly tottering to ruins or else remodeled and covered with tall and ghastly sheds for the storing of coal.

Grass now flourished on most of the piers where once many men had coined fortunes. The rows of long-unused casks had become the playhouses of children; great iron pots lay around; clumsy old anchors rusted away in solitude under the sun and the storm. Cats and bats made their homes in the long, low buildings that had been the pride and joy of Old Chetford's former magnates.

Abandoned ships were growing old at the wharves. A dozen of these veterans of the Pacific were there in all stages of neglect. The once-famous names of the Old Chetford whaling fleet might still be read by careful scrutiny, while the figure-heads of women, birds, and statesmen still clung—now grotesque forms—to the ancient bows. Some of the hulks still boasted masts, but from most the serviceable material had been stripped away, leaving them mere floating tombs of dead ambitions and decayed grandeur.

Tuckerman's Wharf, although unused and the last berth of one or two of the whalers, was neither unkempt nor decaying. Someone's care had kept the planking in a reasonable state of security, fought down the weeds, and given the approach to the water a fictitious air of the conducting of business.

Someone had also expended a great deal of attention upon one of the old craft tied up at the south side of the wharf. Its sides above water were painted black, and its deck was as clean and fresh as if holystoned yesterday. It had no masts, but a trim flagpole was fastened at the bow, and from its top the flag of the Union fluttered bravely in the soft spring breeze. On the stern the name *Harpoon* was bright with gold leaf on raised wooden letters.

On this particular day a passerby might have heard the rollicking strains of an old sea ditty, and had he stopped to listen, the sound of boisterous laughter. The voices now and then cracked and the laughter died away in a wheezy chuckle, but at any rate the noise was human and distinctly cheerful.

So thought an odd little man who happened to reach the entrance to Tuckerman's Wharf just as a particularly loud shout of merriment flung itself out upon the air. He stopped and listened attentively.

The odd little man was very small, trim, and youthful. A tiny, black, round-topped hat was perched over his chubby face, and he wore an abbreviated blue jacket with sleeves that seemed on the point of shrinking up over his elbows. His white flannel trousers were skin-tight until they reached the knees, from which point they descended to his neat enamel shoes in baggy folds. His grizzled hair was plastered down, and from this possession alone could his age of about fifty be guessed.

Hank Donelson walked slowly down the wharf, then paused. Shaking his head thoughtfully, he retraced his steps toward the street when another burst of laughter reached his ears. With a strange little smile that just lifted the corners of his mouth, he turned for the last time and, running briskly to the gangplank of the *Harpoon*, quickly made his appearance in the cabin.

A rousing chorus greeted Hank's entrance. "Ahoy, there, shipmate," "Hello, my hearty," "Drop anchor, you lubber," and other phrases of the sea told him how sincere was the welcome. Without answering, Hank walked to the head of the table where a giant-framed, white-haired old man was sitting, and, taking a hitch in his trousers, stood at stiff salute.

"I begs to report, Cap'n."

"Ay, ay, Hank, my boy," said the fine old fellow, "How happens it you're here? Didn't you say yesterday you were going to take down a stove for Tilly today?"

Tilly was Hank's maiden sister, whose love for her vicious old parrot was only exceeded by her contempt for the "shiftless old gabbers," whose club was the cabin of the *Harpoon*. To Hank she was not a pleasant topic for discussion, and he shifted uneasily in his seat, as if he half expected her grim face to appear.

"Well, to tell the truth, Cap'n," said he guiltily, "I *did* sorter promise to take down that stove, but Tilly sent me out to buy some birdseed, and as I was goin' along I heard the boys down here, and—and here I am. Brown sugar in mine, Cap'n, thanky, and not a very powerful lot of water."

Then Hank, as the newest arrival, was introduced to a frank and hearty young man who commanded a coasting schooner hailing from another port. As the nephew of Captain Sykes, he was received with a certain amount of respect and consideration, but he was made to feel that he was not the equal of the men who scoured the northern seas for whales three long years at a time.

> She dashed past them without a word and entered her own little cabin, the door of which she shut with a bang.

"How do I happen to be living in this ship?" said Captain Stewart, in answer to the young sailor's question. "I'll tell you, lad. For twenty years I commanded the old *Harpoon*, and I got to be part owner in her. Those were the days when five hundred ships hailed from this very port, and the catch was worth fifteen million dollars a year. Think of that, my boy. I was in a fair way to be rich, when all at once somebody struck the cursed kerosene in Pennsylvania, and that was the end.

"The others took the spars and rigging and other stuff for their share, and I took the ship, for I loved her like a wife. I made a home here for Abigail and me, and here, please God, I'll stay till I'm piped to quarters up aloft."

The old man's voice trembled impressively as he finished his little story. Just then, the listeners were startled by the sudden appearance of Abigail Renier in tears and a torn dress. She dashed past them without a word and entered her own little cabin, the door of which she shut with a bang.

The visiting mariners looked at each other and then at Captain Stewart. Evidently there was to be no more jollity on the *Harpoon* that day.

Old Artemas was the first to find words:

"Squall, eh? Better run for port, hadn't we, Cap'n?"

Their host nodded. "Yes, messmates, that's about it. I'll have a little patching up to do, and you wouldn't care to be here."

The little company dispersed, and the old man sat down in his favorite chair.

"Abby, dear," he called gently, "come out here and see your grandfather a minute."

The door slowly opened, and the young girl appeared. Then with a swift movement, she threw herself on her knees at her protector's feet, sobbing pitifully.

Startling Revelations

hey formed a curiously contrasted pair, this massive, white-haired man who might have been likened to a mountain crag crowned with snow, and the lovely girl, giving pretty promise of womanhood. The one, in his more than threescore and ten years, had seen many lands and sailed all seas; the other had never ventured far from her little cabin.

Now as the old man bent a kindly arm around the girl's sob-shaken figure, he gazed at her with a great tenderness. Abigail, with a little petulant gesture, shook off the encircling arm and seated herself on a bench. Affectionate as she was, she had lately conceived a distaste for "babying," as she called it. Her love seemed to be kept more in reserve. She dried her tears resolutely now, and looked steadfastly at her grandfather.

Captain Stewart had often seen that look of mysterious concentration on her face, and had wondered what it might forecast, but until today he had never feared for her future. Up to this time her childish griefs, though many and often tumultuous, had always been banished by tender words and comforting caresses.

But now her burst of passion had in it something of maturity, something not to be dispelled by a kiss.

And this change he dreaded with all his heart, for he thought he saw something of Abigail's fascinating, brilliant-minded, yet reckless and weak father. As she sat gazing into his eyes, the old man was sure he traced a resemblance to the one who had inspired the only deep hatred of his life. He shuddered at the discovery.

Neither spoke for some time. "Come, come," the captain at last said tenderly, "what's the matter with my little girl? And a shower, too? Tell me all about it, Miss Petticoats."

"Don't, Grandfather," she returned, with a sudden upflaring of passion, "not that name today."

"And why not today, Abigail?" queried the old sailor in much bewilderment.

"They would laugh if they heard you."

"They? Who? What 'they' is there for us to mind?"

"The girls at the mill. They taunted me about my red dress and this ribbon," and she snatched the dainty bit of silk from her hair and threw it impetuously on the floor.

"Why, I'm sure they're very pretty," faltered her grandfather.

"Pretty!" echoed Abigail scornfully, "Yes, they *are* pretty, but what right have I to wear them? A 'wharf rat,' they called me."

"A wharf rat? I don't understand."

"You would if you had heard them jeer at my home— 'water-soaked old hulk,' they called it."

"But it *is* our home, Abby, our own," and here was the first suggestion of age in the tremulous voice. "You have been happy here, haven't you?"

There was pathetic anxiety in this question.

"Yes, oh yes, indeed," returned the girl earnestly, with a lingering glance about the cabin. "Who wouldn't be happy with such a dear old grandfather and such a love as he has for me?" And Abigail fairly flew to the old man, clasped his seamed neck with her warm arms, and kissed his silvery hair.

Then, indeed, the old cabin glowed. He wanted no better thing in life than this girl's trust and affection.

"What was it started the storm, my dearie? Tell me all about it."

In a few swift sentences Abigail described the trouble at the mill, the attack on Mrs. Copeland, the panic of the horses, and her share in averting an accident. As the old man pictured Abigail clinging to the bit-rings and dangling before the legs of the runaway animals, Captain Stewart's lips muttered a prayer of thanksgiving that this day did not end in the blackness of despair.

Then the eager girl, with flushed cheeks and sparkling eyes, told of the rich old woman's attentions and questions; how she had said she was coming to see the master of the *Harpoon*, and how—most remarkable of all—she had said that Abigail must be rewarded.

"Not that I wanted or would take any reward," said the pretty narrator naively, "but of course I couldn't help wondering what she meant."

The story of her return to the mill, of the minister's rebuke of the crowd, and of the insults of Big Bess was quickly related. Abigail freely confessed to the scratching of her tormentor's face, and when gently reproved, spoke in broken, almost-whispered words of the slurs upon the memory of her mother.

"And I know I have nothing to be ashamed of for her, have I, Grandfather?" she concluded earnestly.

"No, child, nothing," returned the captain gravely. "Those who may say you do speak through malice. See here, Abigail."

Thus speaking, the old man took down from one of the upper bunks along the side of the cabin a beautiful little sandalwood box, neatly inlaid with figures of mermaids and flags, the work of his youthful days on shipboard. Even Abigail had never been permitted to peep into its mysteries. Unlocking the casket, he drew out a thin, gold locket and opened it.

"There is the face of your mother," he said.

Abigail gazed long and silently at the miniature of the fair-haired young creature who smiled so innocently from the encircling gold. A world of tender wonderment dwelt in her eyes as she kissed the picture.

"I knew she was good," she said with a sigh and an affectionate smile.

"It is for you to keep now," said the captain. "I have long cherished it, but it rightfully belongs to you. Never part with it, and always remember to defend her name, as you have done today. Would you like to hear why you may always defend her name?"

"Yes!"

"Ever since you were born, Abby," he began gently, "I have known that someday you must hear your mother's story. From year to year I have put off telling you, partly because you were too young to grasp the full meaning of its sorrow, and partly because I did not wish to cast the least shadow on your happy girlhood. But somehow you've stopped being a girl today, and besides, you've heard something that makes it my duty to speak.

"Twenty-two years ago, your mother was the light-hearted, happy girl whose face you now see. She had never caused us a single tear. She was purity itself and the soul of honor and truth. All her emotions were on the outside, but she loved us well, and we were proud of our child and hoped for a bright future for her.

"One day there came to Old Chetford a French nobleman who had been driven out of his country for a time—Adolph Renier, Count Fornay. He was on a visit to some of his countrymen here, and he brought with him his son Francois. The younger Renier was a handsome man with gracious manners and fascinating ways.

"At some social event—for we Stewarts were well-considered in those days, Abigail—he met your mother and was charmed by her prettiness and simplicity. He pressed the acquaintance in headstrong French fashion, and your mother—well, how could she help being attracted to such a man? I saw that she was losing her heart, and determined to put an end to things before it was too late.

"I called on the Count and told him what I feared. He smiled and said that it was only a passing fancy on his son's part, that it would amount to nothing. And in any event, a marriage with my daughter would never be recognized by himself or his family. I told your mother a part of this, and entreated her never to see him again.

"But I didn't tell her all," continued the old man with a sigh. "If I had, she might have been spared much suffering. But then," he added with a bright smile, "then I shouldn't have had you, dear.

"I'm afraid I didn't count on the waywardness of young blood as I should, for one day I came home to find a letter from your mother telling me that she and Renier had been married over in Mill River. I went there and found that everything was straight and legal, and that your mother was the wife of Count Fornay's son.

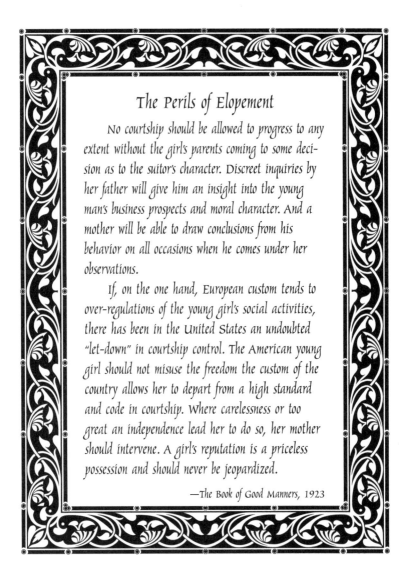

The Perils of Elopement

No courtship should be allowed to progress to any extent without the girl's parents coming to some decision as to the suitor's character. Discreet inquiries by her father will give him an insight into the young man's business prospects and moral character. And a mother will be able to draw conclusions from his behavior on all occasions when he comes under her observations.

If, on the one hand, European custom tends to over-regulations of the young girl's social activities, there has been in the United States an undoubted "let-down" in courtship control. The American young girl should not misuse the freedom the custom of the country allows her to depart from a high standard and code in courtship. Where carelessness or too great an independence lead her to do so, her mother should intervene. A girl's reputation is a priceless possession and should never be jeopardized.

—The Book of Good Manners, 1923

"Well, dear, I tried to put the best face on everything then, and when my Alice went away to France with her husband, I gave them both Godspeed and hoped for good things to come."

As this story proceeded, Abigail's dark eyes glowed with the fire of romantic enthusiasm. She was the daughter of a high-born father! This was ample repayment for all the little wretchedness she had undergone that day. What an armor against the slanders and innuendos of a crowd of factory girls!

"For awhile I got letters from France," the old man went on, "telling at first of happiness and pleasure. After a bit the letters grew fewer and fewer, and those that did come had a tone of disappointment and sorrow that nothing could hide. Then they stopped altogether.

"About this time I came to live on the old *Harpoon*, and for several years after your grandmother's death, I was here all alone, except for the daily visits of Hank—God bless him.

"I was torn with anxiety, and wrote again and again to France, but no answer came. 'Twasn't *her* fault, as I found out afterwards. Finally I determined to go over there myself and find my girl. I couldn't bear the terrible uncertainty any longer.

"The night before I was to leave the ship—Hank had promised to stand watch until I came back—it was black and stormy, but I paced the deck thinking of Alice and wondering if I should find her alive. So near she seemed, even after the years, that I almost fancied I could hear her call, 'Father!'

"I turned to go below, a big lump in my throat, when again that cry—

"'Father!'

"It wasn't imagination, Abigail. I rushed forward and caught her in my arms—my dear girl had come back to her old father with her heart broken and her strength all gone. She fainted dead away, and I brought her down here, kissing her white face and calling her back to me.

"The next day she told me everything—how her husband had made a pretty plaything of her for a time, and then had tired of her and turned to his old life of drinking; how he had neglected her and had at last openly insulted her by flaunting another woman—he even brought her to his home once, the villain; how he had finally cursed her and told her that their marriage was not recognized in France, and that—well, Abby, I won't say more. At that she left him forever.

"I swore by the Almighty that I'd go to France and kill him, but she showed me how foolish it was to think such things and brought me back to reason.

"Six weeks after she reached home you came into my life. Within a year you were all I had."

Abigail's eyes filled with tears, no less at the history of her mother's ruined life than at the pitiable appearance of her grandfather. To see that giant frame shaken with emotion and that fine head bowed with grief was new and strange and terrible. She would have comforted him in her childlike fashion, but she instinctively felt that his sorrow would best wear itself out.

Presently his old kindly smile came back.

"And so, 'Miss Petticoats,' you know the whole story except how you really got that nickname. Your mother used to call you 'Mon petit coeur.' I didn't know French then, and asked her what she meant.

"'My little heart,' she said, and I laughed and told her that 'Miss Petticoats' was as near as I could come to the jargon, and 'Miss Petticoats' you've been ever since."

"And I—oh, think of it—I hated the name when you spoke it a little while ago," said the girl gently. "I shall love it forever now for *her* sake."

"And when you grew old enough to hold a needle, the name seemed to fit you, for you know how you have made clothes for yourself from your mother's dear old finery. Your knack of making pretty things was not from your mother, for she could never learn to sew well."

"Is it from—him?"

"I fear so, dear, but let us trust that it is all. You *will* be a good woman, Abigail?"

"If I can," returned the girl in a faraway tone. She was not thinking of the future; her whole impressionable soul was filled with the romance of the dead. She rose without more words and went to her cabin, holding the precious miniature to her heart.

But the captain's thoughts were all of the days to come, as he sat alone smoking a comforting pipe. The irrevocable past was buried long ago. Abigail was his world now, and her coming life a mystery he dared not attempt to solve.

But of one thing he was certain: the girl could not grow to womanhood in this fashion. Something must be done, and the kindly old man pondered long and earnestly upon what that something should be.

~≪V≫~

Beauty
Provoketh Thieves

rs. Sarah Copeland's mansion on Bristol Street was one of the notable houses of a notable avenue of great estates. Bristol Street was the main artery of the upper city, the channel, as it were, of the blue blood of the oil magnates' intensely self-satisfied descendants. From the region of cotton mills on the north to the tossing waters of Curlew Bay on the south, it stretched its long, beautiful course, bordered on either side by deep lawns rising gently to the houses of stately size and architecture.

Mrs. Copeland's house was a very fit abode for the lady herself. It was stately rather than beautiful, being built of stone and having a front of immense granite pillars, which, under a dull sky, gave it the appearance of a temple rather than a New England dwelling. Everything bespoke wealth, but wholly in the minor key; the owner would as soon have worn diamonds by daylight as to have permitted any ostentation about her dignified premises.

Her charity and good works were not of common knowledge or public trumpeting, for she was not the sort of Good Samaritan who stops the world by the roadside to show what she has done. She gave to deserving need in her own way, and scarcely confided to her little finger when her thumb and forefinger dived into her purse for some helpful object.

"As for me," she would say to her friend, the Reverend Ralph Kane, "I'm not going to leave money to help fat trustees get fatter. I shall give what I give while I'm alive and able to see that the money goes where I want it to. Those who try to help themselves I'll help."

She had long been versed in all the unfeminine mysteries of finance, and her money had grown like the traditional snowball. She knew the stock market also, and not to her sorrow, for she was cool, calculating, shrewd, and unemotional in all her dealings. Her operations were sometimes on a scale that would have astounded her neighbors of Old Chetford, had they been taken into her confidence, but only Ralph Kane knew much about her business life. They had been thrown together in charitable work, and from the very first, the woman liked the man's honesty.

"Rev. Kane is the only minister I know who doesn't seem to imagine that he's the one man who has actually been selected by the Lord for the kingdom of heaven," she once told somebody. She liked him because she believed that conscience—not the opinions of others—guided his conduct of life.

Shortly after noon of the day that had brought Abigail Renier and Mrs. Copeland together in so unusual a fashion, a slim, fashionably dressed young woman ran lightly up the stone steps of the house in Bristol Street and rang the bell. A hatchet-faced, solemn butler opened the door.

"Is Mrs. Copeland in, John?" asked the lady.

"Not at present, ma'am, but she's expected soon. Will you come in and wait?"

"No, I think not. Tell her that Mrs. Worth-Courtleigh called, please."

She turned to go, but the sight of a tall, well-knit, manly figure coming up the driveway caused a reconsideration.

"On second thought I think I *will* wait, after all," she said, and entered the house. "No, not there, John. The drawing room is so formal"—with a little pretense of a shiver—"I prefer to wait in the library."

"Very good, ma'am," returned the well-trained servant, with just the suspicion of a shrug from his thin shoulders. With the utmost ceremony he ushered her into a restful, beautiful old room finished in dark walnut, from whose walls looked down the choice spirits of genius.

Now Mrs. Worth-Courtleigh was not a literary woman, nor yet noted for her love of books, but she picked up a large volume that chanced to be on the library table and began turning its pages nervously. Even John, the butler, seemed to understand that she was somewhat out of her accustomed sphere.

"Anything further I can do, ma'am?"

"Nothing, thank you. When Mrs. Copeland returns, please let her know that I am here."

"I will do so, ma'am," and the butler closed the door noiselessly, the shadow of a smile flitting over his gaunt face. That evening below stairs, he almost became cheerful and related to his chosen confidant that "Mrs. Worth-Courtleigh wanted to wait in the library this afternoon, instead of the drawing room.

I took a look at the book she picked up and bless me if it wasn't upside down."

Mrs. Worth-Courtleigh had waited till the door was closed before she threw the book impatiently upon the table. She then rose and paced restlessly from fireplace to window and from window back to fireplace again.

How could she detect in her own face that something, spiritual rather than physical, that might have been called repulsive?

She was undeniably a pretty picture in her agitation. Masses of reddish hair were piled high on a shapely head in the mode of the period, and the cream and pink complexion that is the compensation for such tresses was saved from dullness by a pair of lustrous gray eyes that sometimes darkened to violet. Her mouth was large but finely curved, and her nose thin and well-shaped. It was not a common face, nor was its owner's temperament easily recognized, except that one would have readily believed that under the stress of emotional abandon she would go to almost any length.

Her husband was a middle-aged lawyer of sober habit and judicial turn of mind. He had succeeded admirably as the legal adviser of great corporations. The money he made was freely turned over to his pretty wife to give her the luxuries she had enjoyed as a girl and to help her ambition to become the leader of Old Chetford's fashionable set. He loved his wife deeply, but he was too engrossed in his profession to study her daily life critically. It was enough for him that she was an ornament to his home and a woman much sought after and admired.

Mrs. Worth-Courtleigh's unrest increased as the minutes passed. "He will surely come here," she said half aloud. Then she caught sight of her own fair reflection in the great gilded mirror over the marble fireplace.

"I am not changed for the worse, am I? Of course not," she asked and answered in the same breath as she studied her features. How could she detect in her own face that something, spiritual rather than physical, that might have been called repulsive?

She heard a familiar step in the hall, and, with a little deepening of her rose-leaf coloring, she dropped into a chair.

The man for whose coming Mrs. Worth-Courtleigh had waited with such agitation was a fair-haired, well-favored young fellow of perhaps twenty-four or five with a rough-and-ready style that made him popular. Being Guy Hamilton, and Mrs. Copeland's only nephew, he considered his status in the world as quite secure, and he took that world as his own particular oyster to be opened with a golden lever. In this process he obtained from life all the pleasure that could possibly be extracted.

As he came face to face with Mrs. Worth-Courtleigh in the room he had come to consider almost his own, he raised his brows in well-bred surprise. But his greeting was conventionally polite.

"Why Mrs. Worth-Courtleigh—don't rise, please—I scarcely expected to find you here. But it is a pleasure to see you anywhere," he said, with the smooth ceremony habitual to him when in the society of women of his world.

The large gray eyes flashed fire.

"If it is such a pleasure, *Mr.* Hamilton, I am surprised that you have deprived yourself of it so long. Since when have you taken to denying yourself any self-satisfaction, however small?"

"Come now, Lucy, don't sneer, that's a good girl. It hurts me and doesn't improve you."

"Ah, you do remember my name, after all!"

"Remember your name? Really, why shouldn't I?" he queried with a light laugh.

"Your formality, somewhat unusual in private as you will admit, would indicate that you had forgotten, and forgotten other things beside a name."

"There, there, Lady Imperious, be your own sweet self," and with flourish he raised a little gloved hand to his lips and kissed it.

"But, Guy—"

"Now, now, Lucy, don't scold. I'll admit I've been beastly unsociable, but the fact is I've been deucedly busy, and—"

"Busy! *You* busy!" A smile of scorn, of fast-rising temper curled Mrs. Worth-Courtleigh's handsome mouth into something not at all attractive. "I fear I shouldn't care to know the business you have been engaged in for the past month or two."

"By George," cried Guy, "I wish Parks could paint you with that expression. Queen Elizabeth—royal wrath—all that sort of thing, you know."

"First you neglect, and then you ridicule me," she retorted passionately. "I—wonder—who—she is."

"She! What she? What are you talking about?" queried the man in astonishment, real or affected. The woman wondered which.

"The 'she' who is keeping you from me. If I knew, I believe I'd—kill her!"

Despite his rule never to be troubled at anything, Guy felt a very unpleasant sensation about his heart at the words of the woman he had thought he knew so well. Evidently he had but just begun to reach the depths of her nature.

"By Jove," he said with a low whistle, "I almost think you would."

"If I didn't actually," she went on swiftly, "I would figuratively—she should be made to suffer."

"But there is no 'she' at all," he protested earnestly, "at least, no particular one. I can't be a woman-hater, you know, and shun them all. Don't you see that it would make you too noticeable?"

"What do I care?" she asked fiercely.

"Well, I do. I must protect you, if you will not protect yourself. Think of the meddling fools who would delight to toss your name about. And there is Aunt Sarah; when she looks at me with those eyes of hers sometimes I imagine she knows the whole story. But you know, Lucy"—he changed his tone of levity to one charged with all the pathos he could summon up—"whatever expectations I have in the world are fixed in her. It is only the lack of money that keeps you and I from never parting."

A tenderly wistful look softened the face of this woman who had just been uttering the fiercest threats.

"If I could only believe you, Guy Hamilton," she said.

"Don't talk of 'belief' between us two," he returned soothingly. "Of course you may."

"But you have—have loved," and the speaker seemed to choke over the word, "so many women."

"But that was before I met you," he whispered tenderly.

Mrs. Worth-Courtleigh seized one of his white, handsome hands with both of hers and held it passionately to her cheek for a moment. As for Hamilton, he was on the point of giving the lady some further reassuring token when the sound of wheels was heard on the driveway outside.

"Aunt Sarah," he said, striding to the door with the vigorous alertness that was part of his fascination for women, "she's getting out now. Pull yourself together, Lucy, for she's got an eye like a hawk."

He stepped into the hall, and in another moment the visitor heard his voice in an almost caressing tone:

"Aunt Sarah, Mrs. Worth-Courtleigh is waiting to see you. She is in the library."

A Woman's Intuition

s Mrs. Copeland entered her library accompanied by the solicitous Hamilton, Mrs. Worth-Courtleigh noted that the old woman was not her usual cool and collected self. Her hands trembled a little as she removed her black bonnet, and her mouth twitched noticeably. After greeting her visitor with something of stately ceremony, she began the story of her adventure.

"The brutes," exclaimed Hamilton sympathetically at the recital of the assault upon her by the mill people.

"Well, not quite that, I think. Do you expect them to draw fine distinctions when they are confronted by the hard fact that ten cents is to be stripped out of every one of the few poor dollars they grind from their wretched lives? How would you like to have your allowance cut down a tenth? Perhaps I'll do it as a lesson in economics."

Hamilton shuddered at the bare suggestion. Already he was harassed by demands he could not meet, and he had seriously considered asking his aunt for an income "more fitting for a man in his walk of life," as he had proposed putting it.

In terse but picturesque style, Mrs. Copeland described the flight of the frightened horses and the bravery of the mill girl who had stopped them.

"Just think of that slip of a thing dashing out and clutching a pair of runaways by the bit," she went on with enthusiasm, "and hanging on like grim death till they halted! Of course I called her to the carriage and had a little talk with her."

"What was she like?" asked the melodious voice of Mrs. Worth-Courtleigh, who had been greatly interested in the story. "Was she pretty?"

"Well, yes. Pretty enough for her own good, I should think. But that wasn't the chief thing about her."

"What, then?" queried Hamilton, in a politely bored tone.

"Pride. Hot, passionate pride. The kind that will carry her to a brilliant future or to destruction."

"Destruction, most likely," observed Hamilton, "it's the way of the breed." The "breed" was to him a pretty species of game in whose preserves he thought himself entitled to poach. If his affairs resulted in disaster sometimes, there were ways by which the facts could be kept from too-wide publicity. He believed thoroughly in the power of the guinea to "help the hurt that female honor feels," and he prided himself on the fact that no one could call him miserly in dealing with such matters.

"I'm not so sure about that," returned his aunt.

Mrs. Worth-Courtleigh's animated face showed that this discussion was quite to her liking. She seemed to desire to continue it, which filled Hamilton with impatience.

"But you say you spoke only a few words to the girl," she persisted. "How could you get such an insight into her character in that little time?"

"My dear, you belong to a class of society taught to wear a mask to fit every occasion. You mustn't forget, however, that there are those who don't study your books. On the faces of the untutored you can read the soul."

Hamilton swallowed a glass of wine and, after a suave apology, lit a cigar. He blew a ring or two into the air with graceful deftness, and then lazily returned to the skirmish.

"Not always a safe guide, I'm afraid, Aunt Sarah. You remember that handsome servant I had last winter. His face was a regular church certificate of moral character, and I'd have trusted him with the Bank of England. As I didn't happen to have that, all the fellow got away with was my new overcoat and some silver souvenirs. I repeat that it isn't safe to judge by appearances."

"Depends a good deal on the judge, Guy," retorted his aunt. "You were never noted for your perception. And, furthermore, this girl isn't of the common kind."

"Who is she?" asked Mrs. Worth-Courtleigh.

"Abigail—something or other; some French name. Her grandfather's name is easier to remember—Captain Stewart. Do you know him, Guy?"

"Yes. A fine old sea dog he is, too. White hair, big frame, red face, devil of a temper, but straight as a string. Lives in a ship at Tuckerman's Wharf, and hates the cotton mills as a cat hates water."

"Amen to that," cried Mrs. Worth-Courtleigh.

"Well," said Mrs. Copeland with great decision, "I'm going to see the girl and her grandfather, and find out what can be done for her. She interests me."

If Hamilton had felt little enthusiasm for the newly-discovered heroine before, he now hated her as cordially as anyone unknown to him could be hated. Although he had never been granted the happy privilege of seeing Aunt Sarah's will, he had long regarded himself as the Copeland heir and had managed his affairs with that definite goal in view. He had no illusions as to any speedy entrance to his kingdom. He was content to wait with a calm fortitude, buoyed up by a generous allowance and the privilege of doing nothing.

"Well, Aunt," he began, "I appreciate your goodness of heart, as I have cause to do. And the girl may be all you think her, but is it prudent of you to lower yourself by going into questionable localities for charitable work? Can you not send her some little present that will please her fully as much as a visit?"

"Lower myself! Rubbish!" almost snapped his aunt. "Can a lady lower herself by going down to the wharves of Old Chetford on a respectable mission like mine? How can any good ever be done with such sentiments as those? If the Samaritan had waited for the wounded traveler to come to him, he would never have been immortalized in the New Testament. I am going down to see Captain Stewart at the earliest opportunity."

He had taken the wrong tack altogether, Hamilton realized, and he determined to run no risk of another mistake today. He looked at his watch.

"By Jove, I have an engagement with Claybourne at the club in ten minutes," he said. "I must be off." And he picked up his hat and cane and sauntered into the hall.

"I, too, must be going, Mrs. Copeland," said Mrs. Worth-Courtleigh with a pleasant smile. "I trust you will soon recover from your adventure. Come and see me, do."

Mrs. Worth-Courtleigh and Hamilton walked down the path together and along Bristol Street to the corner where Mrs. Worth-Courtleigh was to turn, the man moodily thinking of the youthful intruder into his peace of mind, and the woman of the one thing that had been uppermost in her heart for days. When he stopped for an instant to bid her good-bye, she was overcome with emotion.

When he stopped for an instant to bid her good-bye, she was overcome with emotion. "Guy, look at me," she cried passionately.

"Guy, look at me," she cried passionately.

He gazed into her fine eyes for an instant, then flinched before the absolute mastery of their search. Skilled in concealment as he was, he found that no man can endure that kind of ordeal before the woman he is deceiving.

"*Is* there no other?" she asked tremulously.

"Now, Lucy, don't be silly. You will attract attention. Of course there is no other."

With a sigh, half of satisfaction, half of doubt, she turned and left him.

As he proceeded toward the club, Hamilton mused on the unpleasant way circumstances have of disturbing the comfort of mankind.

"Confound Lucy," he thought, "who would ever have supposed she would kick up this sort of a row? What in the world would she do if she knew about Louise?"

The Attawam Club was a trusted institution in the lives of the wealthy younger set of Old Chetford. With the addition of an enormous piazza for summer lounging, the Attawam members possessed a clubhouse in which they felt legitimate pride. A famous old negro cook had recently been installed as chef, and the "Committee on Bar" was always composed of men whose genius along liquid lines was undeniable.

When Guy Hamilton reached the billiard room he found his friend, Captain Claybourne, idly practicing some fancy shot in which he excelled. The captain was a rather short, middle-aged man with a smooth-shaven face and iron-gray hair that he brushed down above his ears. He had inherited some money with which he managed to lead a very well-ordered existence. He held himself aloof from the hurly-burly of life, and delighted to give the impression of being a philosophical spectator of the world.

"Ah, dear boy," he said in his drawling voice in response to Hamilton's greeting. "Glad to see you so well set up today. I am, indeed. Shall we have a little game of billiards—with spirits attached?"

"Anything you say," gruffly assented Hamilton, in no very good humor with himself or mankind, "only I would amend by requesting that we have the spirits first."

This being duly attended to, the game proceeded. But after a badly-beaten half hour, Hamilton threw down his cue in disgust and dropped into a big leather chair. He drew up a little club table on which was a siphon of soda and a decanter of brandy, and prepared to make himself comfortable for the rest of the afternoon. The gallant captain took a neighboring seat.

"Claybourne," exclaimed Hamilton suddenly, "do you know that women are the devil?"

The older man looked at his friend with an expression of mock wonder.

"My dear boy, is that a recent discovery? Don't you think it high time you learned the part of wisdom and let them alone, as I do? Let 'em alone, and they'll let you alone, and then you'll have a paradise without any rotten apples."

His well-knit figure and finely-chiseled face gave him the appearance of a trained athlete who was used to measuring distances as well as souls.

"Who talks of paradise in the Attawam?" asked a clear and jovial voice as the Reverend Ralph Kane swung into the room. His well-knit figure and finely-chiseled face gave him the appearance of a trained athlete who was used to measuring distances as well as souls.

"Hullo, Kane," said Claybourne, with more than his usual cordiality. Hamilton nodded nonchalantly. "Glad to see you. I want someone worth playing billiards with. The youngster here is decidedly off-color today. Paradise, eh? Ah, yes, I was merely remarking how the ladies brightened up this dull world of ours. Play you a hundred points, ten or no count."

"I'm yours," returned the clergyman, throwing off his coat and selecting a cue with much care.

As the game progressed, Hamilton's mood brightened somewhat. Perhaps the gentle breeze that came in through the open windows laden with the incense of spring had a share in the process. Or, possibly, the little club table may have contributed toward his greater cheerfulness, which took the form of rallying the minister.

"Should think your parishioners would raise the very deuce at your coming up here, Kane," he ventured. "Club and the cloth don't mix very often, you'll admit."

The minister laughed as he made a beautiful and difficult shot.

"Well, I won't deny that there was a little warmth in the breasts of some of my people when I joined. But they soon found that I preached just as well and helped just as many poor souls as I had before. In fact, I think I always do better work after billiards than at any other time."

The subject of billiards and the Reverend Ralph Kane had been a standing joke in the Attawam since the memorable Friday night when the faithful of the Third Congregational Church had assembled in the vestry for prayer meeting and had awaited their pastor's coming in vain. At last old Deacon Snow had arisen and declared that he thought he could find Rev. Kane. A few minutes later the venerable church pillar had appeared in the billiard room of the club and remarked to one of the players gently:

"Brother Kane, the meeting is waiting."

The minister, in astonishment, had pulled out his watch. It was nearly eight o'clock.

"I declare, Deacon, I'd forgotten all about it," he answered amid a general roar of laughter.

Today, however, there was nothing to mar the clergyman's enjoyment of his game, and he played with a sure touch and an accurate eye that gave Claybourne an anxious quarter of an hour.

While the afternoon was thus wearing away, Mrs. Copeland was at the desk in her private sitting room looking over her accounts and business correspondence. The desk was a beautiful old piece of dull mahogany from colonial days, and everything upon it was in scrupulous order. Any trifling with this sacred spot was keenly resented by its owner. There was a dark story in the servants' hall to the effect that a cat which had once invaded its precincts and upset a bottle of ink there had never been seen again.

Today Mrs. Copeland found trouble in going through her papers. Her eyesight seemed less keen than usual, and she had to call in the help of a maid to read a particularly illegible signature.

She was compelled to confess that the management of her large affairs was becoming a difficult task. She thought of Hamilton, but immediately decided that no help could be expected from him. His distaste for concentrated work would render him of little real use. And could she trust him? She disliked saying no, but dared not say yes. In her heart he was a disappointment, with his idle and careless style of living. But he was her only sister's child, so she kept her feelings to herself.

"Bless me, it's past the time for my nap," she cried as she looked at the clock. "After that I shall be better able to reason things out."

She lay down on the great horsehair sofa and threw a light knitted shawl over her shoulder. In a few minutes she appeared to be dozing serenely.

So thought the maid who went about on tiptoe in the performance of some little task. Her surprise was great when from the lips of the warm-hearted old lady came this self-query:

"If I am wrong about that girl, what is the value of woman's boasted intuition?"

~VII~

Men
of Good Works

n the vocabulary of Mrs. Sarah Copeland, there was no such word as delay once a certain course had been decided upon. And so early that evening, she went to see Ralph Kane to learn from him what he knew of Abigail Renier.

The minister's study, to which she proceeded with ready familiarity when told by the housekeeper that Rev. Kane was out but might soon return, was a room of queer paradoxes, perhaps unorthodoxes.

"It's all just like him," thought Mrs. Copeland, as she waited there in the evening glow. "Tobacco jar holding down a sermon, fishhooks for bookmarks in the concordance, and *Vanity Fair* hobnobbing with Jonathan Edwards. But he's a man," she said aloud, "and when a minister's a man he can make men of others."

At this point in Mrs. Copeland's reflections a slight knock at the door was heard, and in answer to the lady's summons a figure entered quite in keeping with the tapping. It was a wee scrap of a girl, hatless and barefoot, with great black eyes and a tangle of tight curls not often harassed by the brush.

"Well, I declare," said Mrs. Copeland.

"Please, mum," began the child, "Mrs. Brown sent me to get a book in here and to tell yer that the minister ain't a-comin' home cos he's got a meetin' down to the Coffee House."

"What sort of a meeting, child?"

"They calls it a meetin' fer 'good works,' but I don't see nothin' in it, cos no works is good."

The pathetic pessimism in such a morsel of humanity interested Mrs. Copeland at once.

"What's your name, little one?"

"Susy Brent, mum, an' I works in Number Two mill."

"Poor little chick. Where do you live?"

"Nowheres, mum."

"Why, child, you must live somewhere."

"Nope. Ma says we don't live; we just don't die."

The logic of this statement was not to be disputed by Mrs. Copeland, who well knew the grim horror of some of the mill people's lives. She gazed at the little girl for some time in deep thought.

But Susy now considered it her turn to act as inquisitor.

"An' who are *you*, mum?" she asked.

"I am Mrs. Copeland—Mrs. Sarah Copeland."

The morsel was surprised, but still not to be turned from her course of investigation.

"The one wot lives on Bristol Street? The one wot's so rich?"

"They call me so."

The child surveyed the woman with the critical eye of precocious youth. Then her glance rested on the costly gloves in which Mrs. Copeland always took such pride. She pointed to the well-shaped hands.

"Those. . . . May I just touch 'em once?"

"Touch what, child?"

"Those—those kids."

"Why, what a—certainly, little one."

The girl crept up shyly and with almost devout admiration stroked the soft leather once or twice. Then she shrank back.

"Yer see, mum, I ain't never been so near a real lady before," she observed, as if feeling that her conduct was odd and needed an explanation, "an' I thanks yer very much, I does." Then, having presented a slip of paper on which was written the name of the book the minister wanted, and having received it from Mrs. Copeland, she vanished into the gathering darkness.

The Coffee House toward which Mrs. Copeland now went was originally a ship chandler's shop on the water side of Harbor Street. It was the property of the lady herself, and she gave it rent-free to the organization of which Rev. Kane was the head. And not only that, but she had borne all the expense of fitting up the interior and made up any deficiency in its running cost. With its tiny restaurant where the best of plain food could be had for the lowest possible price, the Coffee House was filling the lives of the mill people and sailors who cared to come with delights they had never dreamed of before.

Once a week there was a little talk on some topic of practical moral value, at which Rev. Kane and many of his humble friends made brief and pointed remarks. The subject for this evening was thus announced by a placard hung on a big anchor near the door:

* * * * * *

"GOOD WORKS" MEETING TONIGHT.
GOOD WORKMEN WILL TELL
WHY GOOD WORKS PAY.

* * * * * *

The Coffee House looked very bright and cheerful as Mrs. Copeland turned into Harbor Street, with its powerful Liverpool masthead light hung over the door and the smaller red-and-green lanterns at either side of the entrance. The windows glowed pleasantly and the sound of a strong voice could be heard inside.

In fact, the meeting was well under way, and Rev. Kane was talking to the assembled crowd. The recreation hall had been stripped of its tables to make room for rows of comfortable chairs. Mrs. Copeland took a seat in the rear and viewed the scene with great satisfaction.

Of the little audience that faced the speaker, some had come for amusement only, others to jeer inwardly if not outwardly, believing with Susy Brent that "no works is good." A few had been drawn in by a liking for the hearty, humanity-loving young minister and a real wish to better their conditions. They all, as it chanced, were listening intently, as most people did listen when within reach of Kane's musical voice.

"My friends," he was saying, "these are practical talks on practical matters by practical men. Men who work or have worked all their lives will show you why good works are the only works worth one's while. The meetings are not to be religious except in the intent to make you better men and women and children. The talks will be short and you can all understand the speakers, for they will say what they mean in simple words. Between talks there will be music, and after it's all over there will be a bite of something to eat."

A ripple of applause, evidently for the final promise, interrupted the speaker at this point. He smiled, for he knew human nature.

"You will readily understand," he continued, "that the music and the luncheon are not what you are chiefly invited for. You've got to listen to a few little speeches, and you've got to keep order. I'm a trifle touchy on that point. I'll have no policeman loafing around here, but if occasion requires I'll be my own officer."

The reverend's audience was quick to see the man of resolute action behind the cordial exterior. Had anyone doubted his prowess, Mr. James Anderson, the Copeland coachman, could have furnished information as to certain exercises with stuffed mittens in the stable loft behind the parsonage.

"And now," said the minister, "we are going to hear from a man you all ought to know and many do know. He is the brave old whaler, the good citizen, the honest man, Captain Phineas Sykes."

The jolly and rotund sea dog was hailed with a storm of approval as he arose from his seat and made his way down to the platform. He cleared his throat with the sound of a small foghorn, pulled his fringe of whiskers, and launched his address.

"Messmates and landlubbers," he began in a tone he would ordinarily have used in shouting orders during a storm at sea, "I ain't goin' to spin yarns nor yet do any sky pilot business. I'm here jest to tell ye what I've found to be the best thing in my toler'bly long v'yge an' that is the vally o' good works, an' good works ain't in no way possible without obejence to orders.

"When yer sure that yer orders comes from the quarterdeck an' is all right, jest ye obey 'em so well that yer messmates can see that there ain't a better man aboard ship then you be.

"Tain't allus easy to understand the why an' wherefore o' orders, I know, mates. When I was cabin boy on the ol' bark Henry Clay nigh on ter sixty years ago, there was plenty of 'em I couldn't see the use of. The fust mate would shout an' bellow until I thought he was clean out'n his coconut. But arter a while we'd scud away under full sail at a clip no other durned whaler in them days could hold a candle to.

"I wants ter say that ye've all got yer stations an' duties on the great ship o' life. Do whatever comes to yer with all yer heart an' soul, an' yer'll be better an' happy fer it as sure's my name is Sykes. Thankee hearty fer yer kind attention."

"That's the sort of thing that will do good," said Kane to himself. "It's a breeze off the ocean right into their stifling souls. I'll push it home with a tune."

Accordingly the orchestra began the first mission work of its career. It had evidently not been constructed with a view to sacred use, for its first offering was a Strauss waltz. But what it lacked in devoutness it made up for in volume and beauty of tone, and the minister was not disposed to object to its worldliness as he saw the evident delight of his people.

And now Mrs. Copeland's astonished eyes beheld the trim figure of her coachman, James Anderson, proceeding down the aisle.

"Well, it's true that wonders will never cease. He's a good fellow. I'll raise his pay tomorrow," she thought. Thus was virtue its own unexpected reward.

It was evident that public speaking was not Mr. Anderson's forte, but he was "in the ring" as he afterward expressed it, and determined to make a good fight.

"Ladies and gentlemen," he started, choosing his words with great care, "we all must do good work if we want to amount to anything in this world. We're like horses, we are. Of course we can't all be two-ten trotters, but even if we're draft horses we can be good ones and be respected in the stable. We—er—that is—I don't know as I've got anything more to say."

"Go on, James," said Rev. Kane in a whisper, "you're doing first-rate."

"Well, as I was saying, when we get into the ring—the track, I mean—we want to be always on the lookout to jab the other fellow on the point of the jaw—no, no, to beat all the other horses, and to land on his stomach—that is, to come in under the wire, and give the knockout—well, ladies and gentlemen, I may as well admit that I was a prize fighter once, and when I get excited all the old lingo comes back to me. But I want to tell you, just the same, that good works pay and I know it."

"You're a liar!"

"Who said that?" James shouted.

"I did," came the answer in thick tones, as the burly figure of Peter Grimes, the weaver, rose from a seat near the door. "An' I mean it, too."

Anderson started from the platform, but Rev. Kane was quicker. Before the men in the audience had time to become excited or the women to scream, the minister seized the big weaver by the coat collar, twitched him skillfully into the hall, and, with a supreme effort of strength, shot him accurately through the open outside door and down over the steps, where he fell in a sprawling mass on the sidewalk. Having proved that he would be his own policeman, Kane calmly walked back to the platform and reopened the meeting.

After two or three more brief and picturesque addresses and a tune from the evangelized orchestra, the "bite to eat" was set forth in a rear room, and Mrs. Copeland found an opportunity to speak with the minister on the subject that had so filled her mind.

"What do you know of Abigail—what's her name?—the granddaughter of Captain Stewart?" she asked with her usual abruptness.

"Much that is good," was the reply. "She is refined, brilliant, charming—much superior to any mill girl I know of. Her unusual qualities have interested me for some time."

"Would she make a good secretary for me? Could I trust her? How about her education?"

"I think she would be entirely satisfactory. She was nearly through the grammar school when she went into the mill, and she has read and studied a great deal since. As for trusting her—well, I'd trust her."

"That's enough," said Mrs. Copeland.

"But I doubt," the minister continued thoughtfully, "whether she would accept anything that smacked of assistance."

"I'll smooth over all those little matters," said the lady with a smile. "Besides, in a year's time she will be made valuable to me if education will do it."

Then she went home under the escort of her coachman, who was secretly rather annoyed at the honor, for he had hoped he might meet Peter Grimes on the way and have the pleasure of landing his left on some susceptible portion of that public disturber's anatomy.

~VIII~

Mrs. Copeland Visits the *Harpoon*

ature was in her most tender and caressing mood the next morning as Mrs. Copeland went in search of the *Harpoon*. Birds were madly attempting to sing one another down in the noble elms of Bristol Street; the air was fresh and laden with the balm of the young season; dandelions and violets and lilies of the valley ran riot along the street edges, and all life seemed to share the subtle intoxication of the drink of May.

Mrs. Copeland herself felt great buoyancy and a hope for the future. A serene night's rest had strengthened her determination in regard to the girl, and the good report made by Rev. Kane was now added to her own strong bias in Abigail's favor.

As she neared Harbor Street, she looked up with reminiscent affection to a little hall over a grocery store. There she had learned to dance, and there had swirled the silks and satins of the town's elect. Although it was now a cheap billiard room, and although the beefy-faced proprietor was sitting at a window smoking a very rank and dirty pipe, she smiled pleasantly at him and actually nodded for old times' sake.

She had some difficulty in finding Tuckerman's Wharf, for many of her landmarks had long since disappeared, but at last she entered the neat gateway and stood a moment to survey the scene.

The water of the harbor was rippling merrily under the clear blue of the cloudless sky. A few gulls wheeled lazily across the vista, and now and then a tiny tug snorted into view and out again with absurd energy. Far down to the south the air was smirched by the tall clouds of smoke from the mill chimneys.

"Thank Heaven, they haven't got up here, at any rate," exclaimed Mrs. Copeland, as she drank in the loveliness of the immediate view. Stockholder though she was in the great industrial barracks, she kept her aesthetic opinion of them in a quite separate recess of her nature.

Tuckerman's Wharf seemed deserted this morning, so far as she could determine at a glance. There were no signs of life aboard the *Harpoon*, and Mrs. Copeland had finally made up her mind to stroll away for awhile, when a queer sight on the end of the pier attracted her attention.

The figure she saw was covered with reddish-brown calico, standing straight as a ramrod and looking almost as slim. Indeed, it seemed that a strong puff of wind must inevitably pick it up and deposit it in mid-harbor. An immense blue sun-bonnet surmounted the top of the structure, and its occasional nodding proved that there was a human head somewhere within its recesses.

"Gracious, can that be Abigail Renier?" exclaimed Mrs. Copeland with a shudder. Then she dismissed the thought with a smile.

"Too thin altogether. And too stiff," she said. "But I'll go and find out *who* it is, and perhaps she can tell me something about the *Harpoon* people."

As a matter of fact, the woman on the pier was Hank Donelson's maiden sister, Tilly. Hank had outrageously and in a wholly indefensible manner disappeared shortly after breakfast when there was half a cord of wood to saw, and Tilly had steered straight for Tuckerman's Wharf to hale the culprit back to duty. But for once she had been mistaken, for she could find neither Hank nor anyone else on the *Harpoon*. Being of a frugal mind, and needing something for dinner, she had borrowed some fishing tackle and bait from Captain Stewart's supply and was now engaged in enticing her next meal from the incoming tide.

She looked around suspiciously at Mrs. Copeland's approach. "Be you a-lookin' for someone?" she asked, adjusting the neck of a clam on her hook and lowering it with infinite caution to the water.

"Yes, for Captain Stewart."

"Cap'n Stewart? Well, he ain't here."

"This is the *Harpoon*, isn't it?"

"Yes, that's here right enough. 'Twouldn't a' been, though, ef Cap'n Joel could a' taken it with him."

"Does he love it as much as that?" asked Mrs. Copeland with a smile.

Tilly pretended to have a tremendous struggle with a flounder that she had just pulled out of the water. Then she said, "Yes, I 'spose you call it love. An' if he must love anything, it'd better be a ship. *That* can't talk back."

"Your experience of love must have been bitter, my good woman."

"H'umph! Don't know anythin' about it; don't want to. Never even seen much of it in other folks!"

"Indeed? But pray can you inform me when Captain Stewart will probably return, or is there anyone else who can do so?"

"Well," returned Tilly dubiously, "that's him a-comin' down the wharf."

As Mrs. Copeland turned and went to meet the old man, she saw that Abigail Renier's grandfather was no common sailor. She was filled with admiration at his splendid frame, and she liked his frank and honest face at first sight. She held out her hand cordially and introduced herself.

"I am Mrs. Sarah Copeland," she said. "Perhaps your granddaughter has spoken of me."

"She has, ma'am, she has, and I am proud and happy to meet you. If I can be of any service—"

"You may be of great service to me and to your granddaughter. It is about her that I wish to talk to you."

"Will you come aboard my home, ma'am? I can make you comfortable in the cabin, and perhaps show you some interesting things. And mebbe you'll smile, but I can think better down there than anywhere else in the world."

"By all means, Captain. I have heard of your snug quarters down here and I want to see the whole of it. So prepare to receive a very appreciative guest."

The captain, with inborn stately courtesy, led her across the gangplank and they disappeared down the companionway together.

During these proceedings the fish at the end of the wharf had been toying with Miss Tilly's bait, for that lady had been watching the captain and his visitor with distrustful eyes. She shook her head ominously and registered a vow that she would not leave the premises until "that woman" had taken her departure.

Courtesy and curiosity struggled for mastery in the honest captain's heart as he drew the chintz covering from a rare old ebony armchair he had picked up in his voyages, and offered it with much ceremony to his guest. He saw the look of real pleasure in Mrs. Copeland's face as she surveyed the unique relics of his long life on the ocean—the beautiful and costly ivory carvings; the delicately colored shells, tinted by the magic of the sea; the great glowing branches of coral flaming out in the dim light. He was proud of his floating parlor and glad that a woman of culture had come to see it at last.

And he was curious—there was no denying that. Something for Abigail's advantage was in the wind, but what? Money? She would never take it, nor would he allow it. A present? That would be permissible, perhaps; it depended on the nature of it. He dared speculate no further, but pulled himself together to receive the coming proposition.

IX

Love's Mightiest Test

aptain Stewart, I am a business woman," she began. "When I talk business I use business directness."

"Yes'm," he replied rather feebly.

"Your granddaughter has done me a great service; I am in her debt."

"She has told me the story. The service was nothing to mention," said the captain earnestly. "Although, if I do say it, Abigail is a brave girl."

The glow of affection in the fine blue eyes found an answering of admiration in the gray ones. Each thought of Abigail in different ways, but to each she was the dominating figure of the interview.

"As I have already said," continued Mrs. Copeland, "it *was* a great service, and I must repay it."

"We are not rich," broke forth the old sailor with rugged emphasis, "but Abby and I do not want pay for doing our duty."

"'Abby'? That's the girl's pet name, I suppose?"

The captain admitted the fact with a bow.

"Too harsh for a pet name—altogether."

"Mebbe, ma'am, mebbe; but there's another."

"Ah, two of them? She is fortunate. What's the other?"

A shade of embarrassment passed over the captain's face as he replied, "Miss Petticoats."

"Miss what?"

"Miss . . . Petticoats."

"What rubbish!"

"Well, ma'am, you see 't was this way—"

Now Mrs. Copeland knew the habits of sailors. She would not have been averse to a reminiscence under ordinary circumstances, but this was not an ordinary visit. So she good-naturedly cut into what she felt was about to become a long story.

"That's the way, I believe, you seafaring men begin what you call a 'yarn.' Well, I'll have it on another occasion. Today I'm pressed for time. . . . Your granddaughter has done me, a stranger, a great service. How can I repay it?"

The captain rose abruptly at this second mention of payment, and drew himself up to his full height of six feet, two inches. He felt no shame now in the presence of this fine lady. One of the powerful elements of his character had been stung into action as by a rankling dart. He would put an end to all this talk of recompense, and at once.

"I have said, ma'am," said he sternly, "that the Stewarts accept no pay for freely-given service. You are my guest, and courtesy demands that I hear what you wish to say, but I ask you kindly not to mention the word pay again in connection with the duty Abigail couldn't have shirked."

"Ah, Captain Stewart," returned the lady with some amusement, "it isn't hard to see where your pretty granddaughter gets the pride she so carefully cherishes down in her hot little heart. But believe me, I meant no disrespect. I am abrupt because— well, I have my reasons. I am greatly interested in your grand- child. Tell me about her."

Under the warmth of this request all the good old man's resentment melted in an instant. This rich and cultured woman wanted to know about his beloved Abigail? Why, that very request in itself was reward enough for the girl's service. He would tell her everything without reserve, tell her of Abigail's devotion to those she loved, her scorn for those she hated; tell of his own hopes and fears for the girl who was now at the beginning of womanhood.

With rough eloquence, inspired by the subject, he held Mrs. Copeland's deepest interest for nearly an hour. He poured forth the story of his daughter's ruined life, Abigail's coming and the growth of certain traits from both her par- ents in her young heart. He dwelt tenderly upon her warm affection for himself, her love for the old ship, her scrupulous pride in dress and person, her newly inspired reverence for her mother.

By well-timed interruptions and judicious questions, Mrs. Copeland had no difficulty in obtaining a complete summary of Abigail Renier's mental, moral, and physical characteristics, and, making all due allowance for the strong bias of a doting old man, it was still perfectly clear that no common girl lived here in this ship.

"She works in the mill?" asked Mrs. Copeland, when at length the captain seemed to have exhausted his fountain of eloquence.

"Yes, for nearly three years now. She *insisted* on it."

"Doubtless," was the dry rejoinder. "Then she has no education, I presume."

"Beg pardon, ma'am," the captain replied almost indignantly, "she has a very good education indeed."

Then he explained how he had learned French from a French sailor years ago so that he might read the books his daughter had brought back from Paris, and how he had taught Abigail when she was very young.

"See here, ma'am," said he proudly as he threw back a curtain and brought to view a large collection of volumes arranged on shelves fitted into several bunks, "she has read these, every one."

"M-m, well," observed his visitor dubiously as she noted the titles of some of these cherished books, "I should say that a few of them, at least, might just as well be left unread by a girl of Abigail's age."

Somewhat crestfallen, the captain tried another tack.

"Here is some of her writing and here a lot of her sums," he said, as he dragged into view a pile of papers covered with arithmetic problems. "She's always been a master hand at figuring."

The time had now arrived for Mrs. Sarah Copeland to strike.

"Captain Stewart," she said incisively, glancing about the cozy cabin, "as a sensible man, a man of the world in a way, you must see that it is impossible for your granddaughter to grow to womanhood under these surroundings, comfortable as they are. She is evidently a girl of great refinement, high aspirations, and a great deal of brilliancy, but as yet her character is unformed. How and by whom are you going to form it?"

"You are right, ma'am, I don't doubt," replied the old sailor. "I have loved her and been good to her and done what I could for her, but I couldn't be a mother to her. Abby has needed a woman's companionship, and it's been a great loss to her that she hasn't had it. A man's an anchor, but a mother's a rudder, so to say."

"I'm glad you recognize the situation, Captain. Furthermore you must perceive that the drudgery of the mill and the companionship of sailors—excellent men, I have no doubt—are not fitting for such a girl as she. I'm not a snob when I say that she's made for better things."

"True, ma'am, true," said the old man thoughtfully. Mrs. Copeland had skillfully penetrated a weak spot in his armor.

"Now here is what I have to say. I want Abigail to come and live with me, to help me with my correspondence and accounts, and otherwise to be a companion to me. In return she will have a home, clothing, and education. Think for a moment, and then give me your answer."

For a little time the cabin seemed to swim before the sight of the old sailor. The magnitude of the offer, with its enormous possibilities for the years to come, overpowered him. He seemed the helpless victim of some terrific stroke of fate.

Finally, through the fog that seemed to surround his faculties there dawned the realization that this would mean separation from his one joy in life—his pretty, loving, clever Abigail.

"But, ma'am," he finally found words to say, "Abby—to leave me? And I, an old man—to be parted from her always? I—oh, ma'am, I can't do it, I can't indeed."

"Now Captain," said Mrs. Copeland kindly, pitying his distress, "you may reassure yourself on that point entirely. It doesn't mean parting at all. Abigail will come to see you often, and you can come to see her any time you please."

"Well, ma'am, I shall not stand in my dear child's way. I'm an old hulk that'll soon be broken up. She's just ready for launching, you might say, all new and trim and taut. The hulk has no business getting in the way just as the new boat's going to slide into the water. You have my consent, ma'am, and there's my hand on't."

The lady took his big, rough paw and shook it warmly. Then she asked suddenly, "You love your grandchild, Captain?"

"I can't tell you how much, ma'am."

"Then listen to this, and never forget it: the mightiest test of love is sacrifice."

In the silence that followed, voices were heard on the wharf above.

"I say, Abby Renier, have you seen anythin' of my brother Hank?" came in shrill, rasping tones.

"No, Tilly," was the musical reply, "I haven't, but I *think* he's up at Norton's store talking with the new clerk."

"New clerk, eh? Is he—is it a woman?"

"*She's* a woman, and a mighty pretty one, too," said the tantalizing voice, and the next instant Abigail dashed down the companionway in her breezy fashion, and came to a sudden halt as she saw her grandfather's guest.

"How do you do, my dear," was the pleasant greeting. And then with no more preliminaries, "I have just made a proposition for your future. Your grandfather will tell it to you."

In a very few words the old man outlined the offer that had come to her. She, too, was dazed for a moment, but as the full significance of it all dawned upon her, she broke into a passionate storm of protest. She threw her arms about her grandfather and implored him not to send her away.

"No, no, little girl, there'll be no real sending away," reassured the old man, "you're to come here and I'm to go there as often as we like, and everything will be as right as a trivet."

"And think carefully, my dear," said Mrs. Copeland in her most convincing tone, "think of the advantages you will be sure to get in such a new life. You must regard your future, for there will come a time when—"

"Ay, ay, ma'am," broke in the sailor bravely, "when the last bo'sn's whistle calls the old man aloft, you mean. It can't be very far off."

At this not overly cheerful conversation Abigail burst into tears, and sobs shook her body as the storm a young sapling. Then she rose defiantly and faced the two who seemed to be conspiring against her peace.

"I won't go. I won't. No one shall make me," she cried.

The captain looked at Mrs. Copeland, and in her eyes he thought he saw the request to be left alone with the weeping girl for awhile. So he blundered over to the pipe rack and then up to the deck. And strangely enough—for the sun was still shining in a cloudless sky—he seemed to have difficulty in seeing to fill and light his pipe.

Left alone with the pretty picture of despair in the cabin, the stern Mrs. Copeland did a thing that would have caused her acquaintances on Bristol Street to regard her sanity with suspicion.

She went to the side of the weeping girl, drew her gently to a seat, and placed the beautiful head on her breast with the tenderness of a mother. For moments that seemed hours to both, no word was spoken. But the sobs began to grow calmer, as an angry sea under a gentle rain, and finally they ceased altogether.

The elder woman broke the silence.

The captain took his stand on the prow of his beloved vessel and communed aloud with himself.

"Dear child," she said in a tone no one then living had ever heard from her lips, "do you know why it really is that I want you to go home with me? It is because my life has been incomplete since nine years ago when I stood beside the new-made grave of a girl of about your age—my only child. You are not afraid of me now, are you, Abigail?"

The tear-dimmed eyes were raised slowly. They saw that the stern features above them had relaxed into a smile that had something almost unearthly in its faraway tenderness.

"You will help brighten an old woman's life, will you not, dearie?"

Abigail looked at her fixedly, a strange light in her eyes. Then, without a word, she softly kissed her benefactress on the cheek. And with a little sigh in which regret and happiness were mingled, she let her head fall on the breast that was so seldom guilty of such manifest emotion.

Abigail spent the evening overhauling her small stock of fineries, although it had been decided that she should not take up her residence at Mrs. Copeland's until the following week.

As for Captain Joel, he consumed incredible quantities of tobacco as he sat at ease in his cabin watching the lithe young figure flitting to and fro at her task. Far into the night Abigail heard him pacing the deck overhead with measured tread. When the glimmering in the east began to note the coming of a new day, the captain took his stand on the prow of his beloved vessel and communed aloud with himself.

"Joel Stewart," he said, "you had sealed orders from Alice to do the best you could for her child. Now that the right course has been worked out for her by a safe pilot, you want to dispute the reckoning and steer a wild course with no compass but your heart. You mean well, but you're twisted on latitude and longitude by your affections.

"Overhaul your rigging, old shipmate, and sail the little one into a safe harbor. Remember that 'the mightiest test of love is sacrifice.' Now turn in, you old barnacle, and when it's your watch again, see that you come up smiling for duty."

X

Society
Amuses Itself

obert Worth-Courtleigh came home to dinner with a pleasant anticipation of an evening of quiet literary browsing, good cigars, and a big leather armchair in his pretty modern house on a "new" street. Mrs. Worth-Courtleigh, having inhabited one of the ancient residences until her marriage, absolutely insisted on "something fit to live in."

Worth-Courtleigh himself would have been content anywhere with his pretty wife, his library, and his cigars. He was a heavy man with a face of granite and a voice that seemed a perpetual threat. He wore a short, bristling gray beard and the steely glint from his greenish eyes, added to his other formidable attributes, was enough to make the stoutest witness quake under his cross-examination.

People called him brutal in the court room, but that was the fault of his aggressive physical qualities, and not of his heart. Mrs. Worth-Courtleigh knew his true generosity and humanity, as he had never spoken a harsh word to her, nor shown himself other than a gentleman. They had drifted into a pattern of indifference mainly through their great divergence in tastes. Although had she chosen, the wife might have turned the husband toward any sort of mutual enjoyment. She would make no such effort, nor would she attempt to change her desires to match his.

"Robert is a rock," she once confided to one of her many dear friends, "and I do not propose to play ivy to His Massiveness. My tendrils reach higher."

Worth-Courtleigh met his wife at dinner and kissed her in his formal fashion.

"What's all this rumpus in the house, my dear?" he asked between spoonfuls of soup.

"Rumpus, Robert? I don't understand."

"Flowers, lots of candles in the music room, a general air of festivity."

"Why, Robert, it *can't* be possible."

"What can't?" he asked helplessly.

"Why, that you have forgotten that tonight we give a musicale for Madame Smythe."

"Who?"

"Oh, come Robert, don't pretend ignorance. Jane Smythe, then, if you like that better. She's just back from Paris, and has a b-e-autiful technique. Solfeggio says she's sure to be heard from in grand opera; and I have the honor of bringing her out. It's absurd in you to have forgotten it."

"Well, Lucy, I must throw myself on your mercy. I've been fearfully busy of late, and even have an engagement tonight with some of the mill officials."

The wife's quick instinct took alarm. She cared little for her husband's society, but his presence at such an event was another affair altogether. As a showpiece, it was imperative.

"Now, Robert," she entreated with the sound of tears in her voice, "I depended on you to help me out tonight. It's a *very* delicate affair, indeed, and you must stay in. Do cut the horrid mill people out for once, and give your wife your evening."

The charming woman who would not be ivy then acted very like that plant. She went to her burly husband, and twining her warm, soft arms around his neck, put her red lips up for auction, the price of which he well knew.

"Well, well," he said hastily, "I'll stay. But don't expect me to join in the idiotic talk of a lot of your guests. I'll be on exhibition as a dummy, and that's enough."

After dinner Worth-Courtleigh retreated to his library to fortify himself before the ordeal of an evening of coat and society small talk.

It was Mrs. Worth-Courtleigh's ambition to become the prophetess of a new social cult in Old Chetford. She dashed into the work of entertaining with abandon. Her dinners were revelations to the descendants of the whalers and the Quakers; her dances things of beauty and great cost; her patronage of out-of-town geniuses pleasant and profitable—for them, at least.

She had begun to be mentioned in the society columns of the Boston papers, and when one gushing writer called her the "Madame Maintenon of Old Chetford," her cup of happiness was full. This very writer had been brought down from the metropolis after a little practical persuasion, and she was even now closeted with Mrs. Worth-Courtleigh over instructions as to what names should appear in next Sunday's "paragraph."

"It is *such* a delightful experience, my dear Mrs. Worth-Courtleigh," she cooed in her vivacious fashion, "to visit your dear, archaic Old Chetford, and see the descendants of an ancient aristocracy at your feet. What an inspiring thing it must be to have social power."

They had come down to the drawing room, and Mrs. Worth-Courtleigh had taken her position beside a splendid stand of palms, cactuses, and orchids in readiness to receive her guests. Behind this sheltering screen stood the jour-nalist. This arrangement had been made for the convenience of the lady in jotting down the names of specially distinguished guests, and it also fur-nished her opportunity for making running comments on the various persons as they entered the room.

The reference to Guy Hamilton, marvelously accurate in its intuition, aroused all her resentment, all her jealousy.

"Who, pray, is that pert, overdressed young woman?" said the voice behind as the first arrival was transferring her filmy wraps to a maid in the hall, "rather pretty, but *would* the world cease to turn if she should happen to faint away?"

In considerable amusement Mrs. Worth-Courtleigh replied, "Isn't this Madame Smythe, my chief guest of honor, the lady to whose voice you are to pay tribute, Mrs. Rushton?"

Nothing abashed, the woman in the background went on with her rapid fire.

"That putty-faced little man with the hair dragged out over his ears—who's he? Captain Claybourne? Fine old family? Appearances *are* deceptive. And that tall blond fellow who looks like a refined lady-killer, and—ah, there's a handsome chap for you. Gracious, I believe he's a minister. What a pity. Who is he?"

"Reverend Ralph Kane," answered Mrs. Worth-Courtleigh with little ceremony. The earlier reference to Guy Hamilton,

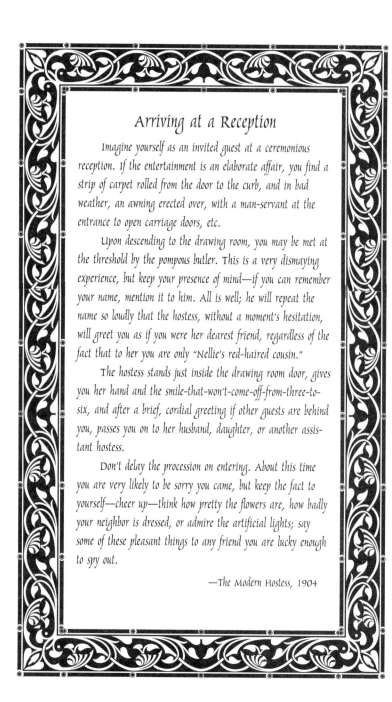

Arriving at a Reception

Imagine yourself as an invited guest at a ceremonious reception. If the entertainment is an elaborate affair, you find a strip of carpet rolled from the door to the curb, and in bad weather, an awning erected over, with a man-servant at the entrance to open carriage doors, etc.

Upon descending to the drawing room, you may be met at the threshold by the pompous butler. This is a very dismaying experience, but keep your presence of mind—if you can remember your name, mention it to him. All is well; he will repeat the name so loudly that the hostess, without a moment's hesitation, will greet you as if you were her dearest friend, regardless of the fact that to her you are only "Nellie's red-haired cousin."

The hostess stands just inside the drawing room door, gives you her hand and the smile-that-won't-come-off-from-three-to-six, and after a brief, cordial greeting if other guests are behind you, passes you on to her husband, daughter, or another assistant hostess.

Don't delay the procession on entering. About this time you are very likely to be sorry you came, but keep the fact to yourself—cheer up—think how pretty the flowers are, how badly your neighbor is dressed, or admire the artificial lights; say some of these pleasant things to any friend you are lucky enough to spy out.

—The Modern Hostess, 1904

marvelously accurate in its intuition, aroused all her resentment, all her jealousy. She clutched her heart and leaned for support a moment against one of the friendly palms.

Nothing of this was lost by the keen intelligence behind the screen.

"Aha," said the woman to herself, "is there something between the parson and my fair hostess? No, he is scarcely her style. Who is it that has floored her so? I have it—the big, light one I called a lady-killer."

The approach of Madame Smythe and the duty of introducing her to the rest of the party brought Mrs. Worth-Courtleigh to her usual state of self-possession. In a little while Worth-Courtleigh himself appeared and obediently went through a task he detested as thoroughly as he did his clawhammer coat.

The chatter of gathering crowds, the swish of skirts, the belly laughs of the men, the little shrieks of amusement from the women, the rippling notes from the piano as someone touched it carelessly, and all the subtle odors of refined femininity—none of these things touched the emotions of the big-brained lawyer in the least. But he knew that they were a part of the bread of life to his young wife, and he tolerated if not encouraged them.

The presentation of the singer having been duly made to the assembled crowd, about three-quarters of whom had known her well since childhood, the conversation became general and little groups collected according to their tastes. After a time, in similar throngs they proceeded to the music room and found seats.

After a melodious tribute from an imported male quartet, Madame Smythe appeared, and then the "Jewel Song" from

"Faust" was underway. A small Italian played the accompaniment wonderfully well, bringing out the charmingly halting and uncertain rhythm and the wild lilt of exhilaration in so masterful a fashion that the young woman could hardly have sung it ill had she chosen.

From all about came murmurs of admiration and expressions of ecstatic delight. "Charming," "So soulful," "Spontaneous as a bird" were some of the spoken comments—especially near Mrs. Worth-Courtleigh. It was well for that lady's peace of mind that she could not hear other whispered opinions wherein Madame Smythe was set down as an upstart without a voice and she herself criticized for presuming to force such a fledgling into the favor of Old Chetford.

Something of the happy light fled from Mrs. Worth-Courtleigh's face when during one of the intermissions, Guy Hamilton sought her out.

"So you still care to honor me with your presence?" she said, looking straight into his fair, handsome face—"That is, publicly."

"Publicly or privately, your honor is my first care," returned Hamilton in his most correct manner.

Scorn and disbelief brimmed into her eyes.

"Then why have you not—ah, Robert, playing truant again?" she turned to greet her husband and Rev. Kane.

"I must protest, Mrs. Worth-Courtleigh," said the minister with a laugh, "we could hear the prima donna to excellent advantage in the library. I'm an ordinary sinner, you know, and I have come to beg absolution."

"By the way," said Kane, "where is Mrs. Copeland? I surely expected to find her here."

"She sent her regrets. Some special work prevented her coming, she said."

"My aunt has been very busy of late," volunteered Hamilton, "preparing for the reception of a new protégée she has discovered—a mill girl, I believe, and said to be pretty. She stopped my aunt's horses during a little trouble with the mill people the other day, and Aunt Sarah would have it that she was a heroine. Knew which side her bread was buttered on, I presume."

Mrs. Worth-Courtleigh's luminous eyes pierced Hamilton's mask of indifference and saw his anxiety at the threat that had come into his life in the person of an ambitious young girl. Nor was she entirely alone in her penetration, for there were several of Hamilton's intimates who were well aware of the growing insecurity of his foothold in his aunt's house.

"How delightful for your aunt and—you, Mr. Hamilton," she said smiling sweetly. "It is always so charming to see one of high station stoop to befriend one of the rabble."

"I trust she will not regret her kindness," sneered Hamilton, "but I'm afraid it's like trying to make the silk purse—you know. What guarantee is there that this girl and her grandfather are not fortune hunters and adventurers?"

"I'll tell you what guarantee there is, Hamilton," said Kane in his ringing tones, "the guarantee of as honest an old sea dog as ever lived, the guarantee of a proud and scrupulous girl, and, if that is not enough, the guarantee of Ralph Kane."

Guy Hamilton smiled sarcastically. A gleam of light was beginning to penetrate his mind. He bowed to the minister with elaborate ceremony.

"Pardon me, Rev. Kane, for wounding your feelings. I was wholly unaware of your interest in that quarter. My deep concern for my aunt is responsible for my prejudice, perhaps."

"Keep your concern for yourself, Hamilton," said the clergyman pointedly, "you may need it."

That ended the Abigail Renier discussion, and after more singing by Madame Smythe and a noisy performance of the Twelfth Hungarian Rhapsody on the part of Arpeggio, a dainty supper was served, typical of Mrs. Worth-Courtleigh and all her belongings. Soon the good nights were said, and a little later the guests of the recital had become its critics, according to the pleasant social custom of abusing whatever may be devised for our entertainment.

"A stupid evening," decided Mrs. Worth-Courtleigh as she was preparing to plunge within her dainty sheets, "I didn't have ten words with him alone—I wonder if that girl, that Abigail, is really as pretty as they say she is."

"If Hamilton harms, or tries to harm, one hair of her head," thought the Reverend Ralph Kane before going to bed, "he shall answer to me."

～ XI ～

'Twixt Smiles
and Tears

hen Abigail returned to the *Harpoon* in the early sunset, she stood for a moment on the bow. A rich glow spread across the water, transforming its islands and shores into kingdoms of dreams. The girl's eyes filled with tears, more, perhaps at the beautiful scene than at the sorrow of separation. The final breaking of powerful ties was yet to come.

She smiled when Hank Donelson's head darted from the companion.

"Now, Miss Abby, jest ye come below and give me a bit of advice on a point of importance. Will ye, now?"

"Why of course, Hank," she said pleasantly. "Lead on, you dear old boy."

Almost bursting with pride, the sailor conducted Abigail to the after-cabin, and then into an ordinarily unused section of the hold amidships. She stood at the entrance for a moment filled with the innocent amazement of girlhood. Then she gave a little cry of delight.

"O-O-h, *Hank*, how lovely! You never did all that yourself!"

"Yes'm," he admitted, trembling with delight, "Is it—is it swell?"

"Elegant! And what is it all for? Why—yes—of course. For me! A good-bye party. You're a bad boy to go to all that trouble. It's a perfect vision!"

From end to end and overhead the hold had been festooned with streamers of red and white, Abigail's favorite color combination. A masthead light was brilliantly glowing at either end, while along the sides a dozen red-and-green lanterns shone most cheerily. A long table was set forth for the feast. The cloth was a brand new ducksail, and the candles were stuck in shells of all sizes and hues. An immense pyramid of freshly boiled lobsters formed the centerpiece.

Abigail hurried to her cabin to put on her best outfit for the great event, and had just emerged when the guests began to arrive. Hank, as master of ceremonies, received the company at the gangplank with wonderful civility, and shouted the name of each as he or she boarded the *Harpoon*.

All the old salts who had known and loved Abigail for years were on hand. Captain Sykes, Artemas Slickersley, and a few other of Captain Stewart's cronies were resplendent in their choicest land togs and well-greased hair. The young skipper, Captain Sykes's nephew, came too, with frank and honest admiration for the lovely heroine of the occasion shining in his eyes.

Rev. Ralph Kane, escorting two or three of Abigail's mill friends, arrived a little later. All the guests paid their respects to Abigail, who stood, blushing and radiantly happy, in the after-cabin, and then—

"Smash my binnacles, if that ain't Tilly!" cried Hank as all the visions of playing lord of the feast vanished in a twinkling. How his sister had learned of the celebration he was at a loss to know, but here she was, an embodied kill-joy. Probably she would drag him back to the dullness of their little kitchen. His infantile face puckered as if he were about to cry.

But, wonder of wonders, Tilly calmly descended the companionway with an absolutely gracious expression on her face. She carried a big bundle in her arms, and she greeted everyone pleasantly. The bundle, being stripped of its paper, proved to be a cage, within which perched her parrot, Nicodemus. The bird looked with wonderment at the unusual sight.

"Now then, messmates, all amidships," cried Hank, offering Abigail his arm with gallantry. The little procession of honest souls passed to the gay supper room. Such lobsters, all agreed, had never been seen; such chowder had never been tasted on the old *Harpoon*; such clams and scallops simply couldn't have been found anywhere else; and as for the plum-duff with brandy sauce—well, that triumph of culinary art would have caused the fancy cooks of the Hill to hang their heads. And there was ice cream, contributed by Rev. Kane.

Throughout the celebration, Captain Stewart occasionally grew silent, for upon him was the heaviest blow to fall. "Love's mightiest test" kept singing itself in his soul, and he knew that by the measure of his grief was measured also his manhood.

Tilly, slipping quietly away, soon returned bearing Nicodemus in his cage. She hung him from one of the under hatch-rings so that he was brought into direct line of view with the members of the party. Then he startled everyone, except his mistress, by screeching:

"Good-bye, Abby; good-bye, Abby. Good luck, good luck, good luck!"

"Oh, you old dear," cried Abigail, "you taught him to say that, and you brought him down on purpose. Oh, everyone is so kind. How can I thank you all?"

"I'll tell you, Abigail," said Kane, rising in his place, "You can best show your gratitude in your new life by never forgetting these old friends, as true as any you will ever have—"

"As if I ever could!" broke in the girl rather indignantly.

"Remember that the world is large and you a small part of it, and yet you may make that part of wonderful value. Be brave, honest, upright and true . . ."

"I do not believe you will," he continued. "Remember that the world is large and you a small part of it, and yet you may make that part of wonderful value. Be brave, honest, upright, and true, and—I will not say that you will necessarily be happy—you will deserve to be happy. We all trust you and love you, Abigail; you have our heartiest Godspeed."

"Speech, Abby, speech," quavered old Artemas Slickersley.

"Shall I?" she whispered to her grandfather, blushing prettily.

At a nod of approval from the old man, she began, this child who tonight saw the whole world through the rose-colored glasses of happy anticipation.

"Dear, good friends, all of you," she said, "I am going away, but not out of your hearts at all. Oh, you will see how I shall think of you when I come into my kingdom. I shall be a great lady someday, and everyone will love me for the good that I shall do. No more taunts, no more insults; the world will be glad that Abigail Renier is living."

"Poor little girl," thought Kane, "when the disillusioning comes what a crash there will be."

"But it *is* hard to say good-bye to the old ship," she continued. "I've lived here all my life and I love every timber and nail in it. You'll all come here very often, won't you, and tell the *Harpoon* how sorry you are that Abby has gone? And tell my dear grandfather that I shall never cease to love him and—that—I—oh, Grandpa, Grandpa!"

She broke into sobs and threw herself into his arms. He soothed her with a few words and brought her to a realizing sense of her duty to the guests. She looked about, smiling through her tears.

It was then that Captain Phineas Sykes arose to the opportunity. Dragging out a large box from under the table, he proceeded to untie its strings clumsily and put the cover in readiness to remove at the proper time. He got upon his feet and waved his right arm at Abigail.

"Miss Abby—Abigail Renier," he began. "This 'ere gift ain't much to brag on, but our hearts is in it, Abby."

Saying this, he pulled out from the box a big shoulder-cape of bright yellow fur, and waved it triumphantly before Abigail's shrinking eyes. Its hideousness was all too apparent, yet after the first shock the girl's warm nature rallied bravely, and she saw the love and devotion before everything else.

With a sincere smile she thanked the unsuspecting old sailors in a few pretty words.

There were songs and toasts and yarns in reckless profusion before the evening had wholly worn away. The ditty that aroused the greatest enthusiasm was one that had been ingeniously revised so that it declared that although "Jack has a gal in every port, my Abby's the one fer me."

At last came the farewells of the company. The old sailors kissed Abigail, and the youngest wished that he might, but contented himself with a hearty handshake. Then one by one they went away, the lights were put out, and the fragrant darkness of the May night claimed the *Harpoon* for its own.

～XII～

At New Moorings

ittle sleep came to the eyelids of the excited girl in the cabin of the *Harpoon* that night. A transition so stupendous, so full of promise she honestly believed had never come to a young woman before. She tried to project herself into the years to come; she saw herself well-dressed, well-groomed, like some of the girls of the aristocracy she had envied. She loved good clothes, not from any birdlike desire to merely flaunt fine plumage, but because shabbiness hurt her as something unclean.

She felt too, with a strange throb of gladness, that her character was to be molded by influences and persons fitted for that task. She knew herself thoroughly, and now that she had heard the story of her birth she felt that she better understood the contradictions in her personality. She was old enough to appreciate the effects of Gallic blood on simple New England stock, and she saw in a new light her pride, her rash impulsiveness, her warm affections, and her love of truth.

Reviewing the events of the past week, she knew that she would not have gone to Mrs. Copeland's as a dependent; the mere thought fanned her pride into hot indignation. No, she was going because *she* could grant a favor, *she* could become of value, *she* could make the grand lady in a sense dependent on her. She would improve herself, truly, but in that very process she would become more and more necessary—perhaps an object of pride to her new mentor.

But in the great sea of the future one light far outshined all others. It was the call of duty to clear her mother's name of every cloud, however filmy. Since hearing the story of the tragedy from her grandfather, it had become Abigail's passion to exonerate her mother's unjustly spoiled reputation. Ah, she would carry out her part at any cost—that she vowed with all her strength.

How she could become the instrument of justice for her mother she did not know, nor did she much care. She realized, however, that the higher she climbed in the social world, the more crushing a blow she could deliver when her moment arrived. After all these sleepless dreams the girl fell into a dreamless slumber in spite of her resolution, to be aroused late in the morning by her grandfather's knock and his cheery call:

"Come, Abby my girl, this is the day you set sail."

∽⊱⊰∾ ∽⊱⊰∾ ∽⊱⊰∾

Mrs. Copeland's reception of Abigail was characteristically cordial and direct. "My dear, you are welcome. This is your home now as well as mine. I hope you will be happy in it. When you are not, tell me so frankly."

This she said as she met the girl at the door. Hank and the captain had accompanied their idol to the very steps, bringing her few little belongings with almost ludicrous care. Nothing could persuade them to enter, however, and they immediately went down the path together, waving a final farewell.

Abigail gulped down the threat of a sob, then turned to Mrs. Copeland with one of her radiant smiles.

"I am sure I shall be happy in this beautiful place and with you," she replied. "And when you are not glad that I am here, tell *me* so."

"I shall, my child. Now come to your room."

To Abigail's rather exotic color sense, the dainty white and blue of her chamber seemed wan and emotionless at first, yet she recognized the perfect taste that ruled there as well as all over the house.

From the dim and cramped interior of the *Harpoon* to the airy brightness of the mansion was a change that drew out all the buoyancy of the girl's nature. She sang the old French songs with a brilliancy that attracted the attention of more than one caller.

"Who *is* that girl with the delicious voice?" asked an out-of-town friend one day at the sound from upstairs.

"That's my new secretary, Miss Abigail Renier. She does sing well, doesn't she?"

"Like a thrush. Is she as pretty as her name and her voice ought to have her?"

"M'm, ye-e-s, I am inclined to think she is."

"Then why not exhibit her?"

"Not yet," replied the wise old woman, "you spectators might be inclined to criticize the picture as unvarnished. Her day will come, though."

Abigail's first week in her new home was busy. First of all came the dressmaker, an object of awe and admiration. She was a fat and bustling little woman who knew where all the skeletons of Old

Chetford's first families were kept, and was prone to make them dance merrily. More than once Mrs. Copeland's raised finger and pursed lips gave her silent warning that the sound of the rattling bones was not good for the young girl's ears.

The dresses themselves surprised and rather disappointed Abigail. Her delight had always been in the primary colors shown by the women of the Latin races. These clothes were simple, pale, undemonstrative; she feared she would look insignificant in them. But when she put them on one after the other in their completed state, she knew at once that they brought her beauty into greater prominence than ever. This was her first lesson in good taste, and she never forgot it.

Other branches of the girl's education were entered upon without delay by Mrs. Copeland, whose rule it was to act today as if you were going to die tomorrow. An old clerk named Samuel Henderson, who had once been in the employ of Mrs. Copeland's husband and was now living comfortably on a pension, was engaged to give Abigail instruction in the fundamentals of business and finance. It required very little persuasion to obtain the services of Rev. Ralph Kane for a couple of hours two days in the week in order to instill into her mind the essentials of history, biography, and literature. In all of this Abigail showed a tenacity of memory, a grasp of the meaning of things, and a breadth of view that fairly startled the young minister.

One afternoon their talk chanced upon Walpole's famous dictum that "every man has his price."

"Do you believe that, Abigail?" asked Kane, half expecting an indignant repudiation of any such doctrine.

"Yes, I do," she replied frankly, "only you mustn't make it merely money. I think that there is some way to reach anybody in the world and persuade him to do things he does not believe are right. Even you—"

She left the sentence uncompleted, but the depth of her gaze, full into the minister's eyes, started his blood a little and gave him a strange sense of helplessness before this strong character. As he went home he wondered how she would have finished the sentence, and in the quiet of the evening in his study that wonderful look of hers haunted him.

. . . He wondered how she would have finished the sentence, and in the quiet of the evening in his study that wonderful look of hers haunted him.

With such a world of delightful novelty to occupy her, Abigail was very happy. She missed her grandfather, of course, but that fine old fellow came up to Bristol Street later in the week to see how the girl "liked her new moorings," and she had little chance to feel homesickness.

Abigail quickly won the allegiance of the Copeland servants by her kindness and lack of offensive superiority. She had the good sense to avoid familiarity with them, and she did not go to the other extreme of presuming on her position to order them about needlessly. John, the hatchet-faced butler, was made her slave by a little incident which he described in the servants' hall to an admiring audience.

"You see, Miss Abigail," he related, "isn't what you might call bang-up on the way the quality conducts itself at the table, and she knows it. So today she comes to me, and she slips a dollar into my hand and says to me—

"'John,' she says, 'I feel that I've been making dreadful mistakes at the table, and Mrs. Copeland is too kind to correct me.

Now I want you to watch me at dinner and when I do anything wrong you just clear your throat, and I'll see what I'm doing and correct it.'

"Well, she starts right in taking her soup off the point of her spoon, and I clear my throat. Then she tips up her plate, and I clear it again, good and loud. Then she takes a piece of bread and butters it away up in the air, and I gives another old whopper. Pretty soon she makes so many mistakes that all at once Mrs. Copeland gives me one of them awful looks of hers and says—

"'John, you may leave the room. If your throat is in such a condition as that, you'd better go to bed and have a doctor.'

"Then Miss Abigail speaks right up, and says—

"'No, Mrs. Copeland, it's not his fault at all; indeed, it's not. It's all mine. I got him to clear his throat when I made mistakes in eating, and oh, dear, I made so many that he had hard work to keep up.' And I thought she was just about to go off into tears when Mrs. Copeland gives a rousing big laugh, and everything ended jolly. She's a brick, that gal is."

Guy Hamilton's attitude toward the newcomer in the household was studiously neglectful and superior. His disgust for his aunt's "visionary scheme" was limitless. Of course, this feeling was never expressed; he professed the greatest unconcern as to the girl and did everything in his power to solidify the impression that she was merely engaged for a little clerical labor, and of no threat to him.

He rarely spoke to Abigail and what he did say was with a fine air of condescension. He thought his best policy was to "keep her down," as he expressed it, and he fondly believed he could freeze her into a sort of menial position.

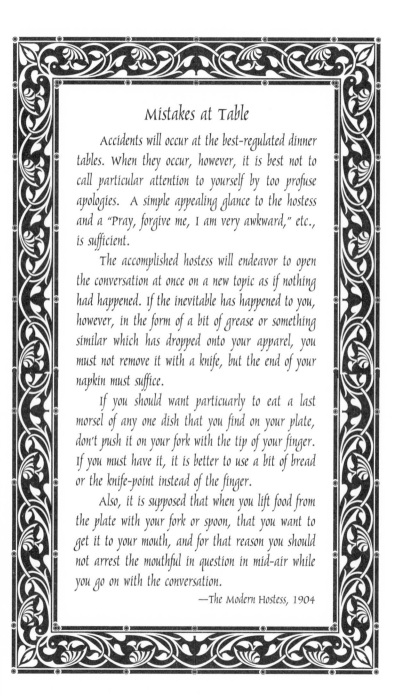

Mistakes at Table

Accidents will occur at the best-regulated dinner tables. When they occur, however, it is best not to call particular attention to yourself by too profuse apologies. A simple appealing glance to the hostess and a "Pray, forgive me, I am very awkward," etc., is sufficient.

The accomplished hostess will endeavor to open the conversation at once on a new topic as if nothing had happened. If the inevitable has happened to you, however, in the form of a bit of grease or something similar which has dropped onto your apparel, you must not remove it with a knife, but the end of your napkin must suffice.

If you should want particuarly to eat a last morsel of any one dish that you find on your plate, don't push it on your fork with the tip of your finger. If you must have it, it is better to use a bit of bread or the knife-point instead of the finger.

Also, it is supposed that when you lift food from the plate with your fork or spoon, that you want to get it to your mouth, and for that reason you should not arrest the mouthful in question in mid-air while you go on with the conversation.

—The Modern Hostess, 1904

One day an incident opened his eyes in a measure. He and Abigail happened to meet in the library for a moment, and at just that particular time the doorbell rang. The butler was out and the maid far off in another part of the house.

"Answer the bell, Abigail, there's a good girl," he said with a sort of patronizing authority.

Instinctively she started to comply; then a sudden thought stopped her.

"No," she said, "I shall not answer the bell."

"And why not, pray?" sneered Hamilton, "Is it beneath you, do you think?"

"What I think is of no consequence, Mr. Hamilton. What I know is that Mrs. Worth-Courtleigh is at the door, and that you may prefer to admit her yourself."

"By Jove," he thought afterward as he tried to remember whether there had been any meaning in her eyes as she mentioned the name of the visitor, "that girl is too sharp for her own good. And perhaps I'd better drop vinegar and try molasses. It never fails with women, never."

A Pirate Craft
Sighted

he slipping away of a year and a half in the life of Old
Chetford was marked by no external changes of great
importance. Another cotton mill had been erected,
and the city was climbing into the first rank of manufacturing
communities; more plate glass had appeared in the places for
retail trade, and a new theater had been constructed out of the
remains of the ancient Episcopal Church on Liberty Street.

But none of these things was absolutely essential to the
drama of human life in the old town.

More noteworthy was the passing to his fathers of the Reverend Dr. Evans, the pastor of the Central Church for over
thirty years. This blow was softened to the hearts of the gentler
sex by the certainty that the good old clergyman would be succeeded by a youthful servant of the Lord, not long from the
divinity school and happily unmarried.

The real, momentous changes, fraught with good or evil,
were taking place in the lives of men and women. The never-
ending building of character, the limitless circling of wheels

within wheels of human personality, the births of ambitions, the deaths of hopes, the loves and hatreds of high life and low—all proceeded in due measure under the hand of God, who neither hurries nor delays His work for all the smiles and all the tears of the world.

Abigail Renier's share in the changes of time had been very great. The bud had bloomed, and the flower was as fragrant and attractive as its early promise had given token. Childhood had stolen away into the mists of memory, and womanhood had placed its sign and seal on her.

The inevitable result of the influences of wealth and refinement were seen in her walk, her bearing, her voice, her gestures. This delighted Mrs. Copeland beyond measure, as justifying her warmest predictions. Her "boasted woman's intuition" had made no mistake, and she gloried in the fact.

"Abigail has certainly made wonderful progress by her own inborn qualities," she said to Rev. Kane one day. "But don't you think that I, too, deserve some of the credit?" she asked wistfully. She felt a childlike desire to be praised.

"You certainly do," he returned with his kindly earnestness, "a part no one can overestimate."

Tears of gratitude came to the stern old woman's eyes. It was her most cherished pleasure to feel that she had turned the strong tide of this young life into safe and happy channels. She loved the girl more than she would have confessed to anyone, even to herself.

Abigail's mental progress had been equally remarkable. She applied herself to her studies with immense energy, choosing, so far as she was allowed, the things that would make her "amount to something."

All the practical elements of finance and business she had drained from old Samuel Henderson, the pensioned clerk, until he declared that his attendance was a waste of time—pleasant, he had to admit, but still a waste.

So now this girl from the "rabble," as Mrs. Worth-Courtleigh had once phrased it, had become an almost indispensable confidant of Mrs. Copeland in the handling of her affairs. All this, with its implied responsibility, had steadied Abigail, toned down her tendency to erratic exuberance. As her grandfather would have put it, she had "taken on ballast."

She would not have been herself had her course through these eighteen months been wholly of smooth sailing. Her warm temper, her pride, ever ready to spring out almost involuntarily, her strong sense of what she considered justice, were sometimes brought plump up against Mrs. Copeland's powerful will and settled convictions with a shock that might easily have meant disaster.

One day, as the two were going over some business matters at the mahogany desk, Mrs. Copeland said with what seemed to the girl a touch of brusqueness: "Abigail, where is that letter I asked you to copy and file?"

"It must be here. I brought it down from my room this morning."

"It isn't, or I shouldn't have asked you."

Abigail caught sight of the envelope on the desk. Hot with indignation that a charge of carelessness should be made against her without investigation, she rose imperiously and, pointing to the packet, said in an angry tone—

"You will find it there, Mrs. Copeland; you've no right to accuse me without looking," and swept out of the room and up to her chamber.

A few minutes later a very penitent Abigail came down again.

"Oh, Mrs. Copeland," she cried, striving to keep back her sobs, "will you forgive me? I—did bring back the envelope, but I left the letter in a book I was reading, and—just found it. What can you think of me?"

Such incidents as this were few, and when they did occur they made Mrs. Copeland's heart warm toward the girl rather than otherwise. She recognized Abigail's firmness in standing on her rights when justice seemed to be on her side, and her instant yielding when she was shown to be wrong, and she was by no means displeased.

Abigail's musical tastes were given every encouragement. In fact, when Mrs. Copeland found what a natural aptitude she had for the piano she insisted on a thorough course of instruction for the girl. With his characteristic flattery, Professor Arpeggio went into ecstacies over his new pupil's cleverness. However, she did play very well indeed.

Once, when a world-famous woman pianist came to Old Chetford for a recital, Abigail sat spellbound through it all, and nothing could induce her to touch her piano for a week.

"But my ears are still full of that wonderful, wonderful playing," she said in answer to Mrs Copeland's remonstrance. "Don't make me spoil it all by listening to myself. I want it to last."

But that was well in the past when, on a bright October afternoon, she was dashing through some tempo studies with a precision and clearness good to hear. An unperceived listener stood in an open piazza window and gazed in wonderment at the girl's flying fingers. At a pause in the playing he pounded his hands together with tremendous vigor.

"Grandfather!" cried the girl as she ran to the window and dragged the beaming old fellow into the room. "How did you ever get up to the window without my hearing you?"

The captain roared with laughter.

"*You* hear *me?*" he rejoined. "What, with all that crash-bang and lickerty-larrup going on in the pianner? Why, I could have brought a whole ship's crew here and you'd never known the difference." Then he added tenderly, "Are you glad to have Fridays come, Abby?"

"Oh—yes!" she replied fervently. "Whether you come here or I go down to the old *Harpoon*, it's always a dear, delightful day. I wouldn't miss them for the world, not even for—this," and she looked about the fine room with eyes full of meaning. "I never would have wholly left you—you may well believe that—but what on earth are you so mysterious about?"

Truly the captain was conducting himself in a rather unusual manner. He shifted uneasily from foot to foot, his face grew red, and his glance constantly sought the open window through which he had entered. Then a curious little chuckle was heard outside.

"It's a gray squirrel, I think," said Abigail, "there are lots of them in the trees."

"Ho, ho, ho," shouted the old sailor. "A squirrel! He, he, he. A *gray* squirrel. Come in here, you squirrel, and show yourself to the lady. Come in, I say."

And there entered Hank Donelson to Abigail's great delight and surprise. Hank had been away from Old Chetford for over a year as mate of a coasting schooner and had just arrived in port. His youthful face and figure were absolutely unchanged. He looked at Abigail with a sort of awe.

"Why, Abby, how you've grown. Why, you're a out and out lady with yer grand new good looks—well, I ain't going to make yer vain, that's all. I says nothin' but I thinks a lot. I'm a kind of scared of yer, for a fact."

"Nonsense, Hank," said the girl as she cordially grasped his hand. "Weren't you my friend in the old days? Well, you are here, then. I haven't changed a bit."

"Now I'll play something for you, Hank," she exclaimed merrily. "What shall it be? Ah, I have it."

Then came the infectious lilt of the "Sailor's Hornpipe," played as Hank had never heard it before. When it came to a song Hank yielded to the inevitable. All three joined in one of the rollicking choruses of *Harpoon* days. The merriment was at its height when the door opened and Mr. Guy Hamilton walked in.

Hank was terrified into silence; the captain more gradually subsided; and Abigail, although she stopped singing, turned to Hamilton with a radiant smile.

"It was for old times' sake, Mr. Hamilton. Did it make a *horrible* noise?"

"Not at all, Abigail. It's pleasant to have the old house waked up now and then. How do you do, Captain? Introduce me to your friend."

Evidently it was one of Mr. Hamilton's agreeable days. He shook Hank's hand warmly, chatted pleasantly with the captain for a moment, and then went and stood beside Abigail, who was still at the piano.

"Sing me the 'Nussbaum,' will you, Abigail?" he asked in a caressing tone, the quality of which was not wholly respectful. "You know how I always enjoy it."

Hamilton had his way, and Abigail sang with all the delicacy of her poetic nature. Then she devoted herself to her grandfather and Hank, and time passed on golden wings for all of them.

As the two old salts were on their way to the hospitable cabin of the *Harpoon* the talk turned, as a matter of course, on Abigail.

"Yes sire, Cap'n, the gal has changed mightily. But somehow or other I'm afraid she's got a pirate craft alongside in that feller that helped her play the pianner."

"Nonsense, Hank, my lad," returned Captain Joel.

Hank said nothing more, but during the rest of the walk he shook his little head and seemed to be engaged in deep thought.

❧XIV❧

A Rolling
Stone

he day for the Camera Club's outing was one of those
beautiful gifts of mellow October for which Old
Chetford is famed above all other New England
towns. The air was spicy and just tempered to the degree for
out-of-door pleasure. It was a day to feel the gladness of young
life, to send the blood along its course in leaps and bounds.

Abigail's spirits were more than characteristically buoyant as
she walked along with Guy Hamilton to the rendezvous of the
club. He was a fine and commanding figure in his fashionably cut
outing suit, and his air was that of a man who knows his social
value and his personal charm. As the unsophisticated girl at his
side stole glances at him from time to time, she was sure that no
one in all Old Chetford could compare with him in the manly
graces, and she felt the pride that is but natural to a young
woman selected by so notable a figure.

At the tomblike old granite City Hall, set in a tiny square
of grass, a dozen or more of the members of the Camera Club
had already assembled when Abigail and Hamilton arrived.

104

Hamilton took special pleasure in introducing his pretty companion to those leading lights of the club whom she did not already know. If she had any trepidation, however, as she was presented to Thomas Harrington—a fat, heavy-jowled banker and the president of the club—she gave no evidence of it.

"Charmed to meet you, Miss Renier," said Mr. Harrington pompously, adjusting his eyeglasses the better to examine her face. "We've all heard, of course, of Mrs. Copeland's protégée; I trust you will enjoy our little trip. I warn you against my friend Hamilton, however. He's a dangerous fellow, very dangerous indeed. Ha, ha, ha!"

And he shook his fat sides and dug Hamilton in the ribs, much to the latter's disgust.

Others of the Hill set were on hand, notably Captain Claybourne, who had permitted himself to be brought by Miss Mehitabel Anastasia Postlethwaite, a maiden of maturity, who wore a bundle of little brown curls at the back of her head and had written a book of poems.

Claybourne looked uncomfortable. For years it had been an accepted fact that Miss Postlethwaite had been setting her sights on the gallant captain.

The Reverend Archibald Greenacre, with an immense tripod camera, hurried up a little later, preceded by his tall and bony wife whose personal appearance might have suggested a cause for his own meekness.

Mr. Alphonso Emerson, custodian of the Old Chetford Public Library, was very nearsighted and could not see to take a picture, but that mattered little to him; a camera was a good enough peg to hang a club on, and he hailed the new organization as distinctly educational. His wife, a simpering lady with a

The beautiful day, the presence of this unspoiled and charming girl at his side, made him for the moment a man of fine impulses.

youthful taste in dress, was escorted by Dr. Hackett, a jolly old surgeon who had seen service in the Civil War.

The company at last completed by the addition of a dozen more couples of local distinction, a start was made for Fairport. The sight of the twoscore persons armed with hand cameras, which were not so familiar at that time, was especially surprising to the street urchins along the waterfront.

As the company wended its dignified way over the long and unsightly bridge that led across the harbor to Fairport, Abigail stepped from the ranks for a moment and looked down along the line of wharves. Yes, there was the old *Harpoon*, distinct because of its spotless deck, and there, too, floated the flag at its bow.

"Grandfather's in," she exclaimed brightly, "and perhaps Hank, too. Dear old ship! Couldn't we take a picture of it, Mr. Hamilton?"

"No, Abigail, not now," he said rather impatiently. Then, seeing the disappointment on her face, he added kindly, "It's too far off. Perhaps when we come back we can go down and get a good shot of it."

On the Fairport side Abigail and Hamilton, tempted by the autumnal beauty of the fields, left the direct road to the fort at the point and followed a little path that skirted a thicket of glowing color.

Here was Hamilton in his cleanest mental attitude toward women. The beautiful day, the presence of this unspoiled and charming girl at his side, made him for the moment a man of fine impulses. As he looked at Abigail, he could not help a comparison of her with Lucy Worth-Courtleigh; Abigail was a simple, fragrant blush-rose beside a brilliant and overpoweringly intense exotic.

The girl was bubbling over with a pretty curiosity that led her to ask all sorts of questions, as if he were a great repository of fact and fancy. It flattered him, and he answered good-naturedly when he could and with humorous evasion when he could not.

"What about your pictures?" she queried, as they walked along at a swinging pace.

"What pictures?" he replied blankly.

"Why, these," she said, tapping the handsome and costly camera slung at his side.

"Ah, to be sure—pictures—of course. Stupid of me. Do you know I'd forgotten all about them? It would be the proper thing to take a picture, wouldn't it? But what shall it be?"

"That!" cried Abigail, pointing to an opening in the trees through which showed a bit of road and a quaint red farm-house. Beyond the russet arch of the leaves glimmered the deep blue of the bay. It was a vista to delight an artist.

"It *is* pretty," returned Hamilton, unslinging his camera. "I'm a bit rusty on this sort of thing, but I guess I can make it work."

"O-o-h!" exclaimed Abigail, as she looked into the "finder" at Hamilton's request and saw the lovely miniature reproduction of the scene. "Isn't that fine? A little to the right. There! Splendid!"

Her hair brushed his hand as she bent to the camera to take her observation. The just-perceptible contact tingled like electricity. He pressed the little knob, and at the dull click she started up.

"You—we shall certainly win the prize with that; the others cannot hope to find anything so beautiful."

"No? They might if they were here," he replied, with a measured emphasis quite foreign to his usual devil-may-care speech.

"Why, what *could* they see more beautiful than that picture through the trees?"

"Just stand there a moment," he said, pushing Abigail gently into the opening between the trees to a spot where the sun shone brightly, "just stand there, and you can help me win the prize."

> Her hat had fallen back, and her hair was blown into picturesque confusion by the soft wind that came up from the Gulf Stream.

With the light on her upraised, wondering face, the girl looked like a dryad of the autumn. Her hat had fallen back, and her hair was blown into picturesque confusion by the soft wind that came up from the Gulf Stream. She was the incarnation of the bloom of life made more exquisite by contrast with the dying year.

"How can *I* help you?"

Another click, and a light laugh from Hamilton, who replaced his camera on his shoulder.

"No more pictures today," he said jauntily.

"No more? I thought everyone was to take ten."

"Not necessarily, Abigail. The prize picture is here," he said, tapping the black box confidently.

She was not convinced. "How can you tell what the others may find?"

"I don't care what they find; none of them can have you in the foreground."

"Me? What has that to do with it?" she asked.

109

"Everything. You see—upon my soul, Abigail Renier, don't you know that you are a beautiful girl?"

She felt the hot blood mount to her face. No man save her grandfather had ever told her such a thing before, and there was the whole world of difference between his simple-hearted flattery and this bold and disquieting admiration. She raised her eyes and found him gazing at her with an expression she could not fathom, but was sure she did not like.

Again and again he kissed her until an incoherent murmur warned him that she was coming back to consciousness.

She took refuge in that woman's way that is as old as time by changing the dangerous subject to one commonplace.

"Don't you think we had better be going on?" she said. "It is quite a distance to the fort."

"As you please," Hamilton replied stiffly, as with something very like a sigh he followed her toward the roadway.

A stone bank was directly across their path, and Abigail stepped upon it with little care. Her one desire was to return to the party and so be rid of the awkwardness that had so suddenly arisen between them.

"Wait! Let me help you," said Hamilton, as he stretched out his hand toward hers.

"Oh, no, thank you. I—"

She was interrupted by a dull grind as one of the stones on which she was standing became dislodged and rolled to the ground. She tottered for an instant, striving to regain her balance, and uttered a sharp cry of pain.

"You're hurt," cried Hamilton, springing toward the swaying girl whose face had gone pale.

"Yes, I'm afraid I *am* a little—I'm such a nuisance. What—"

The world closed in around her, and she would have fallen had not Hamilton caught her in his arms.

"Fainted, by Jove," he exclaimed, gazing down into the white, lovely face in the hollow of his arm. "Abigail! Abigail!"

But Abigail made no sound.

Then this courtly man of the world, this darling of society, this first gentleman of Old Chetford, bent his head and kissed the unresisting lips. As ice will sometimes give the same sensation as fire, so Abigail's cold mouth inflamed his passion. Again and again he kissed her until an incoherent murmur warned him that she was coming back to consciousness.

The sound of wheels from a passing carriage startled him. He realized that the occupants must have witnessed the tableau in which he had been the only active participant, and he wondered who they might be. He had little time for speculation, however, for Abigail had revived and he knew she would need immediate attention.

"It's—sprained—I believe," said the girl, as she tried to put the foot on the ground, and cringed with the hurt. "Oh, dear, I have spoiled your day by my carelessness. I'm *so* sorry."

"Never mind my day, Abigail. Perhaps it's not spoilt after all. Lean on me and we'll get to the red farmhouse somehow. There I can hire some kind of a rig, I guess, and take you home. Come now. There's a brave girl."

"I always thought Guy Hamilton was not exactly the right sort," said Robert Worth-Courtleigh to his pretty wife as they rode along toward the fort. "Who was that girl?"

"She?" replied the lady with a bitter smile. "She's that young upstart that Mrs. Copeland is making such a fool of herself over."

"Oho! The girl she has practically adopted. Captain Joel Stewart's granddaughter. I always understood she was not of the common kind."

Mrs. Worth-Courtleigh made no reply, and as they drove on to the point, he failed to notice that her hands were clutched so tightly together that she was obliged to remove her torn gloves when she reached the scene of the Camera Club's festivities.

But before she arrived at the fort, Lucy Worth-Courtleigh had outlined her plan.

☙XV☙

Gossip
at the Clambake

he constituent parts of the Camera Club had swept
down the road toward the ruined fort without com-
ment on the absence of Abigail Renier and Guy
Hamilton. In fact, the various oddly assorted couples were
quite sufficiently engaged with one another to preclude any
thought of deserters at this time.

Captain Claybourne, for instance, was inwardly groaning as
Miss Postlethwaite was making him the recipient—the very
first, she gushingly assured him—of her "Lines to a Stranded
Dogfish," written during her summer at Quitno Beach.

Miss Nelly Nevins, the schoolgirl to whom all life was a
joke, succeeded in raising dark thoughts in the breast of
Librarian Emerson, her partner. They two chanced to be the
rear-guard of the company.

As they neared their destination, Claybourne became as
uneasy as his philosophical mind would permit over the continued nonappearance of Hamilton and Abigail Renier.

He had been suspecting for some time that Hamilton was not wholly oblivious to the charms of his aunt's protégée, and as the young man's closest friend he had warned him in vague fashion once or twice, always to be met with a laughing disclaimer that did not convince him. The proximity of a pretty young woman was to him always a position of danger, and he knew Hamilton's inflammable nature.

The thud-thud of a horse's hoofs and the rumble of a passing carriage interrupted his musing. Claybourne caught a glimpse of Mrs. Worth-Courtleigh's face. It was set and hard, and bore traces of some unpleasant experience. He wondered if she had been quarreling with her husband, and ended, as usual, by thanking God that he had no wife. Poor Miss Postlethwaite!

Having reached the fort, the camera-armed company broke ranks and entered upon the work of the day. The rocks, the trees, the bay, the city opposite, the ships sliding out of the harbor, the far-off islands, were lured into the little black boxes from every conceivable point of view and with all degrees of skill, varying from the cleverness of Tom Harrington, who was an amateur of great ability, to the wretched, misfocussed attempts of Mr. Emerson. Then they photographed each other in groups and pairs and ones.

"Where *is* dear Mr. Hamilton?" asked Mrs. Emerson at last. "Our pictures will never be complete without him in them and that pretty Renier girl—what can have kept them?"

Mrs. Worth-Courtleigh surveyed the group through half-closed eyelids.

"Really, I think his time is quite fully occupied," she said, in an indolent tone. "He is more pleasantly engaged than he could possibly be down here."

"Nonsense, nonsense," puffed Harrington, growing red in the face at this implied slight on his cherished club. "Hamilton enjoys photography thoroughly; he told me so himself."

Mrs. Worth-Courtleigh laughed with the irritating manner of superior knowledge.

"There are many things he enjoys better, Tom."

"Such as what?" persisted the president of the Camera Club.

"Oh—er—now that I think of it, I believe I saw Mr. Hamilton and that girl together in the field as we passed the red farmhouse—do *you* think she's pretty, Tom?"

A sudden hush fell upon the company. This speech from a woman of Mrs. Worth-Courtleigh's standing, a speech so unmistakable in its virulence, astounded most of them who knew of the friendship between the lady and Hamilton. Even the heavy-witted Harrington saw a great light.

"Whe-e-ew," he whistled under his breath, "so that's the jig, is it? Well, I warned her against him this very morning. Deep girl. The joke seems to be on your Uncle Thomas."

"Come on, people," he cried to his band of enthusiasts, now turned into a set of scandalmongers, "let's go down to the water and see the bake."

There is a fascination in watching the preparations for and the cooking of a clambake known to no other culinary process. With ever-sharpening appetites, the club folk gathered around the fragrant pile to watch the progress of events. Captain Sykes and Artemas were plied with questions.

"Now, Captain," said Harrington with his best air of patronage, "we want you and Artemas to stand up by the 'bake' and be photographed. We are all going to snap you at once."

"But we ain't got much on fer clothes, Mr. Harrington. If we'd a-known—"

"No, no," cried the ladies, "just as you are, by all means. You are *so* much more picturesque."

"Well, all right," said the captain good-naturedly, though a little in doubt as to whether he had been complimented or not. "Fire away."

The members formed a semicircle, and all got their cameras in position. The captain and his thin mate stood at either side of the steaming pile and set their faces into wooden smiles. When Mr. Harrington gave the signal, forty clicks resounded like the firing of some midget battery, and the deed was done.

Captain Sykes lifted an edge of the canvas and took a long, professional sniff. Then he poked about a bit until the red claw of a lobster appeared to view.

"Just five minutes more," he declared.

In the meantime stakes had been driven into the ground nearby, and cross-pieces nailed on them. Over these were placed long boards, and a rude but substantial table was the result. This was now spread with coarse earthen dishes and cups and pewter eating utensils. Artemas had made coffee in a gigantic pot that had once helped cheer a crew of whale hunters beyond the Arctic circle.

"Haul off," came the cheery cry from the captain.

"Ay, ay, sir," piped Artemas, and in a minute or two the luscious treasures of the deep were uncovered.

There was a rush for seats and a great rattling of plates, knives, and forks. Some of the men served as waiters, bringing up the clams in immense breadpans and the lobsters in little wooden trays. The Reverend Archibald Greenacre, who conceived the idea that he ought to be helpful, was among the most enthusiastic of the servers. But when he took his place at the table to indulge in his favorite creature comforts of clams and melted butter, his wife whispered to him with her air of authority—

"Archibald, Mrs. Worth-Courtleigh tells me that she saw Mr. Hamilton kiss that girl of his aunt's. I don't know whether to believe her or not, but it's our duty to find out. Take Worth-Courtleigh aside by and by, and ask him. *He* tells the truth, anyway."

The clergyman's heart sank. He was a gentleman and had little taste for such an errand. But his wife's personality was so much stronger than his own, and her income so much larger, that he had fallen into unquestioning obedience. So, after the feast had been eaten and pronounced the best in Old Chetford's history, he sought out Worth-Courtleigh, who was alone by the water smoking a cigar.

"Greenacre," said the lawyer, after hearing the rector's mission, "what I saw or did not see I conceive to be no one's business but my own. When I enter the profession of gossips, I shall withdraw from the bar—and my practice is quite large at present. Have a cigar."

But he wondered at his wife's injudicious dropping of the story, entirely innocently, of course, and he sighed to think what trouble her thoughtlessness might arouse.

~XVI~

A Shattered Idol

ept within the Bristol Street mansion for the next week or so by her sprained ankle, Abigail found herself a very cheerful prisoner. Guy Hamilton was careful to see that she was provided with the rarest of flowers and the daintiest of sweetmeats, which warmed her instinctively. He himself devoted much time to her pleasure, and talked and read to her with all the ability he possessed.

He looked upon himself as somewhat to blame for her accident; he even experienced a feeling of shame sometimes as he remembered the kisses he had pressed upon her lips under circumstances which he would have been quick to condemn in anyone else. He admitted freely now the fascination of the girl, yet something kept in restraint his impulse to openly love her.

"Confound it," he said to himself one day, as he watched Abigail's lovely profile half-eclipsed by a book she was reading, "I want her, and yet I can't tell her so. What's the matter with me? I never was troubled in that line before."

Then the face of Mrs. Worth-Courtleigh rose into his mental perspective, filled with passion, as he knew it would be should he declare for another and a purer allegiance. He knew that he would be a coward before the fury of a woman scorned.

"Oh, Lord," he thought, "why do we men always get into these infernal messes? Why can't we all be Claybournes, with his 'let 'em alone, and they'll let you alone'? I'd like to cut the whole business, and I might if it weren't for the money."

His uneasiness had been greatly increased that same day by the receipt of a little envelope whose perfume he knew. The note inside read—

> Meet me at two this afternoon at H—without fail. There
> is something of great importance I wish to say to you. L.

He cursed fate again, but he knew he would obey; he felt that in back of the curt command was a threat. He would face the music and learn the worst at once.

He little knew of the struggles that tore the heart of Lucy Worth-Courtleigh before she decided to send for him. Ever since the fleeting sight of that kiss in the fields, her wrath had made such sport of her that even her husband noticed that something was amiss and anxiously asked if she were ill.

In the seclusion of her chamber she chewed the bitter memory, until at times she could have screamed aloud. Pride urged her to let him go with scornful silence; but the jealousy borne of a powerful infatuation spurred her to meet him face to face and see if there were any glimmer of excuse for his conduct.

And so, at the appointed hour, this leader of Old Chetford's "modern" set and this hero of social romance found one another.

The place of their rendezvous was a public house at the northern end of Bristol Street known as Howard's. It had once been the home of a rich old recluse, and even now it looked like a private estate, set far back from the street in a heavy growth of trees and surrounded by a high and dark stone wall. Its reputation for good fare was unimpeachable, but the women who had occasion to visit the place generally did so heavily veiled.

In a little private parlor of Howard's there arose a violent scene between the two, so violent that the landlord had to come and gently beg for less noise. Mrs. Worth-Courtleigh threw all caution to the wind and railed at the unfortunate Hamilton.

"So you have found a new toy to take up your time, have you?" she said when he entered the room. "A new woman to kiss, another to add to your string of conquests, you liar. You'd deny it, would you? Well, I saw you put your lips upon that nameless creature from the wharves, over in Fairport that day. Dear little innocent! She believes you, of course, trusts you implicitly, relies on your honor, and all that. Faugh!"

Staggered at this revelation of her knowledge, Hamilton shifted and stammered in a dazed and helpless fashion that fed the woman's wrath the more. He could not tell the truth about the incident of the kisses, and thus clear Abigail, for he knew that would turn ridicule upon himself and make his transgression all the more unforgivable.

He rang for brandy, drank a large draught, and then stared stupidly at the handsome vixen as she went on with her bitter tirade.

"Oh, you are very much relieved, no doubt," she cried, "to be free of me and to find fresh material for your peculiar style of wooing. And they say this girl is fresh and unspotted with the world, and all that sickening stuff. I say she's—"

"Come now, Lucy. Abigail's a good girl," he remonstrated.

"Bah! Tell me that about a girl who lets *you* kiss her in a country byway. She's of vile origin, and she doesn't belie her stock—But you!" she cried with passionate pleading, "How could you do it, remembering me? How could you, how could you?"

Something—perhaps the sight or the influence of the brandy—suggested a means of escape to Hamilton. He accepted it with gratitude.

"Well, I'll tell you the whole truth, Lucy, and you'll see that I—that you have been treating me very unjustly. I'm ashamed to say it, but the fact is that before I started on that infernal camera expedition I went to the club and got to drinking. I drank altogether too much and wasn't myself at all. What I did in the field I hardly remembered afterward. Do you think I could forget you in my right mind? Never, Lucy. I swear it."

This bit of diplomacy on Hamilton's part was well-timed. Mrs. Worth-Courtleigh's anger had passed its climax, and in the reaction came tenderer thought of the man who so filled her horizon. Partly because she wished to, and partly because it seemed plausible, she believed the story and gradually came to her normal frame of mind.

To clinch the advantage and make her quiet, if nothing more, Hamilton added a lot of vows and declarations of devotion, which would not hurt him, and would do wonders for her peace of mind.

She went home completely mollified as regards Guy Hamilton, but more determined than ever in her hatred of Abigail Renier, who, she reasoned, must have taken advantage of her escort's condition with some deep intent of bettering herself—

perhaps a future marriage. That, she felt, she could and would prevent.

Hamilton sought the sheltering fold of the Attawam Club as soon as the interview was over. He felt that he needed some antidote against the nerve-racking experience of the afternoon, and, as usual, he relied upon alcohol to supply the remedy.

"Oh, hang it, don't make it so hard for a fellow. Don't you know, can't you guess that I love you?"

He drank heavily there, but no resulting joy came. Instead there was only a sodden discontent with life and its burdens. He remembered a new French romance at home in the library, and he determined to go and read it that he might forget his woes.

Without seeing anyone he went directly to the library in search of his book. There he found Abigail, who had been assisted to a seat near the window and was now reading by the last rays of the declining sun. She turned to him with a bright smile and a cheerful welcome.

With the wrath of Mrs. Worth-Courtleigh still ringing in his ears, he looked at this embodiment of purity and truth and felt, even through his drink-dulled brain, a deeper emotion than had ever yet stirred within him. Coupled with this was a sensuous admiration for the girl's warm and radiant loveliness.

He steadied his voice as best he could, and began to talk to her in a vein he had rarely used before. He spoke of her gifts, of her opportunities for storming the fortress of life; he led her to talk of herself, of her aspirations, of her visions for the future. In all this there was on his part a persistent coupling of him and her that she could not fathom. He spoke of *their* future now.

"But why—why should you speak so of me—of yourself?" she asked in large-eyed wonder.

"Oh, hang it, don't make it so hard for a fellow. Don't you know, can't you guess that I love you?"

Had the aristocratic roof of the Copeland mansion fallen about her ears, Abigail could have scarcely been more astonished. Keen of perception though she was, she had seen nothing before now to suggest such a thing. Hamilton had been too impersonal, too much an ideal standing quite beyond her, to dream of as a lover. Now she heard, but did not credit her senses.

"That *you*—love *me*?" she gasped.

She was so startled that when Hamilton drew her closely to himself, throwing an arm about her shoulder, she made no effort to release herself.

"Is it such a surprise, Abigail?" he asked hoarsely, bending his head so closely to hers that their faces almost touched.

At that moment she knew the truth.

She slipped from his grasp and faced him with an air of defiance.

"Abigail! Have you no word for me? I love you—love you. You must know what that means."

"Mr. Hamilton, I am truly sorry. But I fear you are not quite—not quite yourself today."

"Not quite myself, eh? Well, how can a man be himself when he's in love?"

"I mean that you have been drinking," she answered steadily.

"Well, and what if I have?" he asked with a harsh laugh.

"Nothing, except that the words you have just used were evidently inspired by liquor and not by your heart. They are an insult, under such circumstances, which you must not repeat."

By the aid of table and chairs she made her way to the bell-cord, and before Hamilton had fully realized what she was doing, rang for the butler. That mournful figure, after a significant glance at Hamilton, assisted Abigail to her room with elaborate ceremony.

There, in its pure seclusion, the girl wept in youthful fashion over the fall of her cherished idol. She had hitherto admired Guy as a "gentleman," a title which to her stood for a mystical sort of being, the human symbol of nobility of nature and the perfection of courtesy.

And now! As with her childhood doll, she had found that her ideal was stuffed with sawdust. He had become as common as the commonest by his insult to her pride. To be made love to by a drunken man! It was incredibly vile, something of which she felt she ought to purge herself, like the Hebrew women of old. Love? She knew nothing of it, and if this were one of its manifestations, she wanted never to hear of it more.

Being left to his own gloomy reflections in the library by this girl who, strangely enough, was not honored by his advances, Hamilton tried to read the French romance. But the flirtations of the type of heroine in which he usually delighted had no power to charm him now, and at last he tossed the book into a corner and quit the house for the club.

There he found a rather congenial crowd, and again drank more than was necessary. Yet he could not shake off the thought of Abigail's haunting eyes and the vision of her proud face.

"By Heaven," he said to himself, "I almost believe I'd have asked her to marry me."

~XVII~

God Almighty's Gentleman

inner that evening was not a lively meal at Mrs. Copeland's. Hamilton did not return, and his aunt missed the bits of conversation that usually flew back and forth between her nephew and Abigail.

"Well, well, my dear," at last exclaimed the old woman in a sort of mock consternation, "what's happened to your tongue? Off its hinges, I daresay. Ah, it takes Guy to make it wag, not a crusty old creature like me. Odd he didn't come in to dinner. John said he went out not half an hour before the bell rang. Did he say anything to you?"

"No—not about dinner," returned the girl, whose vivid cheeks she feared would signal something to the keen Mrs. Copeland.

"Nor where he was going?"

"No, not a word."

"It's strange he should go off so near dinner time," said Mrs. Copeland.

"Very," assented Abigail, and the meal concluded with no more light on the whereabouts of the wandering Hamilton.

"Play me something, child," said Mrs. Copeland as she called for lights in the drawing room.

The wretched girl was in no mood for the piano, but she sat down dutifully and opened a folio of music at random.

It chanced that Schubert's "Death and the Maiden" came to the surface, and she began to play it gently.

The tender melancholy of the music, the haunting beauty of its harmonies, and the suggestion of its name were too much for Abigail in her overstrung state of mind. She was the maiden, and the "death" was the death of that maiden's dream of a hero. Tears filled her eyes and she could not go on.

"I—I'm not feeling very well tonight, Mrs. Copeland," she said brokenly. "I don't think I'll play any more, if you'll excuse me."

"Tut, tut," the old lady thought, "nerves! A new thing for Abigail. There's something behind of all this, I'll be bound. But I'll let nature work." Then she said aloud kindly—

"Well, well, my dear, you needn't play any more, of course. Get a good sleep tonight, and I don't doubt you'll be all right in the morning. You want to be, for Rev. Kane is coming, you know."

Yes, Rev. Kane was coming, and Abigail felt a sense of satisfaction at the knowledge. *He* was to be relied upon, in any event. She liked him heartily and honestly, and enjoyed his tuition—which had now come to be more the discussion of equals than she realized.

Once behind the locked door of her bedroom, she sat down with her Tennyson, which was to be the subject of tomorrow's talk, and tried to read. But not even the imagery and beauty of the lines could hold the girl's thoughts for long. The handsome face of Hamilton, changed into something coarse and mean, kept arising before the printed page.

"How *dared* he?" she asked herself. What had she done to give him occasion to believe that she could be treated with less respect than other women? She did not know, of course, of his escapades in lower life. She judged his usual treatment of the sex by what she saw him do in his own sphere. She wondered if all the men of the set in which he shone were as empty and false as he.

Even if he did love her, she mused—and the thought gave her no thrill such as she had learned to know in fiction—he had no right to tell her so in such a fashion and in such a condition. Had he been himself, and had he asked her to marry him, she might have hesitated in her answer. She might have doubted whether the tempestuous love of romance, which she knew she did not have, was of the right sort.

But now Hamilton's condemnation was complete. Forgiveness and forgetfulness, the ordinary cures for the little lapses of mankind, would not come in this case, for the truth was clear to her mind that in that scene in the library was revealed the true Guy Hamilton. Forgiveness can never change a fact; forgetfulness is a glossing that cannot be trusted.

She went to bed early, and after a bit more of self-communion in the dark, fell into sound sleep with the locket in which her mother's face was framed clasped close to her heart. Once she awoke and thought she heard an unusual noise in the hall below. She knew it was Hamilton coming home. Had she seen him, her disgust would have been complete.

Next morning Abigail was up with the sun, humming gaily as she busied herself with the pretty mysteries of her toilet. Her mood matched the crisp and glowing morning, and gone was all the dark melancholy of the night before. As she passed through the lower hall on her way to the breakfast room, she caught sight of Hamilton's hat and coat on the hat tree.

"Good morning, Mr. Hamilton," she said, making an elaborate curtsy to the articles of apparel. "I'll venture to say that you do not feel as well as I do this morning."

The owner of the hat and coat did not appear until Abigail and Mrs. Copeland had breakfasted, and then he made a wry face at his egg and dallied with his coffee.

"What a bumbler I must have been," he mused as he tried to find something of interest in the morning paper. "As I remember it, I almost thought myself in love. I'll square accounts with that girl sometime, and give her a lesson in manners. But no open rupture now; Aunt Sarah mustn't hear of yesterday's affair. If one of us is to leave Bristol Street, it mustn't be me."

Now Hamilton was in great physical need of a "bracer," as he termed it, but he thought it best to see Abigail before he left the house, and test her frame of mind as to himself.

He went to the drawing room, where he found her dusting the piano and arranging the music, dressed in the daintiest of caps and the most fascinating of muslin aprons. Hamilton had to admit that she was a delightful picture. Alas, he moralized, that such a fiery nature should be concealed beneath that fair exterior. He was spared the task of framing an introductory speech, for she was the first to offer greeting.

"Good morning, Mr. Hamilton," she said serenely, but with no trace of interest in her voice.

"Good morning, Abigail," and for the next minute or two the man felt as if he were alone in the room. Then he ventured inquiringly:

"Abigail?"

"Yes," she replied, facing him.

"I—I owe you an apology."

"Indeed?"

"Yes, for yesterday's foolishness. You—you do know it was foolishness?"

"Yes, I thought so."

"I was not—not myself, you understand."

"Yes—I—understand."

"You will pardon me? You will not bear me ill will?"

"What you really mean, I presume, is that I will not tell your aunt."

"Well—I—that is—" he stammered, taken aback by this keen penetration of his thought.

"You needn't be alarmed, Mr. Hamilton. I shall not tell her. I owe her too much to wish to cause her the slightest annoyance."

"You are not flattering to me. You would not keep silent for my sake?" he queried.

"Scarcely. Why should I? You did not for your own. If this is all you have to say, I will go on with my work."

Had Abigail seen the look of malevolence he gave her retreating figure, she would have had still further cause to distrust him. But she went about her task with a song very irritating to Hamilton in his present condition. He was about to say something, he knew not what—something, perhaps, he might have been sorry for, when the door opened and the butler announced:

"The Reverend Mr. Ralph Kane."

Hamilton never felt any special interest in "sniveling parsons," as he called them, although this one could have put him in his place with boxing gloves in three minutes, and less than ever did he care to see Kane at this time. So he bolted from the room without ceremony, giving the clergyman only a nod in answer to his salutation.

"I'm afraid Hamilton has been going it pretty strong again," thought Kane as he passed into the library for his two hours' reading with Abigail. "He looks as if he hasn't a friend on earth this morning."

"Well, Abigail?" he said cheerily as his pupil, or, as he put it, fellow student, came toward him.

"Well, Rev. Kane?" she returned in like fashion.

"It's Tennyson, I believe, this morning."

"Is it?" she said mischievously. "Why, so it is. But I'm afraid I've been a bad pupil, for I have hardly touched my lesson. You will have to do all the thinking today."

According to their custom, he began to read aloud. He had chosen "In Memoriam," and as his fine voice rose and fell in the noble cadences of that noble poem, the girl's mind could not resist a comparison of the two men who a little before had been under the same roof.

Up till yesterday there had scarcely been any points of contact between the two in her thought. The one had been the embodiment of the refinement and the courtesies of life; the other she had liked for his genial personality, had admired for his good works, and had respected for his cloth.

A great shock had changed her point of view completely, just as an earthquake might alter the appearance of a familiar landscape. She found herself judging the two men by that great touchstone, the use of which all must learn sooner or later—the test of character. Applying this rule she knew, once and for all, which was the true gentleman.

Although her thoughts were far away from Tennyson, these lines at last struck in upon her musings with a meaning that fairly startled her:

> And thus he bore without abuse
> The grand old name of gentleman,
> Defamed by every charlatan
> And soil'd with all ignoble use.

He felt sure that no love of literature was responsible for those parted lips and those shining eyes.

"Ah, Rev. Kane," she broke in impetuously, "what *is* a gentleman? What did Tennyson mean by a gentleman?"

He was struck by the intensity of her manner and the look on her face. He felt sure that no love of literature was responsible for those parted lips and those shining eyes.

"A gentleman, Abigail? Why, my dear girl, there are as many standards as there are classes of society. My own is simple enough: first of all he is a man. Then he is a courteous man, who will not wound others' feelings without cause; he loves honor and truth and decency. If he is refined and educated and cultured, so much the better, but these things come last."

"A man first of all!" Ah, that was the keynote of the whole matter, thought Abigail. A gentle man! He who is not a man cannot be a gentleman.

131

"But society—" she began.

"Yes, I know what you are going to say, Abigail. Society has a different scale of measurement. The grace of a bow, the suavity of a phrase—that's the sort of thing that makes its gentleman. But I tell you this, Abigail, that between society's gentleman and God Almighty's gentleman there is a gulf of folly and untruth so wide and so deep that the one could not cross it if he would, and the other would not if he could."

He spoke with the earnestness of a prophet of old, with the eloquence of a man who feels that he has a task to perform for the good of the world. Sham, hypocrisy, untruth—these were the devils he was striving to cast out from the social body.

Abigail drank in his enthusiasm as it were an element of the air. She too had begun to feel his love for humanity, his impelling desire to be of service. She had seen the smashing of one of her idols, but she knew now that it was a false god; let him die. She was young, and the earth was fair and bright. There was work to do, and someday she would do it and do it well. Kane would help her, she believed, and she turned to him with a beautiful look of gratitude that he did not then understand, but which he treasured long in his heart's storehouse.

~XVIII~

The Spirit
of Christmas

uch to her disgust, Abigail went out too soon and strained her ankle by a long walk down Promontory Road. She was immensely exhilarated by the sweep of the wind up from the bay, the shrieking of seabirds and the tossing waters before and around her, but when she reached home she could hardly walk, and next day she was again helpless.

It was very near to Christmas before she was able to leave the house. During this time her relations with Guy Hamilton were unchanged so far as a casual observer could have noted. But there were no more of those intimate discussions that Hamilton had come to find so desirable, no more of the stories of society life she had once drunk in with such eagerness.

Now, in skillful butterfly fashion, Abigail flitted away from danger; she treated Hamilton with a deferential courtesy that was far more exasperating than downright rudeness would have been.

"A battle now and then would signify interest," he thought more than once, "but this politeness is enough to madden a fellow. You can't tell *what* it means."

As is the way of the male, the more distant the girl became, the more ardently he wished for her closeness. He was angry with himself, with her and with all his world. Fits of moody depression trod hard upon his heels. He threw himself into his "affair" with Mrs. Worth-Courtleigh in reckless and tempestuous manner, and she no longer had occasion to complain of any neglect on his part. Yet she felt that Abigail was still dominant in his mind.

"I hate gossip, as you know, and yet— well, the best of us seem fond of it."

The Worth-Courtleigh servants were not averse to discussing the matter.

"An' I think she'll get caught yet," said Mrs. Worth-Courtleigh's maid to her favored suitor, the footman, after completing a tale of special interest.

"She'll not either. Mr. Robert wouldn't believe it, even if he found it in one of his own affidavits."

Mrs. Worth-Courtleigh perceived with great satisfaction that the newest and most entertaining gossip was not of herself, but of Hamilton and Abigail Renier. Scandal never sprains its ankle, and she saw her own innuendoes made on that day in Fairport collect and magnify themselves into a story of definite and dark proportions.

Worth-Courtleigh heard the tale in some roundabout way, and was troubled by it—especially as he remembered what he had seen in the fields—and feared there was some basis for it.

"Lucy," he said to his wife at lunch one day, "have you heard this wretched story about Hamilton and that protégée of his aunt's? Oh, yes, I know what we saw, but that hardly accounts for the stuff now going. Somebody has added to it and circulated the thing till it's everywhere. It's a burning shame, I say."

"It *is* too bad, Robert," she replied earnestly. "I hate gossip, as you know, and yet—well, the best of us seem fond of it."

"I'll admit that some reasonably good people love to talk scandal," he said. "It is a form of their self-conceit to imagine that it makes their own virtues more apparent. But that doesn't absolve them from a share in the dirty work at all. I'd like to hear Kane talk on it just for a while."

"Oh, Kane," she exclaimed somewhat petulantly. "Kane is a saint, of course. He is one of those absurd characters who never does anything wrong."

The lawyer laughed.

"I fancy he wouldn't care to hear you say that of him, Lucy, for he is a man and a good fellow to boot. But there are some things he doesn't stoop to do, and tale-bearing is one of them. I wish I could say that of all my male acquaintances."

Later that afternoon Mrs. Worth-Courtleigh went down to the vestry of Saint Agnes Church, which was directly opposite the Copeland house, to help arrange for the Christmas tree to be given in combination by the parishes of Rev. Greenacre and Rev. Kane. She always felt a sense of saving grace in lending her aid to church work of this more tasteful sort.

It was a pretty scene that met her eyes as she entered. The vestry, with its gothic arches of natural wood, its latticed windows, and its cleverly concealed lights, charmed the vision. It was now made still more beautiful by long festoons of evergreen intertwined through the rafters, caught up here and there with gilt stars. At one end was a hemlock tree of generous proportions, and over it, on a long band of gilded paper, the words:

PEACE ON EARTH, GOOD WILL TO MEN.

Mrs. Worth-Courtleigh was greeted with proper enthusiasm by the group of ladies who were engaged in arranging the toys, filling the candy bags, and trimming the tree. Mrs. Greenacre, Miss Postlethwaite, and Mrs. Emerson were there, as well as other members of both churches. Reverend Greenacre was trotting about from group to group, mildly encouraging the laborers but doing nothing himself. The diffident Mr. Emerson, armed with a little wooden mallet, was breaking slabs of candy into pieces small enough to go into the little bags for the tree.

> All that the gathering had heard blown by the wind of malice seemed to culminate here in this little place of God.

Mrs. Worth-Courtleigh, whose artistic sense was recognized to the full, was given the task of hanging the glittering baubles of red, silver, and gold on the tree. The others knelt and stood about her to hand her the various articles she needed.

"We were saying just before you came," observed Mrs. Emerson with her simper, "that it's too bad dear Rev. Kane isn't married. Of course Mrs. Brown is a good soul, but a housekeeper isn't a wife."

"True," sighed Miss Postlethwaite.

"And they say he has *such* a delicate task," continued the librarian's wife, "in keeping off the women. I hear it's scandalous the advances the eldest Prudover girl—the tall one with the hook-nose, you know—makes on every occasion. They say she even ogles him in prayer meeting."

"It is not good for man to be alone," said Mrs. Greenacre.

"But," interposed Miss Postlethwaite, "if he were to marry, of course he would have to stop those lessons with Mrs. Copeland's secretary—the Renier girl."

It needed but the mention of Abigail's name to turn the tide of scandal-mongering in a new direction. All that the gathering had heard blown by the wind of malice seemed to culminate here in this little place of God and under the mimic star of Bethlehem.

One story was matched by another more atrocious until, finally, poor Abigail had not a shred of reputation left her. It was even hinted that she and Hamilton had disappeared after the Fairport incident, and had not been seen for three weeks. Then Mrs. Worth-Courtleigh deemed it best to interpose. Looking down from her perch on the chair, with a sweetly smiling face, she said gently—

"Oh, but we should not be uncharitable toward the poor girl. We should pity her. There is some excuse for her; her mother was an unworthy creature."

Mingled with murmurs of admiration for Mrs. Worth-Courtleigh's tolerance were expressed desires to hear more of the tale.

"Dear me, who was she? Tell us about it."

"Oh, no. I cannot repeat such stories. But as for her child—well," with a raising of her eyebrows and a shrug of her shoulders, "you know society must be particular, or what would become of it?"

"What, indeed?" was the chorus.

"I have always observed," said a new voice calmly, "that when one woman apologizes for a scandalous story about another, you can be almost certain that she is trying to make her hearers believe it is true."

The newcomer was Mrs. Brown, Rev. Kane's housekeeper, a matronly woman who had befriended more unfortunates than she would care to acknowledge. She had slipped in quietly and had heard much of the talk.

"As for Mr. Hamilton and Miss Renier," she continued, "what real evidence is there that their relations have been anything but most correct?"

"My dear lady," broke in Rev. Greenacre, "when a man stoops to a woman beneath him in the social scale, it is not to raise her up."

Mrs. Brown would have argued this theory to the end, had not the attention of the whole company just then been diverted by the appearance of a queer little figure at the door. It was the morsel—Susy Brent—who had long ago warmed Mrs. Copeland's heart by that chat in Rev. Kane's study. She was a quaint sight with her little woolen cap and shawl and a muff that had done its best service long ago.

"Please, ladies an' genlemen," she piped loudly, "is Mrs. Brown up here? 'Cos if she is I've got a message for her from Rev. Kane. Yes, I sees her now," she added, as she went to that lady without hesitation and whispered something in her ear.

"All right, Susy, I'll see to it," said the lady pleasantly. "Now wouldn't you like to look at our tree?"

The others added their invitation. Here was a chance to patronize a poor fellow being, and they gushed over her rapturously.

If the morsel was at all excited by the unusual scene and the more than unusual attention, she gave no sign of it. She viewed the tree with a coldly critical air.

"Why, Susy, don't you think it just be-e-autiful?" exclaimed the intense Miss Postlethwaite.

"Yes, them green things is very pretty," replied the girl, "but they been't good ter eat, be they?"

"Oh, there'll be plenty of candy by and by," said someone.

"Candy; umph! I guess you don't know poor folkses very well. They'd rather have a bit o' cold meat than gumdrops."

"Don't you go to church?"

"Me, mum? No. Look at me shoes an this—" she said, holding out her pathetically patched dress.

"I should think your mother would make you go," said Mrs. Greenacre severely. "All nice little girls go to church."

"Guess Ma don't set much store by churches. Pa was killed paintin' a steeple."

"Ah, in the service of the Lord," exclaimed Rev. Greenacre with great fervor.

"That's what Deacon Snow said, but Ma, she said she guessed the Lord was pretty poor pay. They'd only give her half wages for the last day Pa painted."

The rector raised his hands in horror.

"Oh, such benighted ignorance, such awful sacrilege, such—"

But his wife dragged him away to attend to some detail of decoration, and his sentence was never completed.

Susy retired into the background to watch proceedings. She was made happy by a bag of candy and a doll that Mrs. Brown appropriated for her sake, and she began to think that it might be well to cultivate churches after all. In the midst of the chatter and the bustle, Mr. Emerson entered from the hall.

"S-she's c-coming!" he stammered.

"Who's coming?" was the general query.

"T-that R-renier girl."

"How can you tell, my dear?" asked his wife. "You can hardly see ten feet away."

"W-well, I know it's she," he said, becoming more composed. "I can tell her by that red cloak with the black braid and frogs." This cloak was one of Abigail's favorite garments; it was, in fact, the only article of her mother's attire she had kept.

In a moment more the girl was in the room, fresh and hearty and smiling radiantly at the little party. She bore in her arms a big box containing Mrs. Copeland's offering for the Christmas tree. She seemed the incarnation of good will and holiday cheer.

"Where shall I put it, Rev. Greenacre?" she asked of the rector, evidently regarding him as the responsible head of the affair.

"Put it on the floor, Miss—er—Renier, if you please," he answered stiffly.

Abigail deposited her burden carefully and turned to speak to the others. They seemed extraordinarily busy over their tasks. Only Mrs. Worth-Courtleigh was looking at her.

"How do you do, Mrs. Worth-Courtleigh," she said cordially. "What a pretty effect you've made here."

The woman stared at the girl with absolute unrecognition in her eyes. She uttered not a word, but after a moment of contemptuous scrutiny wheeled about and went back to her tree.

Abigail was transfixed with surprise. Then she understood; it was a joke, of course, some new form of holiday amusement.

"Oh, I see," she laughed, "you are all pretending not to know me so that I shall have to introduce myself all around. Well, I'm Abigail Renier, at your service, Miss Postlethwaite, Mrs. Emerson, Mrs.—"

The words were frozen on her lips by what she saw. Not one of the women turned, nor paid the slightest heed to her words. They had heard, oh yes, she knew they had heard. She blanched with a terrible anger that made all else in life seem trivial.

"What is the—?"

"What is the meaning of this?" she had meant to say, but at that moment her intense pride asserted itself, and she walked proudly to the door, looking neither to the right nor to the left. As she passed into the hall her red cloak slipped from her shoulders and to the floor, but she did not heed it.

"What did they mean—the spiteful cats?" she said, her intent shifting in a moment. "I'll go back and face them."

Just as she reached the inner door, she heard Mrs. Worth-Courtleigh's melodious voice:

"Well, poor girl, what's bred in the bone, you know. She is not responsible for her mother."

Abigail sprang forward like a wild thing, but encountered the tiny figure of a little girl, knocking her down.

"Why, you poor little mite, did I hurt you?" she asked anxiously.

"No, mum," replied Susy, "I'm used to being knocked around; our house is small for so many."

"Have you a mother?" cried Abigail passionately.

"Yes, mum," replied the wondering child.

"Thank God for her, then, dear. Thank God for her!"

"Take these," said the little voice after a moment's silence. The girl held up the doll and the candy.

"These, child; why?"

"I seed you weren't to get anythin' in there, and I came out to give you them things. No, I don't need 'em, really I don't."

141

Tears filled Abigail's eyes and she gathered the little girl into her arms and kissed her tenderly. Then she released her with something that sounded like "Bless your big little heart, my dear," and ran swiftly across the street and into the house.

❧ ❧ ❧

"Bless my soul, what an excitable young woman," observed Rev. Greenacre after Abigail's unceremonious departure. "She's very pretty, though, and it's a pity she's—she's—! Come Emerson, help me with our motto. The 'Good Will' is a little twisted, don't you think? Run and get the stepladder, that's a good fellow."

❧ ❧ ❧

Mrs. Worth-Courtleigh was one of the first to leave the church. When she reached home she undid a paper parcel, took from it a crimson cloak trimmed with black braid, and threw it violently across the back of a chair.

Then she sat down, wrote a note, and sent it to the Attawam Club.

~XIX~

The Whip
of Scorn

he five o'clock loungers at the Attawam Club that afternoon had something out of the ordinary to occupy their minds and their conversation. It had been snowing fitfully during the day, and the flakes were still lazily pirouetting in the air.

It was not for any special love of beauty nor sentiment as to its Yuletide appearance that moved the hearts of the company. The potent fact was that for years Captain Howard had offered a prize of an oversize bottle of champagne to the first man who should reach his roadhouse each season on runners. It was a seductive prize; those who would have scorned a money reward were delighted if they could bring back the great bottle of champagne to the club and make merry over its outpouring.

So the "Leather Room"—thus called because all its fittings, chairs, couches, tables, wall-hangings, and carpets were of that material—was buzzing with talk of the snow, and bets were plentiful as to which member, if any, would bring the prize back in triumph to the Attawam.

Guy Hamilton, who had spent most of the day in these congenial surroundings, was one of those most interested in sleighing wagers. He had kept a watchful eye on the clouds and the snow, and his big roan mare was even now standing in a nearby livery stable hitched into a handsome cutter and guarded by James Anderson, the Copeland coachman. In an hour, Hamilton believed, there would be sufficient snow for the trip to Howard's but he kept his belief to himself.

At last he sauntered nonchalantly into the hall in order to make a quick dash for the stable. He was just about to pass the outer door when a messenger handed him a note. He tore it open, read it, swore roundly, and left the club.

"Hang it all," he declared as he drove toward the Worth-Courtleigh's. "Lucy has the most exasperating habit of turning up when she isn't wanted. What's in the wind, I wonder? 'Come to me at once, and take me somewhere!' Pretty message, isn't it, just as I was about to spring a joke on the boys? Confound it, I'll—"

His further reflections were interrupted by the sight of the cheerily lighted Worth-Courtleigh house. He hitched and blanketed his horse and rang the bell. Lucy herself came to the door.

A smile of satisfaction, of triumph even, lighted her face. It pleased her vanity to think that this big and handsome man should be at her beck and call.

But she was keen enough to note that he was in a bad state of mind. He was there unwillingly; perhaps, she reasoned with a throb of jealousy, perhaps because he had intended to meet someone else.

"Guy," she whispered tenderly, "you are not pleased. Have I—have I offended you?"

When Lucy at last appeared, Guy had to admit that even he would not have recognized her.

Then he told her of the wager about the first sleighing, and how her note had ruined his chances of winning the prize. Her spirits rose at once. Surely, no woman could possibly figure in that plan. She cried gaily—

"And so you think I've spoiled your plan? Don't look so sad. You shall have your ride to Howard's, and I'll go with you. That's all the difference."

"You?"

He looked at her wonderingly.

"Yes, why not?" she answered brightly. "My husband is away, you know."

"All the fellows will be there. Always are on the night of the first snow."

"What of that?"

"What of it? Great Scott, Lucy, don't you realize that they'll see you—recognize you, very likely?"

"I'll risk it. It will add spice to life, and spice is what I need just now."

"But—"

"Besides, I'll bundle up so my own husband wouldn't know me. Now go, and I'll meet you at the corner of Bristol Street in ten minutes."

For three-quarters of an hour Hamilton paced his splendid horse back and forth near the appointed place, in no happy condition. The snow was falling rapidly, and he longed to be off for Howard's. When Lucy at last appeared, Hamilton had to admit that even he would not have recognized her. Her face was enveloped in a large white cloud until only the tip of her pretty nose was visible. She wore a long red cloak trimmed with black braid, a garment that seemed familiar to Hamilton, although not exactly connected with her.

She got in and pressed close to Hamilton as he tucked the wolf skin robe around her. Then the rangy mare was given her head, and they dashed up Bristol Street. Past the northern mills, along by the river they sped, she chatting gaily and he answering in monosyllables. Now and then they overtook some sleighers; a "click" to the fast mare and they were far ahead in a moment.

It was a strange ride in the dark, the snow beating on their faces, the wind rushing past their ears, their hearts filled with stormy emotions of widely different nature. It pleased neither of them, Mrs. Worth-Courtleigh perhaps the less. After a few miles of it she said suddenly—

"Wouldn't it be better to turn back now, and drive straight to Howard's?"

"Oh, Lucy," he returned disgustedly, "haven't you got rid of that idea yet?"

"I'm awfully hungry, and it's altogether the best place in town," she persisted gaily.

He pulled the mare almost upon her haunches and swung her sharply around toward the city.

"Well, if you must," he said sullenly.

He cut the roan sharply with the whip, and she sprang along through the loose snow.

Howard's was a blaze of light when they arrived, and the yard about the house was lively with sleighing parties constantly coming from the city. Hamilton recognized several of his club friends who lifted their hats attentively but scrutinized the well-disguised woman with curious smiles.

"I'm safe, safe!" thought Mrs. Worth-Courtleigh with exultation. "They don't recognize me. And this cloak—ah, I can play the game to the end."

They were shown to a handsome private parlor where a fire was blazing and a dainty table was set for two. Hamilton ordered supper, and the pair sat down cozily before the fire and spread their hands to the blaze. Under the influence of a preliminary drink, Hamilton became quite cheerful and forgot the unpleasant things of life. After all, why should he object to Lucy's coming here if she herself did not? It was a jolly place, she was a pretty woman, and a good supper was on the way.

A party of his friends had a room nearby, and he could hear them talking of him. "We all thought Hamilton had cleaned up the prize," said a voice, "when he disappeared so early. But he wasn't here when we arrived. Funny, what could have kept him?"

"A woman most likely," answered someone else, and there was general laughter.

"You see they know you," said Mrs. Worth-Courtleigh, "and it *was* a woman, wasn't it, dear? But they can't guess who?"

After a most satisfactory supper Hamilton smoked a cigar or two, and the pair thought of home-going. But the door of the room occupied by the clubmen was wide open, unfortunately, and the risk of being detected in the glaring light was too great, even for Lucy's self-will. For an hour or more they were prisoners, until at last the striking of the clock aroused the woman to a sense of other danger.

"Eleven! I *must* get home, Guy!" she exclaimed nervously. "We can manage it somehow. Hold your hat before my face, or your arm, or anything as we go by. Now!"

They glided past the open door unheeded, they hoped, for the party of roisterers within appeared too much occupied with Captain Howard's famous Christmas punch to note what was going on in the hall. But they, too, were on the point of breaking up, and they followed close upon the heels of Hamilton and Lucy. They had just time to bundle themselves into the cutter and be off as the others came down the stairs.

"Good night, *gentlemen*," cried Lucy mockingly, "you'll not see us again." She had full confidence in the roan mare, and it was not misplaced. Hamilton took the back streets and left Mrs. Worth-Courtleigh near her home. Then he drove back to the club.

"And now, Miss Abigail, even if you had a chance to explain, you might not find it easy," she said aloud.

A few minutes later Lucy left her house and walked hurriedly to Bristol Street. She crossed over to the vestry of Saint Agnes Church, and after looking carefully about once or twice, tried one of the windows. It yielded to her touch.

"Ah, I thought so," she said. Then she took a parcel from under her coat, slipped off its paper covering, dropped the contents upon the floor inside, and shut the window.

"And now, Miss Abigail, even if you had a chance to explain, you might not find it easy," she said aloud.

When Hamilton reached the Attawam he found that several sleighs laden with his cronies had just arrived from Howard's. The jingling of bells, the neighing of horses, the shouts of stable boys, the peals of laughter, the snatches of song, the outflaring of light from every window in the clubhouse—all gave promise of a notable "night of it." It suited his mood to perfection, and, giving his horse to a club servant, he hurried into the house and ordered a stable boy to call James Anderson, who was downstairs, to take the animal home.

A not-altogether-sober shout greeted Hamilton as he made his appearance in the Leather Room. It was a hubbub of reproaches, of banter, of invitations to drink (which the delinquent seemed to hear most clearly), and of mock-pathetic requests for light on his peculiar and unclubable conduct.

He noted, with a curious feeling of resentment, that Rev. Kane was sitting in the adjoining "Quiet Room" reading as calmly as if all this din were a part of his own library. What right had a parson to come around spoiling sport by his very presence? Then and there all his latent dislike of the minister crystallized into hot and unreasoning hatred.

A servant came in and respectfully touched his elbow. "Beg pardon, sir, but Anderson is in the office and wants his orders."

He went into the main hall, where he found the coachman, whip in hand, ready for instructions. The crowd, not to be cheated of its prey, followed.

"Come, Hamilton, tell us who the darling was."

"Yes, by Jove, tell us, old man."

"We saw you at Howard's.

"Bet anybody I know who she was," blurted a tipsy young fool, the decadent son of a respected bank president. "I know that cloak she wore, he, he, he! I've seen it before, you can bet your life."

"Two to one you don't know," shouted another reveler.

"Here, now, you fellows," growled Hamilton, "quit that. It's none of your business who she was. Understand?"

"Oh, come, Ham'lt'n," hiccoughed someone pathetically, "don' shpoil the' bet. Betsh ish betsh 'tween gen'lemen."

"Name her," demanded two or three in unison.

"Well, I'll take my oath it was that pretty Abigail—what's her name," cried the tipsy youth.

Hamilton flushed angrily.

Find out for yourselves," he said.

At that moment Kane entered the main hall from the Quiet Room. The sight of him roused all the worst elements in Hamilton's nature and completely obliterated any compunction he might have had on Abigail's account. He would humiliate this meddling parson once and for all, and he saw a clear and effective way to do it.

"It will do no harm to deny such a palpable error as that, Mr. Hamilton," said the minister, in precise and measured tones.

Hamilton looked him over contemptuously.

"Why do you interfere?" he asked.

"Merely as a friend in behalf of a woman; a woman who appears to need defenders," returned Kane, with a glance of scorn about the crowd.

"As a friend, eh?" sneered Hamilton. "Well, you may as well understand that I shall not be drawn into this thing, even if you are."

"But Hamilton, don't you see that if you don't deny it—"

"I'll neither deny nor affirm it," shouted Hamilton angrily. "Suppose it were she?"

"*But it was not,*" said the minister with a deep solemnity that would have carried instant conviction to men in their senses. There was danger in his tone; the justice-loving heart of the man was coming to the surface and the clergyman was fading away, but the fatuous Hamilton saw nothing.

"Oh, wasn't it?" he cried sarcastically.

"You cowardly cur!" cried Kane, starting toward the slanderer with uplifted fist.

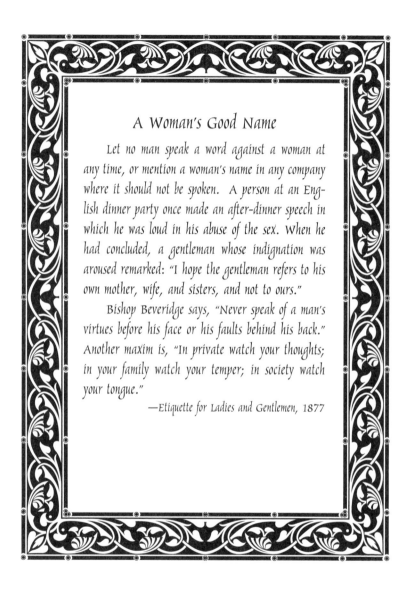

A Woman's Good Name

Let no man speak a word against a woman at any time, or mention a woman's name in any company where it should not be spoken. A person at an English dinner party once made an after-dinner speech in which he was loud in his abuse of the sex. When he had concluded, a gentleman whose indignation was aroused remarked: "I hope the gentleman refers to his own mother, wife, and sisters, and not to ours."

Bishop Beveridge says, "Never speak of a man's virtues before his face or his faults behind his back." Another maxim is, "In private watch your thoughts; in your family watch your temper; in society watch your tongue."

—Etiquette for Ladies and Gentlemen, 1877

Then it was that James Anderson stepped up and laid a restraining hand on the minister's arm. "Don't, sir, don't. It's beneath you. Let me," he said respectfully.

He raised his whip deliberately and struck Hamilton a terrible blow across his fair, handsome face. A livid welt sprang to the surface.

"There's the end of you!" yelled Hamilton, smarting with rage and pain while the crowd rushed in to separate the men. "You'll never use that whip again in the Copeland service."

"Right," exclaimed James Anderson, as with a swift and sudden movement he broke the stock across his knee, "I wouldn't so insult a horse."

~XX~

The Path
of the Storm

bigail went about her little duties next morning with a heaviness of heart that not even the white loveliness of the day could lighten. It had cleared during the night and the sun was shining from a sky of richest blue upon a world as yet spotlessly pure.

A flock of snowbirds swept from tree to tree scattering bright powder from limb and twig, and a few of the venturesome fluttered about Abigail's window sill, perhaps mindful of past favors. But their pretty pleading was unheeded.

The girl was absolutely bewildered by the blow struck at her pride and self-respect by Mrs. Worth-Courtleigh and the others. Women of their rank, she reasoned, would not stoop to such a thing without cause, and she was afraid she had unwittingly done something that merited their displeasure. If so, she could and would make amends. Perhaps Hamilton would find out for her what it was.

But that insult to the memory of her mother! Ah! That was vile, mean, unpardonable. Nothing that she herself had done could justify it. Anger once more ruled her softer mood. But, oh, the hopelessness of it, her own helplessness. She was not an inch nearer the goal of her ambition—to force the world's recognition of her mother's goodness—than she was when Big Bess had shouted her coarse revilings down by the mill. Here in this upper stratum of society she was as impotent as before, yes, even more, for in the old days she had silenced a slander by physical fury.

But what had she done yesterday? Nothing, except walk away like a tragedy queen, as if that would have any effect on women who despised her. She could have cried with mortification and despair.

She threw high her window and leaned out to the glorious air tingling with ozone from the newly fallen snow. Over across the street she saw the pretty little vestry nestling beneath snow-laden branches that seemed bending to give it benediction. Her resentment flamed up anew.

"And they dared," she cried aloud, "in that place they pretend to call consecrated, they dared to humiliate me and lie about my mother. And that 'servant of the Lord,' as he thinks himself—that he should stand there and not say a word for me. Ah, if Rev. Kane had been there—"

A dozen fat little birds, believing that the time for their breakfast had arrived, flew about Abigail's head chirping lustily. She threw a few bits of bread upon the snow.

"You're greedy and quarrelsome, you birds," she said, "but I don't believe you gossip and lie about each other. If I thought you did, I'd never give you a bit of food again."

At that moment she perceived a neat little figure coming up the path. It was that of Nelly Nevins, the prankish schoolgirl. Nelly was an honest and warm-hearted young thing who had become very fond of Abigail in their somewhat limited companionship, and whom Abigail liked in turn for her generous impulses and lack of snobbishness. She was glad to see her this morning, for she felt that the bright girl would be in some degree an antidote for her own melancholy.

"Come right up, Nelly," she cried cordially, "you know the way."

She found her little friend in a very unusual frame of mind. For a wonder, Nelly was ill at ease, and instead of the roguish questions she generally asked Abigail as to how she was getting on in "society," she seemed at a loss for words.

"What would you do, Abigail," she queried at last, "if you were ordered not to do something you wanted to do, and knew was all right to do, and thought you ought to do, and—oh dear, oh dear, I know I'm talking nonsense, but I'm the wretchedest girl—oh, you can't imagine!"

"Why, Nelly, dear," said Abigail, stroking the sunny hair affectionately, "what's the trouble? I didn't know you had a grief in the world."

"I didn't," sobbed the girl, "until yesterday afternoon."

Yesterday afternoon! At that time, too, had come Abigail's most intense bitterness. An evil coincidence, she thought. But if she herself had no comforter, she would be one to Nelly.

"Well, dear," she asked gently, "and what happened yesterday afternoon?"

Then Nelly poured forth her story excitedly. She had been told by her aunt that she must not see or speak to Abigail any more. There had been dreadful stories; Abigail had been shown to be a bad girl, and not fit for her association. Her aunt been very severe and had ordered her to break off all relations with her friend.

Abigail listened with a face as rigid as marble and a heart turned as cold. So this inky cloud of scandal, as mysterious as it was appalling, had already enveloped her best-liked girl companion.

"But," went on Nelly, "I told Aunt that I didn't believe a thing of all the stuff, that I knew you were a good girl, and that I loved you and always would. And I know why they're making such a fuss. The spiteful old cats are jealous because Guy Hamilton speaks to you."

Ah, the light. Cold, cruel, pitiless, but still the light, poured from the innocent heart of a schoolgirl. In that instant the mists rolled away from before Abigail's mind and she saw many things clearly. Not all, for she was as yet ignorant of the origin of the infamous scandal, but she could now understand the scene in the vestry.

"So it is Mr. Hamilton's name they couple with mine," she said in a strange tone that made Nelly's tears break forth again.

The girl nodded her golden head several times affirmatively.

"What do they say?"

"I wouldn't listen to them. I said they were horrid to talk about you."

"You are a dear, good girl, Nelly. I wish I had more friends like you."

"But what can I do?" asked Nelly plaintively. "If I cut you, I'll lose your respect and love, and if I don't they'll send me away to boarding school and forbid my writing to you. So I promised I'd not come here to see you any more. That's better than being sent away where I wouldn't be able to see you even *accidentally*."

"You have done perfectly right, Nelly, and now that I know the reason, I shall not be a bit offended at whatever you do.

We'll leave it to time, dear, and it will come out all right in the end."

After her staunch little friend had gone, Abigail quickly decided on her course of action. She went down to the library and rang for the butler.

"Will you ask Mr. Hamilton to come here a moment, John?" she said to the prim servant.

"He's not down yet, Miss."

"Please go to his room, then, and say that I wish to see him at his earliest convenience."

"Yes, Miss."

When the wondering Hamilton appeared, looking rather worn from his previous night's experience, the girl opened her attack without ceremony.

"There is scandal connecting my name and yours, Mr. Hamilton; do you know what the cause of it is?"

In a dazed sort of fashion he pleaded ignorance. It was impossible, he said to himself, that she could have heard of last night's scene at the club. What else could possibly be in the wind?

She persisted. "You do not know, then, that we are being talked about unpleasantly?"

"No."

"What have I done to deserve this?"

"Nothing," he admitted gloomily.

"Then what have *you* done that subjects me to it?"

"I—I have done nothing, nothing, Abigail, I assure you."

Her lip curled with scorn, and he saw a look in her eyes that he instinctively felt meant grave danger to himself.

"I feel that you are not speaking the truth, Mr. Hamilton. I shall confide in your aunt this morning."

He felt his house of cards tumbling about his ears in an instant. Once that keen old woman interested herself in this affair, trouble would follow as surely as night the day. It was a catastrophe he must avert.

"You—you will tell her?" he asked pathetically.

"Go away with me to a big city— New York. No one will know you there. We can change our names. Come Abigail, you know I love you. Give me your answer."

"Everything that has occurred; all that I have heard."

"No, no, Abigail, there's a good girl. I wouldn't do it if I were you. It will cause her a great deal of pain."

"Perhaps, but I am to be considered now. I owe it to myself, my grandfather, and my mother that I am cleared from this awful suspicion."

Rage for her obstinacy mixed with passion blazed up within him, and he lost all sense of proportion, all power of self-control. He seized her roughly by the wrist. "Listen to me, Abigail," he exclaimed vehemently, "it's a nasty mess, but really I'm not responsible. We can't live it down in this beastly country town. We might as well be hung for sheep as lambs. Let's go away together."

"I—don't—understand."

"Go away with me to a big city—New York. No one will know you there. We can change our names. Come, Abigail, you know I love you. Give me your answer."

All the pent-up emotion of Abigail's hours of brooding burst forth in a torrent the like of which she had never known before. This was the crowning degradation—to be made little of by such a man, to be talked to like a girl of the streets.

"Love me!" she cried, "You! And you again insult me!"

He would have uttered some further protestation, some new plea for his baseness, but the words were frozen on his lips by the appearance of his aunt, grim and terrifying, on the threshold. For him the world seemed turned topsy-turvy; for Abigail an angel of light had come to be her companion.

"I will give you your answer," said the old woman icily. "Leave this house, and never enter it again. Your belongings will be sent to you."

"No, no," exclaimed Abigail in dire distress, "Let me go, Mrs. Copeland."

For reply her benefactor folded Abigail to her arms and stroked her temples compassionately. In this act of affection Hamilton saw the end of his hopes and of his life of ease. In the terror that struck across his soul, he humbled himself before them both.

"Hear me, Aunt Sarah," he pleaded, "before you judge me in such a way. I have meant well by Abigail. I have indeed. I have been crazed by drink and—and trouble. I am willing to sink all personal pride and marry her. Yes, I will give her my name, and she shall lord it over them all if she wishes. What more could a man do?"

"You have heard, my dear. Shall I speak for you?" asked Mrs. Copeland.

The head on her shoulder nodded an assent.

"Then I tell you, Hamilton, nephew of mine though you are, that I would rather see Abigail dead at my feet than your wife. Now go. My house can be your home no longer."

Hamilton went out like one in a trance. He strode down the path and into the street with no object in view, except, perhaps, to find a friend in his hour of need. Friends? They would be few enough once the story of his downfall should be made public. Even Claybourne would very likely turn him a cold shoulder. He directed his steps toward the club in the chance that that worthy might be there; he would tell him all his woes and take advantage of his valuable advice.

After Hamilton's exit, Abigail's overtaxed brain gave way completely under the accumulation of trouble that had borne down upon her. Mrs. Copeland sent for Dr. Hackett in a great hurry.

"The girl's been overworked," said the bluff old physician, "and has been subjected to a great nervous strain of some sort. Let her get a good night's rest, and she'll be all right in the morning."

Reassured by this statement, Mrs. Copeland went away to an important engagement, leaving Abigail lying down in care of one of the housemaids. After a little while Abigail dismissed the servant and lay, with half-closed eyes, trying in some fashion to peer into her own future. As in a dream she heard the doorbell ring, and then became aware of the presence of John, the butler. He mentioned the name of Hank Donelson, and her wandering faculties came home in an instant.

As she rose to greet the honest little sailor, Abigail was filled with dread by what she saw in his face. The grief that was so plainly pictured there spoke of still another calamity on this terrible day.

"What is it, Hank?" she asked nervously, "is anything the matter with—with—"

"Now, Miss Abby, don't be scared," he said gently. "It may not be so bad afater all. But yer Cap'n Joel has been struck down at the wheel."

"At the wheel? I don't quite know—"

"Yes, Miss Abby. He was readin' a little note when all at once he got dizzy-like, an' fell over in his chair. The doctor says it's a stroke. Will ye come down as soon as ye can?"

Without a word Abigail put on her coat and hat, and beckoned Hank to follow. Then together they left the house, and hastened to the old *Harpoon*.

~XXI~

Captain Joel
Sails Away

s Abigail walked to the home of her childhood, she thought of the determination she had felt that very morning to leave the mansion on Bristol Street forever and return to her grandfather, for a time at least.

She had tested "society"—or, at any rate, certain eminent members of it—and she had found how insincere, if not evil, was its heart. How mean and shallow they all were compared with the staunch old friends of her girlish days. Only Mrs. Copeland was true, but even with her affection and confidence, Abigail had now begun to feel like an interloper in the house.

She had been the cause of the expulsion of the old lady's only near relative, had aroused the bitterness of hate between those of the same blood. Oh, what a miserable failure she had been.

Her one consolation was that her valuable experience in business and finance under Mrs. Copeland would make it very easy for her to earn a livelihood for herself and her grandfather.

As she hurried into the entrance of Tuckerman's Wharf, her eyes sought first of all the little mast at the bow of the *Harpoon*. Thank God, the flag was flying and at the top of the staff. She was met on the deck by Dr. Hackett, who could not find it in his heart to deceive this pretty young creature.

He told her how serious such an attack was in an old man, that there was a chance for his partial recovery, but only a slender one. He accompanied her to the large cabin and called old Captain Sykes from the smaller compartment where Captain Joel lay on the bunk that he would not have exchanged for the softest bed in Christendom.

Abigail crept into the little cabin as quietly as possible, but the old man heard her, and he turned his dimmed eyes to her face. She saw in them the light of recognition. She summoned all her self-control that she might appear calm.

"Grandfather, it is I, Abigail," she said softly, approaching the bunk.

The old lips trembled into a smile, and the captain nodded his head slowly.

It was the girl's first coming face to face with serious illness, but her woman's heart told her what to do. She smoothed the pillow under the snowy head and rearranged the bedclothes deftly. She took the rough hand in hers and was rewarded by a feeble pressure of love and gratitude.

The captain began to mutter indistinct phrases in delirium. She bent over to catch his words, terrified at the weird manifestation which seemed to her as the touch of another world.

His grip on her hand suddenly became strong and vicelike, so that she could have cried out with pain had not a greater agony possessed her. After a little his babbling became intelligible.

164

"After, after him, messmates," he cried, trying to raise himself upon his poor, palsied elbow. "Give me the long dart—a-ah—well struck, my hearties. So much more prize money for us all—Struck?—Who struck?—Who struck my Alice to the heart? Eh? What coward killed my girl with his vile hand?—There—that's his face—Oh, I know you, Francois Renier, you spawn of hell!"

In her fright at this awful vehemence, Abigail could think of but one thing to do to calm her grandfather. She drew the little gold locket from her bosom, opened it, and held the face of her mother before the old man's eyes. He smiled with a touch of almost-celestial sweetness.

"Yes, Alice, my dear, dear girl, I know you are pure and good. The world may have its say; we'll live and laugh at it—Miss Petticoats, too—what funny French—for a funny little tot—There, there—She can walk—Come to your old grandpa, and we'll ride-a-cock-horse."

Then suddenly this mood changed, and the captain with a supreme effort almost raised himself to a sitting posture. His face was distorted by anger.

"She do wrong—my innocent darling? How dare they? How dare they say it? Let me go and face them, and I'll—"

As he fell back exhausted, Abigail gave a little cry of horror. She thought that the angel of death had already come, and she threw herself upon her grandfather's breast.

But the end was not yet. Dr. Hackett, who had heard the noise, hurried down and reassured the girl. The old man sank into sleep from which he would probably wake, the physician said, fully conscious and rational. But this did not mean hope, he added. He would return in an hour; meantime Hank and Captain Sykes would be on deck if they were needed.

As Abigail looked about the larger cabin she was filled with remorse at the changed appearance of the room. Not that things had altered a great deal, but there was a lack of that divine something which comes from the touch of a woman's hand. She felt that she had been a deserter, had left an old man to his loneliness—and for what?

She was going about sadly putting things to rights when a bit of crumpled paper on a bench attracted her attention. She would have thrown it into the fire had not an envelope on the floor nearby stayed her hand. All at once she remembered what Hank had said—that the captain was reading a little note when he was stricken.

Mechanically she turned the envelope over and looked at the superscription. In full, round hand it read—

> Captain Stewart,
> The *Harpoon*,
> Tuckerman's Wharf

She looked again at the paper and saw that, folded once as it lay in her hand, it just fitted the envelope. Anything connected with the loved old man was of solemn interest to the girl, and she opened the letter with a feeling of awe. The words that met her eye were seared into her mind a with a red-hot brand.

> *If Captain Stewart loves his granddaughter, he will take her from the Copeland house without delay. Her conduct with Mrs. Copeland's nephew is the scandal of the town.*

166

Stung to madness as she was by this new attack, this horrible assault from ambush, it was some time before she fully realized the full impact of the words. "The scandal of the town, the scandal of the town" kept singing through her tortured brain.

At last her reasoning faculties began to assert themselves, and first of all came the natural wonder who had stooped to such unutterable vileness. She examined the note with some care and found that she did not know the handwriting; it looked forced and unnatural, and was evidently disguised. No clue was to be gained from the envelope.

She took the letter to the cabin lamp and gazed at the words as if she would extract their secret. Happening to hold the paper between herself and the light, she saw embedded in the very fabric itself the letters "A.C."

Then the paper had come from the Attawam Club; she knew that, for she remembered once hearing Hamilton say that the club had its stationery made to order and with the watermark of its own initials.

"Who could have done such a thing?" she asked herself over and over again. If she herself must be made a victim to someone's unreasoning hatred, was it necessary to wound the heart of a simple and inoffensive old man?

This thought filled her with a new terror. Now she understood Hank's remark to the utmost. It was this dastardly letter that had struck down her grandfather and was probably to carry him to his grave. As she thought of what it meant to be bereft of her brave and tender-hearted old protector, she could have killed the unknown author and cheerfully have suffered the penalty.

A movement in the bunk attracted her attention. Crushing the letter in her hand, she turned and, looking into the little room, saw her grandfather feebly trying to beckon to her. She was at his side in a moment.

"Abby, dear," he whispered.

"Yes, Grandfather, I am here. I shall always be here now. I shall not leave you anymore."

"No, dearie, you will not leave me; I am the one who is going. My course in this world is pretty near sailed. I'm going to start on the great v'yge."

"Oh, no, no, Grandfather, you mustn't say such things," sobbed the girl.

"The orders have been given. I'd like to stay for—for you, but the Captain says not."

He tried to raise himself up and looked about anxiously as if in search of something.

"What is it, Grandfather? What do you want?" asked Abigail.

"I—I—dropped a scrap of paper in the cabin a while ago. I'd like to find it."

"Is it this?" asked Abigail, holding up the letter.

"Yes," he replied with a searching look before which she lowered her eyes. "Have you read it?"

She bowed her head.

"Poor, dear child. Too bad, too bad!"

"Grandfather! You do not—"

"How can you hint at such a thing?" he said sternly. "I a mutineer against my own flesh and blood? Of course I knew it couldn't be, my precious."

"Thank God for that," she exclaimed with fervent tears.

"Abby?"

"Yes?"

"What was that poem you read me the last time you were down here? The one about a pilot, you know. Say the lines about the pilot."

"I hope to meet my Pilot face to face, When I have crost the bar," repeated Abigail, in a voice broken with grief.

"Yes, that's it. My Pilot is waiting for me to get aboard. He's standing there—there—behind you. I can't see you now; so dark, and it's yet early—tell them to light the masthead lantern—I—I—Abigail, where are you?"

"Here, Grandpa."

"There, that's a good girl. You always were a good girl. Kiss me. God ble—"

With a deep sigh the noble old mariner set out upon that last mysterious voyage which mortal hand has never yet charted, and from which no ship returns to port.

Abigail looked helplessly for a moment at the still face before her. Then comprehension gradually crept into her face. She gently forced apart the finger that held the letter and secreted it in her dress. In another moment the full flood of her sorrow rushed in upon her, and with a long cry of agony she fell prostrate upon the floor.

Hank Donelson and Captain Sykes clambered down the companionway with blanched faces. They knew too well the meaning of that scream. From the figure on the floor they looked to the white features in the bunk.

"Joel's sailed away," blubbered Sykes, "an' we weren't here to say good-bye."

Hank said never a word, but with tears rolling down his ruddy cheeks stole up on deck and out to the bow. There he hauled the flag down to the deck, walked slowly around it three times, and then raised it solemnly to half-mast.

A self-appointed and tireless sentinel, he paced the old *Harpoon* until a glow in the east proclaimed the birth of a new day.

~XXII~

A Woman Scorned

he two old sailors had at first thought Abigail dead, as well as her grandfather, when they found her prostrate on the floor of the Harpoon's cabin. They gazed at her with awe, neither of them venturing to touch the beautiful white face or to raise the shapely body from its hard resting place.

Dr. Hackett's bustling entrance roused them from their mournful inaction, his warmly human personality cheering their distressed souls as by magic; so deep was their simple faith in his power that they would not have marveled very much had he restored their friend to life.

The physician's practiced eye saw at once that their duty was to the living—the girl upon the floor. He applied some simple restorative to Abigail, and soon the warm tide of life flowed back, but she awoke to but a dim realization of the tragedy about her. Her brain had yielded to the intensity of the strain put upon it, and she smiled vacuously at her distressed old friends.

"Grandpa is asleep," she whispered, "and we must make no noise; he is so easily disturbed. I think I will go to bed, too."

The arrival of Mrs. Copeland at this juncture relieved Captain Sykes of a great load of anxiety. She had been thoroughly frightened when she returned home to find Abigail gone away in her condition, and had bidden James to drive with all despatch to Tuckerman's Wharf. She now stood as a ministering angel in the cabin of the *Harpoon*.

She led the unresisting girl to the carriage, into which Anderson lifted her with tender respect. There Abigail swooned again, and when home was reached she was in a state of complete collapse.

As the girl's clothing was loosened, the fateful note dropped upon the floor. Mrs. Copeland felt that she was entitled to read it, and she did, to her horror and amazement. She, too, discovered the "A.C." watermark, and her first thought was of Hamilton. She thrilled with shame and indignation that a man could make so vile a thing of himself for the sake of future expectations. But she could conceive of no one else with a shadow of motive, or perhaps a heart black enough, for such a horrible assault.

Dr. Hackett pronounced Abigail's illness brain fever, and he had difficulty in saving her life. For days her faint spirit hovered on the borderland, then came back to earth. During the anxious weeks, Mrs. Copeland played the nurse with a loving patience and solicitude that recalled other days in her life. She came to love the girl more than ever. Few could have withstood Abigail's almost pathetic gratitude and her desire to get well so that she might be of service again.

As the girl slowly came to her strength, the good doctor insisted that she must have complete change of scene and must go from Old Chetford for an indefinite period if her complete recovery were to be expected. The continuance of old associations would be disastrous, he insisted. Mrs. Copeland approved of the idea and went to Worth-Courtleigh's office one day to make arrangements for the care of her property during any length of time she might stay away. She trusted the hard-headed lawyer implicitly, and she gave him full power of attorney to act in her behalf in any business matter.

"By the way, Mrs. Copeland," he said, when the important details had been settled, "I find in looking over Captain Stewart's affairs that the old man assumed some obligations— in Abigail's interest, the poor old fellow thought, I suppose— that must be paid directly. What do you think it best to do?"

"I'll pay it at once; what's the amount?" asked the lady, drawing her checkbook from her satchel.

But even as her pen was dipped in the lawyer's ink, a second thought came to her. She realized that Abigail's peculiar pride might rebel at any payment of her grandfather's debts without her knowledge, and she closed the checkbook with a snap.

"*That* won't do at all," she exclaimed. "I ought to have known better."

"I think," said Worth-Courtleigh, "that we'd better sacrifice sentiment and sell the *Harpoon*. Abigail cannot use it anymore, and it would just about square things up. The other little property of Captain Stewart's I find I am not able to touch for the purpose."

"Well, I suppose that is best," returned Mrs. Copeland with a sigh. "The ways of the world are not the ways of sentiment."

It was during this period that Rev. Kane justified all Mrs. Copeland's faith and regard. He was a tower of strength to the house, and his cheery presence and entertaining chat did much to help Abigail on to recovery. He, most of all, noticed the immense change in the girl. Physically she was wan, listless, and bereft of all her old rounded prettiness; spiritually she was a different Abigail. No more of the old exuberance was visible, yet she was still as kind and considerate as ever. But there was a touch of hardness, a suspicion of pessimism, that he did not like to see. "The crucible of suffering has refined her nature," he thought. "I hope it has not embittered her."

Once when some visitor chanced to mention Hamilton's name, he saw a hatred burn in the brown eyes and set the fine features into something that almost appalled him.

As for the man who had wrought this great change, he had declined to accept his dismissal from the Copeland mansion as final. That his allowance had not yet been stopped he looked upon as a favorable omen, and he made several attempts to see his aunt, but with no success. James Anderson had been temporarily installed as butler during an illness of the solemn John, and Hamilton had little inclination to attempt to force his way into the house. He haunted the club perpetually, but his morose spirit and excesses in liquor caused him to be let alone there. Even Claybourne avoided him.

When Abigail was well enough, Mrs. Copeland told her gently about the proposed selling of the *Harpoon*. She approved the plan for, while grateful for Mrs. Copeland's offer of assistance, she felt that her grandfather would not have wished it otherwise.

At first she did not take kindly to the suggestion of going abroad. She felt that she should stay and face the little world of Old Chetford, that it was beneath her moral courage to run away under fire. She said as much to her benefactress.

"But Paris, child, Paris," the old woman exclaimed.

Ah, Paris! The city of her childish dreams, the vision of her artistic nature, and above all, the home of her ancestors! Perhaps—but she checked herself; from now on she would deal with the hard, common-sense facts of life. Yet in the end Paris won her, and she made preparations for going.

Kane advised the exodus with all the earnestness of his sincere nature. In doing this he was tugging at his own heart-strings, for he knew that with the departure of Abigail and Mrs. Copeland much of his own interest in life would go, too. But he felt it best that Abigail should grow to complete womanhood away from Old Chetford, the scene of such tremendous shocks to her faith in human nature.

One day, at Abigail's request, Kane drove her over to Mill River, and there in a little old church they found the record of the marriage of Alice, daughter of Joel Stewart, and Francois, only son of Adolph Renier, Count de Fornay. The minister witnessed the copy of the record before a notary, and Abigail took possession of the paper. When asked by Kane what she meant to do with it, she would only say—

"The day may come when I shall need it."

Just before Mrs. Copeland and Abigail were to start for New York, where they would sail for France, Hamilton made one last desperate attempt to see his aunt. To his great joy he was admitted to her presence. The old lady wasted no time in greetings, nor did she allow Hamilton to enter upon his intended plea of mercy. Going straight to her desk, she brought out the "A.C." note, and thrust it before his eyes.

"Did you write that?" she asked slowly.

"To whom?"

"To Captain Joel Stewart; they say it killed him."

Hamilton read with ever-deepening astonishment and horror. He began to see the enormity of the crime against the girl, and he was fairly stunned by the discovery.

"Upon my soul, Aunt," he declared earnestly, "I had nothing to do with it—know nothing of it. You surely cannot imagine that I would stoop to such a thing as that?"

She made no reply but looked at him in her cold and searching way. Then she bade him an emotionless good-bye, and he left the house.

He hurried to Mrs. Worth-Courtleigh's with new foreboding heavy in his heart. Could she have done this thing, and, by its terrible consequences, have added to the wrecking of his fortunes? It was almost incredible, but he would have the truth.

The woman's exultant face when he told her of the note and its results was enough. She was self-condemned before a man who was himself no pattern of morality, but who was disgusted nonetheless by such vileness.

"Great God, Lucy," he whispered hoarsely, "you don't mean that you—you wrote—"

"Yes, I did write it. Hadn't I cause? I hated the brat, and I hate her now."

He stared at her in silence for a moment.

"You are worse than I thought you, Lucy," he said slowly.

"Oh yes, of course! Because I have made it uncomfortable for the doll of a girl you are in love with. Ah, that's the truth, and you wince, don't you? So now she's going away, and you're in mourning, coming up here to do the Pharisee over me. You'll have time enough to get used to being without her, for she'll not come back in a hurry, I fancy."

"Yes, time enough," he cried in a storm of anger, "and all through you. But I'll not have time to come here again for, by heaven, I've had enough of you."

And then, despite the pleading of the woman, he left the house of Robert Worth-Courtleigh never to enter it again.

At
Hank Donelson's

he Rev. Kane sat in his study on the Saturday evening after the departure of Mrs. Copeland and Abigail. Gazing at his open fire of big hickory logs, he mused on many things as his eye was held by the flame pictures that danced into view and away.

Chiefly his thoughts were of the lovely girl, whose wan smile as she had bidden him an earnest farewell at the station was vivid in his memory and was long to remain there unchallenged. Of her eventual restoration to health he had no doubt; he only feared that no medicine and no new interests could ever quite bring back the beauty of innocent faith in the goodness of the world that had once so distinguished her. She had changed utterly from a trusting girl to a reserved woman, as a sensitive plant closes at the touch of a rough hand.

"The iron has entered her soul, and it rankles. Poor child. She has a long path of shadows to travel before she gets into sunland again. When she does—well, it will be worth some man's while to be there to see the unfolding of her nature."

He took a last critical look at the sermon that was ready for tomorrow's preaching. "And the greatest of these is charity" stood out in bold handwriting on the first page of the manuscript.

"I'm afraid," thought the clergyman, "that the human shell is quite as much in need of charity as of any other divine attribute. We all agree in theory, but as for practice—ah, we differ as violently as the doctors of different schools, except that we are prone to give as minute doses as possible."

As he read, the vision of that Abigail of other days would come before the written words. He saw her brilliant, vivacious, sweetly imperious as she was, he remembered, when with shining eyes she had asked his definition of a gentleman. The scene of the little festival in the cabin of the *Harpoon*, where she had blushingly announced her intention of becoming a great lady, was still vivid before him. He tossed the sermon on the table and rose to pace back and forth before the fire.

"A proud creature," he mused again, "she even preferred to sell her beloved old *Harpoon* rather than accept help to pay her grandfather's debts—I believe I'll go down to see Hank and find out what's been done in the matter. The cold air will blow the cobwebs out of my brain, anyway."

The Donelsons lived in a quaint little wooden house on a quaint little cobble-paved street near the waterfront. The windows were near the narrow sidewalk, and as Rev. Kane reached the door he saw a queer picture within. Hank's little legs were stoutly spread apart in the attempt to stretch a hooked carpet that was being laid by his sister Tilly, who was doubled up like a jackknife driving tacks.

The sitting room, where this ceremony was in progress, was a tiny, low-studded apartment with white wood wainscoting reaching as high as a man's waist and walls of fantastically stenciled figures of impossible birds flitting about.

Tilly greeted the clergyman with proper respect but no enthusiasm.

"Howdy do, Parson," she mumbled, her speech being somewhat impeded by a mouthful of tacks. Hank was more cordial, hoping to knock off work in honor of the visit.

"Now, you, Hank Donelson," sputtered Tilly through the tacks, "you jest keep right on stretchin' this ere carpet 'cause the best room's got to be ready for Sunday, minister or no minister."

"Quite right, Tilly," assented Kane smilingly. "Business before pleasure every time. Can I help you in some way?"

"Wall, if you want to be useful, just get a chair and put it in the middle of the carpet, then sit on it as hard as you can. When I say 'push,' you put yer heel in an' shove the carpet toward me."

"I'll try," replied the clergyman with due meekness as he took his seat and waited for the word. He was amused at Hank's awkward efforts to drive tacks.

Between hammer taps and Rev. Kane's "pushing forward" on the carpet, there were bits of conversation and, as a matter of course, the talk at last centered upon Abigail. Hank's fear lest she should become "Frenchified" and learn to "eat frogs" was almost pathetic; the simple-hearted little fellow could scarcely comprehend the ethical lesson of the girl's departure. But the shrewder and more worldly-wise Tilly understood, and was not slow in uncorking the vials of her wrath on Old Chetford society.

"Ain't them big-bugs nothin' better to do," she asked angrily, "than to go 'round tellin' lies 'bout a good gal like Abby Renier? There's a lot o' glass houses up on the Hill, an' thin ones at that."

She emphasized her points by vigorous flourishes of her hammer, and once or twice unthinkingly hit Hank's neat little boots as a means of laying special stress on her remarks. He was glad of the diversion that came presently.

It was Susy Brent, the morsel, who suddenly stood in the doorway as if she had arisen through the floor. It was characteristic of Susy that one never heard her approach. She held a cup in her hand and looked appealingly at the angular mistress of the house.

"Come to borry somethin'?" said Tilly sharply. "What is it you want this time?"

"Ma said if yer *could* spare a cup o'merlasses—Billy's been cryin' fer somethin' sweet all day, an'—"

"There, there, child, of course I'll spare it," said Tilly, relenting.

Kane, whose fancy had been taken long ago by the eerie little daughter of the mills, spoke to Susy kindly, and soon had her completely at ease. Something they said must have suggested Abigail to the girl, for she suddenly asked—

"The pretty young lady on the Hill—her as used to live in the *Harpoon*, an' work in Number One—ain't she gone away?"

"So *you* know that?"

"She's gone on a big ship, they say. I'm sorry, I am; she wuz kind to me."

"She is kind to everybody."

"Yes, I guess she is. And everybody had ought to love her, hadn't they? Do *you* love her?"

This matter-of-fact question from a child thrilled Kane through and through. It was more than he had dared ask even himself. Now he felt like crying out his answer: "Yes, I do love her; I love her with all my heart and soul; I shall always love her!" but as men will, he held his peace.

"Well, *I* loves her," said Susy, after regarding him solemnly for a time. "Why did she go away?"

"She has been very ill."

"Spects she got cold at the Chris'mas shindy at the church."

"Oh, you *were* there, weren't you?"

"She went home without her pretty red cloak. How I'd like one," she sighed. "I wuz a-goin' to take it over to her house, but Mrs. What's-her-name took care of it and wrapped it up nice in paper."

"A red cloak?" asked Kane vehemently as a great light began to shine in upon him. "Who took it, Susy? What was her name?"

"I can't remember. But she's the stylish, red-haired lady lives in the lop-sided big house on Thorn Street."

"Mrs. Worth-Courtleigh!" exclaimed the minister, jumping to his feet with an air of sudden conviction.

Susy's surprise at this very unusual exhibition of excitement from a clergyman was cut short by the call of Tilly from the entry:

"Here's your molasses, you mite."

Out in the dark hall a wonderful thing happened to the little girl. Her hands and pockets were filled with cookies, and then she was kissed and pushed out of the front door.

When the carpet had been laid to Tilly's satisfaction, Rev. Kane took Hank out for a little walk. They conversed earnestly together for some time, then separated with a hearty hand-shake.

~XXIV~

Society Is Scandalized

alph Kane's sleep, after his return from Hank's, was vague, confused, and troubled. Once he seemed to be on a vast, gray, windy plain, ever pursuing a phantom with a red cloak. He awoke panting and with a heavy weight at his heart that he at once recognized as an established acquaintance; it would be there many days, he feared.

He knew that Mrs. Worth-Courtleigh was the principal in a deep-laid plot to destroy the reputation of an innocent girl. That night of violence at the club was all plain now. This woman was Hamilton's companion on the sleigh ride and at Howard's, and she wore Abigail's red cloak. That she was able to get possession of the garment was all due to the malice and uncharitableness of church people in a house of God! How did wheels work within wheels for the crushing of a blameless spirit?

Poor Worth-Courtleigh, too! Kane felt that such an honest-hearted gentleman ought to know the truth, and yet he would not have been the one to tell him.

The walk to the church, during which he met many of his parishioners whom he knew had helped circulate the scandal, wrought his feelings to a high pitch of nervous excitement. When he reached the house of worship he was like some prophet of old stirred by the evil of the world to deliver a denunciation from God.

The Third Congregational Church was a plain, square structure of wood, clapboarded and painted white, with green blinds hanging at its small windows. The ground floor was occupied by the vestry, where Kane had occasionally given little dramatic entertainments and had shocked some of the more uncompromising of his flock. The main auditorium above, reached from the street by a U-shaped pair of stone steps, was of antique simplicity.

The church was well-filled, as usual, when Rev. Kane entered the pulpit. The eloquence and originality of his sermons had long been recognized in Old Chetford and beyond, and that he was sometimes considered eccentric, always drew strangers to the Third Congregational. But those who knew him best noticed this morning that there was an unfamiliar look upon his face and a peculiar sound in his voice as he read the hymns.

As the minister rose for his sermon and nervously opened his manuscript—which was merely for occasional reference, as he always preached from memory—his eyes fell upon Guy Hamilton sitting in a pew well in front and to the left. The man was debonair, well-groomed, faultlessly dressed, the perfect picture of a member of high society. He was a visitor with the family of a wealthy merchant, and he sat beside the handsome daughter of the house complacent, self-satisfied, and seemingly happy.

A flood of bitterness swept over the preacher's soul as he saw this woman, radiant and honored, and then thought of the sad-faced girl driven across the seas by the undeserved scorn of some of these very people to whom he was about to deliver a sermon on charity. Charity! What charity had they for her in the hour when she needed it most? He felt that he could not bring his lips to utter the conventional words he had prepared for his flock. He would speak what was within him, let the consequences be what they might.

He thrust his sermon aside and rapidly turned the leaves of his Bible for a moment. He stopped at the Book of Proverbs, and in a voice kept calm only by the greatest effort he read with deep and deliberate solemnity these words—

> *The lip of truth shall be established forever: but a lying tongue is for a moment.*
>
> *Deceit is in the heart of them that imagine evil: but to the counsellors of peace is joy.*

He began by speaking about evil reports, how they traveled on the wings of the morning, and how they were believed more readily than good words. Let one be accused of something bad, he said, and the world accepts it as a new gospel; let good deeds be reported by some kindly soul and people are forever poking about with their muck-poles to discover an improper motive behind the acts.

Then, with ever-increasing eloquence and fire, he described the power of scandal to blight and ruin, even if it dealt wholly in untruths.

"I am firmly persuaded," he declared, "that instead of believing a story false that ought not to be true, society's course is to accept as true everything evil, even if false.

"We have our laws and our jails for the corrupters of the body politic, but I say to you that the worst enemies of decency are the peddlers of malicious tales. And none but those who love to hear scandal like to tell it. Many a man has been hanged, many a woman has been imprisoned, who did less mischief than the coiners of forged stories.

". . . . instead of believing a story false that ought not to be true, society's course is to accept as true everything evil, even if false. . . ."

"The object of scandalous reports is generally helpless, for he has an army arrayed against him, an army of gossip-mongers, whose ranks are ever swelling and whose tents always encompass him about."

In the little pause that followed this period there was an uneasy stirring of the congregation, and the people looked at one another in blank amazement. What had this strange minister of theirs in mind that he should forsake the beaten path of beauty of diction and polish of style for such simple, direct, and earnest admonition? Was this but generalization, or was it the prelude to some tremendous personal denunciation that should shake the church from foundation to spire?

"Oh, men and women," continued the speaker, "I would to God I could adequately picture to you the sufferings of the victim of unjust scandal. Such a victim has just been driven from amongst us. Some of you know the one to whom I refer; the rest are probably aware of the facts, for when scandalmongers triumph they are quick to proclaim their victory. Innocent or guilty, the result is generally the same, if the target of malice is a woman.

"Innocent or guilty," he cried, his fine voice trembling with emotion, "that girl is today an outcast!"

So this was the application! The "victim" was all but named, and few in the church did not know the story of Abigail Renier. Guy Hamilton suddenly became the central figure in the sanctuary, and he flushed deeply as he felt his disagreeable prominence. He cursed the hour when he had allowed himself to be put in the power of this fearless minister who had more than once shown animosity toward him.

Among the others there was a tense silence, a dread and yet an eager desire to know where the thunderbolt of the preacher's righteous wrath would next descend. They were not long in doubt.

"That girl is today an outcast," he repeated in ringing tones. "Were she to enter this church this morning for the consolation of the spirit of God, which one of you would invite her to your pew? How many of you would not gather your garment about you in fear of contamination if she but touched its hem?

"But the man—what of him? If you meet him after this service, as many of you doubtless will, will you fail to smile upon him, to invite him to your houses? Will you, fathers, warn your boys against him? Will you, mothers, close your doors to him when he comes to visit your beloved daughters?

"Yet if guilt there was, why does he go free? And the woman—why is she driven out from among you? If there was no guilt, it was he, not she, who assumed its hideous mask. And yet your smile for him will be as bright as your chilling glance at the victim of his deceit. You will say that youth—male youth—must have its fling. You will plead custom, convention. Shame upon such custom! Horror for such convention!

"I tell you, my people," he thundered, stretching his right arm toward heaven, "*at the judgment bar of God there is no sex in sin!*"

Though there was more of the sermon, somewhat along the lines originally planned, that was the climax, poured out from a man's depth of tenderness for a woman who had been misjudged and wronged. It was a union of love and conviction that no man should have been able to resist.

But there were many, and especially of the more rich and powerful set, who were scandalized beyond measure at what they termed their pastor's unwarranted abuse of society, his pointed insult to a man of position, his almost indecent reference to things their daughters ought never to hear mentioned. As the congregation came out into the brilliant sunshine, the comments on the sermon spoke clearly enough of its unpleasant effect. There were threats of secession, hints at parish meetings, and suggestions of dire discipline for the minister who had dared go beyond his province as a servant of the Lord.

The few who believed him in the right were overawed by the carriages and fine garments of the indignant section, and quietly went their ways on foot.

So, too, went the Rev. Ralph Kane to his study, filled with a grim satisfaction he had not known for many days. He believed that he had spoken—or rather that a higher power had spoken through him—truths that would one day bear a rich fruitage. Of the immediate consequences of his daring he concerned himself not at all.

He sat down at his table to write a letter. Three times he half-filled a sheet, and as many times he tore up what he had written and threw the pieces of paper into the fire.

❧XXV❧

Modern Chivalry

ane was up early the next morning looking after the details of a new plan he had devised to help the wage earners of the city to habits of greater frugality. This was a penny savings bank that he had convinced one of the strong financial institutions of Old Chetford to establish. On his way downtown he met Tom Harrington, who had promised to assist him.

"Morning, Kane," said that sleek and well-fed financier, "hope you're all right after yesterday. Awful row all over town on account of your sermon. You meant well, I know, but I may as well tell you in a friendly way that your position on such matters has created dissention in the church. I sympathize with you in all your efforts to do good, but—"

"How about the penny bank business, Harrington?" asked the minister, wholly ignoring the matter of the sermon. "Can you give me that help you promised for this morning?"

"The bank? Oh, yes, I remember. But to tell you the truth, Kane, I'm not quite prepared to go ahead with the matter today.

I shall want a little time to look into it further. Come around in a week." And the pompous banker strode away to his private office.

The minister's disgust at this easily understood cooling on the part of Mr. Harrington was quickly ended by the sight of Robert Worth-Courtleigh coming down the street to his business. Here was a man he could rely on, he thought, with a feeling of thankfulness that the world was not wholly filled with shams.

"How are you, Kane?" said the lawyer heartily with a warm grip of the hand. "You're just the fellow I wanted to see. I've got the deeds by which Mrs. Copeland gives your association the land and building of the Coffee House and I want you to have them now."

He fumbled in his coat pockets with a perplexed air, but no papers were forthcoming.

"By George," he said, "I've left them in my other coat, after all. But I'll go right back and get them and drop into your study with them on my way down."

"Don't go back on my account, Robert," returned Kane. "Any other time will do. I'll admit that I'm like a child that's been promised a new toy, but I don't want to put you to any trouble."

"No trouble at all, Kane. Besides, I've left some of my own papers, too, and I must have them. I'll see you later perhaps."

When the lawyer reached home he went directly to his desk in the library. Lying upon the broad, clean blotter he saw one of his wife's pretty squares of note-paper filled with her large and bold handwriting. He would have quietly put it aside unread, but that the word "Dearest," with which the epistle began, thrust itself upon his sight.

"Ah, to me," he said softly, "what a queer child Lucy is, to be sure." Then he read on.

"You will be surprised, I know, at my writing you—"

"Well, it *is* unusual. She wants a new dress or a string of pearls, I suppose."

"But I feel that I cannot wait till I see you before I speak—"

"It certainly is pearls."

"I may be doing a foolish thing, but I feel I must tell you. You know that I love you. I have given you ample proof of that, but—"

"But what?" thought the lawyer, with some misgiving, as he turned the sheet.

"I fear that you have never really returned my feelings. But I tell you, Guy Hamilton, I will not be thrown aside like a discarded glove. I—"

Here the letter ended abruptly, and the ink of the final word was scarcely dry.

The first effect of a tremendous shock upon an exceptionally strong man is often that of dazed astonishment and a refusal to credit his own senses. So it was with Robert Worth-Courtleigh. He turned the letter mechanically and dully read it again.

As the full force of its terrible meaning gradually swept in upon his brain, a purple flush spread over his face, then a weakness that made him clutch the desk for support. He sank into his chair and bowed his head on his arm, grasping the letter in one hand as if it were some animate thing whose life he would strangle out.

So his wife found him when she hurried back to finish the note from which she had been called by a servant. The unexpected sight of him at that desk, the thought of what must have happened, threw her into a panic.

"Oh—Robert," she screamed, "how—you—startled me. Are you—ill?"

There was no answer from the bowed figure. She would have thought him dead, perhaps, but that his right hand trembled as it clutched the detestable note. At the sight of the bit of blue paper she knew that the hour of reckoning had struck. She turned to go, with a great desire to postpone the evil moment, but her husband heard her and slowly raised his head.

At the sight of the bit of blue paper she knew that the hour of reckoning had struck. She turned to go, with a great desire to postpone the evil moment.

For one brief moment the drawn and haggard face aroused within her a sharp pang of remorse and regret, such as a woodsman might feel when he has felled a great and noble tree. It was a passing emotion, however, for there followed a flood of defiant indignation as she realized that this man held her at his mercy. His very silence increased her bitterness. They looked at one another like strangers.

"Well," she finally cried, "you have read—have dared to read—my private correspondence."

"Would to God I had not, Lucy," he answered slowly. "Heaven help me, I thought—I thought it was for me."

"A likely story," she sneered. "Well—what do you propose to do?"

"To do?"

"Yes. With me? With him? With everything?"

At this the man within him asserted itself, the lawyer training proved its strength, and Worth-Courtleigh faced his wife with dignity and courage.

"There is but one thing to do, Lucy," he said. "You may— you must stay in this house. There is no other protection for you. But remember you stay not as my wife, but as my guest whose residence with me the law permits. As such your wants will all be provided for, and you will be allowed a sufficient income for the continued entertainment of your friends. You will, of course, never see *him* again or have the slightest communication with him. Should he ever come to my house, I warn you that I would treat him as I would a mad dog."

The fairness of the man she had so foully wronged, his calmness, his generosity, his consideration for her, instead of softening her heart to penitence, or at least to respect, roused all the evil qualities within her. Had he raved in melodramatic fashion, had he cursed and threatened her instead of ending the interview with the sorrowful admission that the wrecking of their home might have been partly his fault because he had left her so much alone, she would have felt less bitterness toward him.

All day long she felt the sting of his goodness rankling within her heart. She denied herself to callers, and paced from room to room in the vain attempt to shake off the burden of her thoughts. Was she to remain in his debt perpetually, to be always humiliated by the idea that she was a tolerated inmate of the house, a prisoner on parole? No, a thousand times. There was, there must be some other way—there was *one* way.

She was relieved that her husband did not come home to dinner. She had determined to plead illness, had he done so, for she could not bear the thought of facing him again so soon. She forced herself to eat a hearty meal, for she felt that she might need the sustaining power of food.

After dinner she gathered together her jewels and a few articles of clothing and put them into a travelling bag. Then she threw on her fine furs—all she could reasonably wear—and left the house. A few moments later she amazed Guy Hamilton by appearing at his apartment near the Attawam Club.

"What on earth, Lucy—" he began.

"We are found out, Guy. Robert knows all!" she cried excitedly, and in a few broken sentences she told him of the discovery of the letter and the life to which her husband had condemned her. The man paled with fear, for he could scarcely believe that the iron-hearted lawyer would fail to wreak vengeance upon himself.

"We're ruined, Lucy," he muttered, "what's to be done?"

"Done, done—don't you *know* what's to be done? Do you think I can go back to that house like a slave? Do you imagine I shall promise never to see you again? Oh, Guy, can you not see that my love for you has brought me to this, that all I have to hope for now is in you, that I am here to throw myself on your mercy?"

She broke down, and wept piteously, and he, by that peculiar species of social chivalry that could rob a man of his wife without a qualm and yet feel impelled to protect the woman when the crash came, offered to do that of which in his sober senses he never would have dreamed.

"Let us leave this miserable town, Lucy," he said gently, "and never set foot in it again. We will go far away, and begin things anew. Now—tonight—we will start, and tomorrow they may do their worst. Will that satisfy you, my dear?"

Joy and triumph and the delight of undisputed possession shone in her eyes. She seized his hand and kissed it passionately, and he smoothed her hair caressingly and felt that he had never loved her as much as at that moment. It was a fine thing to be trusted, to be relied upon so implicitly, and he vowed that he would give her no cause to repent of her faith in him.

That night the pair left Old Chetford on the midnight train. Their flight was a rich field of discussion for the gossips, who imputed to the lady faults of which even she had never been guilty. But the dignified attitude of Worth-Courtleigh and his absolute refusal to say a word about the matter to anyone did much to silence the scandal as time passed. Even at the club the topic at last became stale, and Claybourne ceased to mourn the loss of his friend who, he declared tersely, had fallen a victim of "too much woman."

✻ ✻ ✻

On the evening of the elopement Ralph Kane wrote a letter of resignation to the Third Congregational Church. In it he told his people that he had seen the great discontent aroused by his sermon of the day before and that he felt that his usefulness as a pastor was over. He regretted the severing of pleasant ties, but was fully persuaded it was for the best. He was determined, he said, to do the work of the Master unfettered by church government and church prejudices. He would deal directly with the people, and answer to himself and his God for the saving of their souls.

For this labor he was about to go to some great city to undertake his mission. He bade his loyal friends a tender farewell; as for the others, those whom he had offended, he hoped that they would think of him at his best.

~XXVI~

After
Five Years

n a certain moist afternoon in April, when New York lay steaming under a hot sun, two men descended the steps of a large brownstone house on Fifth Avenue. The house was not of the conventional flat and characterless sort, but was fashioned somewhat in the Romanesque style, with a low, heavy arch over the entrance and various odd designs around windows and eaves.

The men, though friends, were an oddly assorted pair, "cross-matched," as the fair-haired one had expressed it. This gentleman was Horatio Atherton, well-known and heartily feared on Wall Street. Behind the ruddy freshness of his face he concealed the keenness of a vulture in financial matters. He was dressed with great care, and in the lapel of his correct frock coat he wore his favorite flower, a pink orchid. He was a mining expert of high rank, and his specialty just now was the promoting of new ventures in Colorado.

The dress and manner of the other man proclaimed him an artist. He was tall, slender, and dark, and his waving hair was covered by a large black felt hat. His features were beautifully regular, and the perfect oval of his face was well set off by a tiny pointed beard. An impressionist of the impressionists, Philip Dalzell was always striving for a new expression in landscape painting, yearning to depict the "light that never was on sea or land." He was making his way rapidly, for in all his weirdness of coloring and sentiment there was more than a trace of genius.

"Well, Atherton," said the artist, as the two proceeded down the Avenue, "what do you think of the new sensation?"

"She's divine, my boy, divine."

"So you, who went to scoff, remained to worship? I thought it would be so."

"She certainly is the most fascinating woman I ever met," avowed the financier earnestly.

"Take care; what if the imperial Miss Van Horn should hear that speech?"

"She would agree with me."

"But like the speech no better for all that, I fancy."

Atherton stopped a moment to light an enormous and very black cigar.

"Who is she?" he asked between puffs.

"Don't you read the newspapers? Besides, I've told you. The Countess Fornay's light is not under a bushel."

"Yes, but—"

"All I know—all that anybody seems to know—is that she's the granddaughter of Adolph Renier, Count Fornay, who died over a year ago in Paris. His son married beneath him, it is said, in America, and his daughter was recognized only when the old Count was so near the end of a tumultuous life that he thought a good deed or two quite essential to a peaceful hereafter. One thing is certain; she was all the rage of Washington last winter, and the French embassy officials clicked their heels together every time her name was mentioned.

"There is no doubt of her social standing—something one can seldom say—Ah, how are you?"

The artist nodded cordially to a well-favored man who swung past them with firm and athletic tread.

"Who's your good-looking friend?" asked Atherton.

"He's a clerical chap, Kane by name. You'd never think it by his coat, would you? I met him at the Realists' Club."

"Whew! The Realists'?"

"Queer place for a parson, eh? Well, he is not an ordinary parson. He has cut loose from churches, I believe, so why not the Realists' as well as another? He practices his profession in man-to-man fashion; says pulpits are screens between God and the people."

"What a bore he must be."

"Not a bit of it, my boy. He's a practical enemy of the devil, and speaking of that gentleman, he gave 'Satan' Montgomery a tremendous drubbing at balk-line billiards last night at the club."

"Ah, a worldly parson."

"That depends on your definition of the adjective, Atherton. But he does a lot of good in his own way, I'm told. His theory is that cleanliness is not only next to godliness, but comes first."

Meantime the subject of these pointed remarks continued up the Avenue with mingled emotions as he found himself nearing the brownstone house. Only the day before he had received through Robert Worth-Courtleigh this almost-brusque message—

You say that Rev. Kane is in New York a portion of each
month. I shall be there in April, and shall be glad to have
him call.

As he thought of Abigail, he wondered how her mind had
progressed and altered under the potent spell of Paris. Conjecture was a necessity to him, for after the almost-tragic events
culminating in her removal from Old Chetford he had felt
unable to frame a letter that would suit himself or the occasion.
He could not give her comfort; he dared not give her what he
felt. He had at first hoped that Abigail would take the initiative
in the matter of letters, but she had not done so, and the little
that he had heard from her had been simple and kindly mes-
sages through Mrs. Copeland.

Now and then he had gleaned bits of information from
Robert Worth-Courtleigh, who was more or less in touch with
Mrs. Copeland, and had learned that the two had traveled to
some extent, but had lived quietly in Paris for the most part,
Abigail studying art, music, and literature with much thor-
oughness.

One day news of the death of Mrs. Copeland had come to
the lawyer's office, and then to Kane in New York. Then he
would have written to Abigail, but was uncertain as to her
whereabouts. In a week he received a brief note from the girl,
saying that after some months of travel she expected to return
to America. He had arisen each morning after that with the
hope that this day he would hear from her, but nothing further
came. And now she was here—he was to see her within a few
moments.

On his arrival at the big house he was shown to a small
reception room of pink and gold by a foreign-looking flunky in
green livery, who looked at him curiously when he asked for

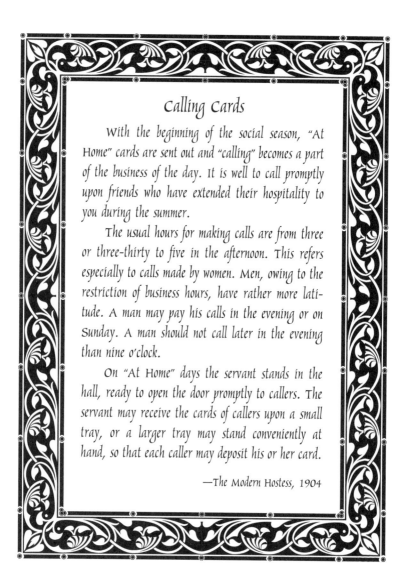

Calling Cards

With the beginning of the social season, "At Home" cards are sent out and "calling" becomes a part of the business of the day. It is well to call promptly upon friends who have extended their hospitality to you during the summer.

The usual hours for making calls are from three or three-thirty to five in the afternoon. This refers especially to calls made by women. Men, owing to the restriction of business hours, have rather more latitude. A man may pay his calls in the evening or on Sunday. A man should not call later in the evening than nine o'clock.

On "At Home" days the servant stands in the hall, ready to open the door promptly to callers. The servant may receive the cards of callers upon a small tray, or a larger tray may stand conveniently at hand, so that each caller may deposit his or her card.

—The Modern Hostess, 1904

"Miss Renier." Across the wide hall in the drawing room, servants were putting things in order after what had apparently been a reception of some sort. Evidences of wealth were not lacking, but he wondered if Abigail's status in the family were not less desirable than in the old days at Mrs. Copeland's. She was secretary or companion, he presumed, perhaps governess.

Here was a tall, lithe, graceful woman instead of the vivacious girl; a cultured, self-poised creature who seemed born to the purple.

He knew that the girl could not be the mistress of much money, for it was a matter of common information that the crash in the Attawam mills and the Oceanic National Bank at Old Chetford, following the suicide of Tom Harrington, had engulfed most of Mrs. Copeland's property, especially as she had decided, at Abigail's solicitation—so Worth-Courtleigh had told him—to stand behind the bank, in which she was a large stockholder, and pay every dollar of its indebtedness.

The flunky returned with the announcement:

"Mad'moiselle, ze Countess, vill be down presently."

He felt a little irritation that his card should have gone astray—should have been taken to the mistress of this fine establishment instead of to—when all else was obliterated by the sight of Abigail Renier standing in the doorway, and the sound of her cordial voice.

"I am so glad, so glad," she said simply.

For the first time in his life, Ralph Kane could not find words for expression. Not one of his visions of the girl had pictured her like this. Here was a tall, lithe, graceful woman

201

instead of the vivacious girl; a cultured, self-poised creature who seemed born to the purple. He would have known her anywhere and yet there was that in her beautiful face which was new and strange—a firmness of the mouth, a depth in the eyes, a latent something more than physical that far removed her from the pupil over whose education he had labored with such heartfelt zeal.

He gazed at her long and earnestly without speaking. He was relieved when she rang for the servant.

"I am at home to no one, Pierre," she ordered.

She faced him again with a trace of her old pretty spontaneity.

"Well, are you not glad to see me?"

"Glad? Surely I am."

"Ah! It was once the American usage to express such sentiments. Perhaps it is changed—*you* have changed," she added suddenly, and was about to say "grown older."

"You have a careworn look. I fear you are working too hard. But you are standing," she said kindly, offering him a chair and sitting down herself.

Kane obeyed mechanically; he was still embarrassed, still under the spell of the new Abigail. What a curious reversal of their positions! In the old days he was the mentor, the one looked up to; now she was the ruler of the situation. At last he realized with vexation that his gaze was still upon her.

"Well, do I stand the scrutiny?" she asked laughingly.

"I—I am afraid I have been very rude."

"Look at me as long as you wish; that, at least, shows some interest. Am I greatly changed?"

"It is more than five years, Abigail—I mean Miss—"

"Why 'Miss'? It is Abigail still or, if you must be formal, be correct. You heard Pierre, I know."

"Countess? I didn't understand."

She absently turned over and over his card which she had brought down from her boudoir.

"I saw that," she said. "You have not heard of the Countess Fornay, then?"

The light of the truth began to dawn.

"Countess Fornay? You—you are—"

"*Je la suis, Monsieur, a votre service,*" she replied merrily.

"But—"

"It's very simple. You recall the marriage records we found at Mill River?"

He nodded.

"'Alice Stewart to Francois Renier, son of Adolphe Renier, Count Fornay,' it read. The son died years ago; the father, my grandfather, died three months before dear Mrs. Copeland left me alone in the world."

Her voice choked with emotion, a manifestation that somehow cheered Kane's heart, as he too felt the loss of his staunch old friend now so keenly.

"I believe," she went on earnestly, "that her death was hastened if not caused by the trouble at the mills and the bank in Old Chetford. The first news of the crash prostrated her, and with each succeeding tiding of disaster she grew weaker, till her life faded out like the dying of a sunset. It grieved her deeply, too, that her fortune should be diverted from me."

"Ah, but that was your own doing, Abigail, your voluntary sacrifice; I have the facts, you see."

"Don't call it a sacrifice, Mr. Kane; I'm not the woman who makes them. It was only that I couldn't and wouldn't allow innocent victims of a man's rascality to suffer if I could help it—and I did help it. But the worst blow of all was when five thousand dollars of the little money remaining to Mrs. Copeland was swept away by Guy Hamilton."

"Ah!" exclaimed Kane, almost jumping to his feet at the sound of this name, which came without a tremor from Abigail's lips. He feared that the flood of bitter memories it recalled might upset her, might create a scene in which he would be but a helpless comforter.

But she looked him bravely in the face from her luminous brown eyes, paying no heed to his interruption. She spoke in a hard and emotionless voice.

"Guy Hamilton forged his aunt's name, and she, for her dead sister's sake, kept silent and let the check be considered genuine. He pleaded that he was on the verge of a great coup in the stock market, that he had only needed the money for an hour to achieve success, when the sudden death of a great financier smashed the market and ruined him. He groveled needlessly, for his aunt would never have prosecuted him."

"It was the act of an ingrate and a scoundrel," exclaimed the minister indignantly. "And they say he is now successful, a lucky operator in the 'Street,' but looked upon as reckless, dangerous, unscrupulous. I hear he is engaged in shady transactions and companies."

"And—that woman?" asked Abigail, with just a deepening of her color and a tightening of her clasped fingers. "The woman he took from her husband?"

"Mrs. Worth-Courtleigh? She tired of him as she had tired of Worth-Courtleigh, and ran away with another man. Hamilton was grateful enough to both of them, I dare say. I have heard nothing of her for several years."

"And now," said the youthful countess with swiftly changing mood, "tell me all about yourself, what you have been doing in New York, what you hope to do, and how the dear old people in Old Chetford—*my* people, you know—are getting along."

He would have ventured a little later to ask Abigail what her plans for the future were, wondering what she intended to do with this splendid and expensive house, but that the chiming of a tiny gold clock on the mantel caused her to rise.

"I hope I do not appear inhospitable, Mr. Kane," she said with a touch of pretty confusion, "but the fact is that I dine at the French consul's tonight, and—well, we women have to dress, you know. I want you to promise to come and see me tomorrow and spend the afternoon. There are many things for us to talk about. Will you?"

He promised with a new feeling of pleasure in his heart, and she saw him to the door herself. There they parted with a warm and friendly clasp of hands that the minister seemed to carry with him as he went his way to the faraway lower parts of the great city.

~XXVII~

The Penalty of Fame

alph Kane awoke early next morning with a pleasant, undefined satisfaction lying upon his consciousness. It slowly took words: "Abigail is here; I saw her yesterday and shall see her again today."

For the moment all vexing questions as to her status in the world and her coming life faded.

After breakfast and a little correspondence were out of the way, he set forth for the Realists' Club where he often went to see if he might obtain some sort of suggestions for the work of the day. He had joined the organization purely on its reputation for embracing within its membership the most mixed set of men who ever touched elbows under one roof. He expected ideas for fresh fields of labor to spring from his association with the radicals he knew there.

In truth there were all sorts of men in the club—decadent poets, dramatists of half a dozen "new" schools, impossible political reformers, ultra-socialists who talked loudly of what ought to be but never attempted to better what was, "symbolists" in art, and a sprinkling of cynical newspaper men and materialistic brokers.

Not too surprisingly, most of the Realists turned out to be idealists of the pronounced sort. Each group worshipped its own special cult with such absolute devotion that any practical work as part of a whole was quite out of the question. So Kane found that, like other clubs, it served as a means to an end: that men without homes might secure imitations and that men with homes might escape from them on occasion. Still he kept up his membership and extracted stray wheat grains from the general chaff.

The minister's life in New York for the past five years had been one of honest endeavor to better humanity as he found it. But he did more than supply a dinner or buy a new coat; he hunted up unfortunates with aspirations for higher things, and he helped them in manifold ways. He cultivated the acquaintance of business men, and made himself a sort of employment agency with free service; he obtained scholarships in various institutions for those he knew would appreciate them. In short—he did the strange, out-of-the-ordinary things he found nobody else doing, and he believed that he was filling his niche in the world as effectually as when he was in the pulpit.

Yet he had not been altogether content in the huge Babylon of a city. Its size precluded any real affection for it; who could love such a heartless giant that rushed unceasingly about its business with no care for suffering?

His regular trips to Old Chetford had been the bright parts of his existence; although he may not have recognized it, his visits to the first recipients of his sympathy, the Coffee House and the hospital, had benefited him as much as those now-flourishing institutions.

The quarters of the Realists' Club were as odd as its members. They completely filled the top story of a tall office building on Madison Avenue, and the view from the many windows was superb. The effect was like that of an immense suite of rooms whose owner had gone mad on the subject of varied decorations. The artists had a room specially devoted to their fraternity, the musicians another, while the authors—saints and sinners alike—rejoiced in a great apartment that contained a dozen private desks.

> She has the holy trinity of beauty, style, and brains, and the greatest of these is—well, first you think it is one, then you are convinced it's another.

The comfortable and well-stocked reading room was the favorite resort of the club gossips, but this morning it was deserted when Kane reached the club. He took up a morning paper and turned to the "Situations Wanted" column, as he was accustomed to do each day that he might by chance find there the cry of some poor fellow whom he could help. Before long Dalzell, the artist, strolled in.

"Good morning, Kane," he said pleasantly. "Saw you going to the Countess Fornay's yesterday afternoon. Do you know her?"

"Yes."

"Lucky fellow. She has the holy trinity of beauty, style, and brains, and the greatest of these is—well, first you think it is one, then you are convinced it's another, and at last you swear it's the third. Of course you've read her book."

"No," replied the minister, greatly surprised, "I didn't know—"

"Wait a minute. Here's a copy right on the table. Behold," and he thrust it with a triumphant air into Kane's hands. The latter turned to the title page and read: *Men and Women: Their Manners and Their Meannesses. Twelve Essays by Miss Petticoats.*

The well-remembered name was like a blow in the face to Kane. With all its sacred associations to be flaunted here under the title of a sensational book! How could Abigail have done such a thing? He read on:

"Translated from the French edition as Reprinted from *Le Revue de Deux Mondes*, by the Author."

"Clever pseudonym, eh?" said the enthusiastic artist. "Clever book, too, and bitter as wormwood. Handles society shams without gloves. Everybody is talking about it, and wondering where she got her insight. By Jove, she's the greatest woman New York has seen for years."

"Who is now receiving the endorsement of your impressionistic ardor, Dalzell?" said a coldly suave voice behind Kane.

"Hello, Atherton, that you? Of whom could I be talking except the Countess Fornay? Pardon me, Mr. Kane; I think you don't know my friend Atherton."

"Delighted, I'm sure," murmured the financier. As Kane shook the outstretched hand, he felt an instinctive dislike for the craftily sensual face that half-concealed a sneer in every smile. He wondered what this man and the frank and honorable Dalzell could have in common. And that he should know Abigail—that made his blood grow hot. Nor was it cooled by the calm tones of the newcomer as he went on—

"The Countess is certainly worthy of your devotion, Philip. She is ravishing."

From the lips of the banker the compliment was an insult, and Kane writhed under it as a dog under a lash. He walked deliberately away from the two and, picking up a magazine, sat down and tried to read. But he could not shut out their conversation; he might have gone to another room, but he was held by a strange fascination.

"She's promised to give me a sitting," exclaimed Dalzell, with a fine air of triumph.

"Not a portrait, I hope," said the blandly sarcastic voice of Atherton.

"Why not, pray?"

A new group of loungers, seeing Dalzell and Atherton, came into the room. It was always taken for granted that there would be something worth repeating when these two wits clashed weapons.

"She has promised to sit for an allegorical picture," declared the artist serenely.

"Then she can't want notoriety, Dalzell, for she'll be swallowed up in your theories."

"I shall paint her as 'The Modern Circe,' but instead of swine as the objects of her fascination there will be men—men of rotundity, both of person and moneybags. Your portrait, Atherton, will be well in the foreground."

A burst of appreciative laughter greeted this thrust.

"There's one comfort," retorted the ruddy banker, "if you paint it, I shall never be recognized."

Then a shout at the artist's expense, and a tentative expression of the opinion that it might not be too early in the day for gentlemen to take a drink.

"Well, anyway," declared Dalzell, "you are at her feet already, though you've seen her but once."

"Nonsense, my boy, it's only a matter of business investments."

This entertaining dialogue was ended by the sudden appearance of a fair-haired, boyish fellow with a fresh complexion and a wholesome atmosphere about him, who dashed up to the group waving a newspaper.

"Here, you fellows," he exclaimed, "have you seen the *Morning Crier?* Here's a whole page about the Countess." And he held aloft a sheet half covered over with illustrations and shrieking headlines. Even from his distance Kane could see the unmistakable likeness of Abigail Renier. The crass baldness of the thing made him shudder.

"Read it to us," cried several of the company.

The youth began the glowing article. With great satisfaction he rolled forth such phrases as "Nobles at her feet abroad," "Welcomed by the most select literary circles," "Another book in preparation."

Inevitably Abigail's personal life then received the attention of the writer's vivid imagination. Upon the one fact that she was the granddaughter of Count Fornay was built a most marvelous structure of falsehood and fancy. After stating that she had received from her noble ancestor a fortune estimated at several million francs, the article proceeded:

"That the advent of this beautiful, titled, and talented woman has set Gotham agog with admiration is not surprising when it is known that for several years she was the open rival of the Grand Duchess of Holstein for the affections of her once-devoted and scandal-free spouse. She—"

"Let me have that paper, will you, Armstrong?"

Kane had jumped to his feet, impelled by an overpowering sense of outrage. He broke into the group and faced the boy with as much calmness as he could command for service.

"Why, certainly, Mr. Kane, if you wish it," replied the young fellow in some astonishment.

The minister crushed the paper in his hands, tore it backwards and forwards many times, and then slowly let the pieces fall upon the floor.

"Gentlemen," he said—and his fine voice had never been more impressive—"that story of the Countess Fornay is a tissue of extravagant falsehoods which are an insult to a good woman and a disgrace to the newspaper that published them."

The company was undoubtedly interested. Here was a parson who was worthwhile; he rushed to the defense of the wonderful Countess Fornay, and he talked as if he were sure of his ground. Others joined the group, and all stood around Kane eager for his next words.

"I knew the Countess Fornay," he went on, "when she was—well, a girl. She has beauty, as you all know. She has also good blood and good brains, and her heart is pure, her character such as you desire for your sisters. She is a woman entitled to the respect and protection of every decent man. Would you, Armstrong, like to have your sister or your future wife the subject of the public gossip of club loungers?"

"No, no, Mr. Kane, I would not," returned the boy with great earnestness. "I am really sorry; it was thoughtless of me," and he shook the minister's hand warmly, making a sincere friend by his honest confession.

"H'm," thought Atherton, as he left for the financial district and his never-ending scheming, "pretty warm defense on the part of our clerical friend. How sits the wind in that quarter, I wonder? I shall make it my business to find out."

After the crowd separated, Kane read a little more, this time in peace, until his watch told him that by going afoot he would reach Abigail's house at about the appointed time.

"How will it all end?" was the question that kept time to his step as he walked rapidly uptown.

～XXVIII～

The Embers
of Hate

he green-clad servant who took the minister's card had evidently received his instructions, for he did not carry it upstairs but threw it into a little silver tray on the hall table, remarking, "Mad'moiselle La Countess gave ordaires you vere to be shown zis vay."

Kane followed him toward the stairs when the sight of a familiar figure made him rub his eyes. No, there was no mistake about it; it was the well-knit frame of James Anderson, who had disappeared from Old Chetford shortly after the departure of Abigail and Mrs. Copeland. The ex-coachman's square-cut face was illumined by a broad smile. He approached and bowed respectfully.

"I thought I couldn't be mistaken, James," said the minister as he extended his hand cordially. "How are you?"

"Very well, sir, thank ye kindly. I hopes you are the same."

"As usual, Anderson, and glad to see you again."

Kane followed his leader up one flight to a dainty morning room, which was just now in a state of delightful confusion

214

occasioned by the presence of several gaily adorned pasteboard boxes and fluffy heaps of silks, muslins, tulles, and other fabrics beloved by femininity. A large, yellow-haired woman in street costume was just leaving the apartment.

Abigail's greeting was kind but her manner, Kane thought, was more artificial than he'd hoped for.

"You will pardon this confusion, I know, Mr. Kane," she rattled on, "but Madame Lafarge has been showing me the superior points of the new gowns her firm has just completed for me. Would you like to view the feminine 'vanities'?"

He nodded as a matter of courtesy, and she, picking up one creation after another, shook each out gaily and held it against her body that the effect might be noted. It was not that she took delight in the pretty dresses, for so did he so far as his masculine mind would permit; it was the apparent shallowness of the new Abigail that troubled him. Finally he said, with a touch of sternness:

"Not much like the old life, Abigail; but I see you have a bit of it in the house."

She looked up from the critical inspection of a ruffle with inquiry in her eyes.

"I mean James Anderson."

"Oh, yes, Mrs. Copeland sent for him to come to Paris on the steamer next after ours. He was an invaluable bodyguard, even if he did sometimes get into trouble through his truly British determination not to learn French." And she laughed heartily.

"I was glad to see him; it was like a breath of the old days. Do you ever miss them, Abigail?"

"Miss them?"

There was a suggestion of tears in the voice, a sudden shifting from gaiety to deep yearning.

"Do you prefer this—this style of life?"

"Prefer it!" she echoed again, with a bitterness of accent that stung him to the very core.

"Then why?"

"You ask why?" she cried, rising impetuously. "Have you forgotten what happened five years ago? Have you forgotten that the kindliest, noblest woman in Old Chetford was driven from her home because she had befriended a young girl and was true to her in the hour of calamity? Have you forgotten that that girl's grandfather was sent to his death by a vile letter penned by a vile man who, under the guise of friendship and respectability, insulted and incited others to insult a girl whose only fault was that she accepted his counterfeit of decency as genuine? Have you forgotten those things, I say?"

"No, Abigail, I have not forgotten," he replied sadly.

"Perhaps you may not have forgotten, too, how the memory of that girl's mother was reviled in the streets; yes, even in the church; how the false accusers of her daughter smiled knowingly and infamously suggested that the daughter of such a woman could not be other than they said she was. I have not forgotten. For five years I have thought and thought of the cruelty of it all. For five years I have schemed and planned that I might fit myself to exact the measure of vengeance that such crimes demand. I care little for myself, but the memory of the dead will not suffer me to forget or overlook their wrong. I have position and the influence of friends. Fate has been kind to me. My birthright came to me almost by accident. Years ago I swore that Old Chetford should one day kneel to me, and that I would turn away in disdain. I tell you, Ralph Kane, that day is near at hand!"

As the fires of this outburst burned themselves away, leaving only the ashes of their wrath, the girl sank to her knees before a great stuffed chair and buried her face in her hands. Then came the needful flood of tears. The minister watched her sob-shaken figure for a minute or two and then gently raised her with quieting words. He was greatly perturbed; here was a soul in distress, such as he had long since vowed to help. But how, in such an instance?

To comfort this beautiful woman who he held so dear was a vastly different thing from solacing his "people" in trouble. He who knew all, who knew even more than Abigail herself, of the injustice of society's attitude toward her, could scarcely blame her for bitterness against the powers that were. Yet he feared for the corroding force of long-cherished desire for revenge upon the soul of this unhappy girl.

He would have given five years of his life for the eloquence that should show her the truth, but he knew her nature well enough, even in its changed form, to be sure that open opposition and direct argument would but add fresh fuel to the flames.

He went to the window for a moment and looked out upon the tide of traffic flowing up and down with ceaseless gaiety under the spring sun. Not far away, where the delicate twin spires of the cathedral pierced the blue, he saw in the street a long line of carriages drawn up against the curb. A bright canopy was stretched across the sidewalk, evidently to be the first avenue into the world of some newly made bride.

With a sigh, he turned from the scene to meet a gaze of intensity from Abigail which he could not fathom. He crushed down all other thoughts and began to put some practical questions to the girl.

"What do you propose to do?" he asked, trying to speak calmly.

"I shall go to Old Chetford in June. The Copeland house—it is mine now—is being renovated, and I shall see to it that those who are my guests while I am there will prove to the gossipmongers that in mere position they are not worthy to tie my shoe."

"And your money, Abigail? You have enough to enable you to live as I find you here?"

"For the present, yes. The Count left me an estate of three hundred thousand francs; of this I have thirty-five thousand dollars left. I hate the money and would not touch it, save for this one purpose. If I need more, I can make it. Indeed, I have already proved this to my own satisfaction here in New York."

Kane wondered how, but did not seek to investigate. Instead he ventured another inquiry:

"You spoke of a letter to your grandfather. May I know about it?"

"Is it possible you do not know? Yet, why should you?"

She told the story, and he, too, felt much of her passionate indignation. But he saw that she had not guessed the authorship of the letter correctly, and his sense of fairness would not allow him to keep silent, even for such a man as Guy Hamilton. Knowing the cloak episode, he was morally certain that the miserable wife of his lawyer-friend had penned the words that sent Captain Stewart to his grave. So, in a general way, he defended Hamilton as a possible victim of unwarranted suspicions, and urged that even the meanest creature was entitled to justice.

He could not help wondering if Abigail had ever heard of the episode at the Attawam Club on that tumultuous night when James Anderson became her champion by proxy. In her present condition, however, he would not have dared interrogate her.

The name of Guy Hamilton, coming from his lips and uttered in tones of attempted charity, was like flame to flax in the girl's heart. An intensity of hatred burned in her eyes, and her face was hardened into something that troubled the minister deeply.

"How I do not know, but vengeance will come. Right, fate, God, everything is on my side. . ."

"Justice to him!" she said with curling lip. "A horse-whip or a noose would be justice, perhaps. But I do not want that kind of justice. He must be reached, as I shall reach him through his selfish impulses. His pride, his self-esteem, must be brought low. I shall find a way. As for that woman—the woman who, while she was trying to disgrace me was paving the road to her own shame—she, too, shall suffer through me. How I do not know, but vengeance will come. Right, fate, God, everything is on my side.

"—No, I know what you would say," she added quickly, as Kane made a deprecatory gesture and would have spoken, "but it would be useless. You are a true friend and a noble man, but you have not suffered as I have, and you cannot realize the truth. You must let me work out my own salvation in my own way."

For a long time after this there was silence between them.

"I saw Hank Donelson the last time I was in Old Chetford, Abigail, and he spoke of you as he always does."

In an instant the clouds rolled away from the girl's mind, and she saw only the brightness of the days far back of her first great trouble. She clapped her hands gaily, and smiled as charmingly as of old.

"And Captain Sykes and Artemas—did you see them, too, dear old barnacles that they are!"

"Yes, both of them; hale and hearty."

"The salty angels! And is Artemas as much of a roistering blade as ever, and is Captain Sykes tired of telling the 'Mozambique' yarn yet?"

"They're the same to a dot, Abigail." Then suddenly: "How would you like to see them?"

"See them?"

"I've been thinking of inviting them to New York for a day or two as my guests. If I do that, would you like to have me bring them up here?"

"Why of *course*, Mr. Kane," she cried delightedly, "and you are so good to have thought of it. You know I cannot go to Old Chetford—yet. Get them over as soon as ever you can."

Kane agreed to expedite matters, and went downtown with a far brighter hope for Abigail than he had yet felt.

That night a letter was sent to Old Chetford on a mission that was destined to bring much joy to the three musketeers of Tuckerman's Wharf.

A Rift
in the Clouds

or several days Abigail was to Kane a flitting and a fleeting vision. He had called once or twice, but found that her time was so fully claimed by social duties as to give little opportunity for friendly chats. Receptions to which she was invited and to which she herself gave, suppers, theater parties, musicales, and the dozens of other frivolities with which the semi-Bohemian set in New York seeks to amuse itself absolutely filled her life almost to the exclusion of personal comfort.

"I am sure she doesn't really care for this sort of thing," mused the minister in his plain little bedroom. "It isn't in her nature to. All these fripperies, I can see, are being used simply as a means to an end. On the whole, I rather wish the life she is leading interested her a little more. It would be better for her nature than that dull hunger for vengeance that's gnawing at her soul."

He thought of trying to enlist her in his work among "distressed souls," but abandoned the idea as impractical for the present. He could do nothing now but wait and hope.

A letter from Captain Sykes, flavored with the breath of the ocean, came to him in due time gladly accepting the invitation to visit New York.

He was greatly delighted when James Anderson hunted him up at his lodgings one evening to talk over old times. He sincerely admired that sturdy ex-prize fighter, and he thought more of him than ever when James, in hesitating fashion, made evident that Abigail's bitterness of spirit had dismayed him profoundly.

As a result of this consultation it was agreed that James, who was now Abigail's courier and agent in many things, should keep a sharp watch upon affairs in the big house.

"That is a bit like playing the spy," thought the minister after James had gone, "but if ever the end justified the means, this is the case."

The next evening, as a dainty card on his study table told him, Abigail was to give an "At Home, with Music." Although this sort of thing had long been foreign to Kane's mode of life, he determined to go. He argued that he might be able to formulate some plan to help her by seeing the sort of people with whom she was surrounded; but the fact was that he would obtain pleasure from her mere presence.

When he reached the Fifth Avenue house on the following night it was aflame with many window lights, and a long line of carriages was crawling along the curb, each stopping for a moment to discharge its butterfly occupants. The music of a string band floated vaguely out upon the night air. James Anderson stood at the steps, dignified and unperturbed, but the French servants within the hall were running about with great apparent excitement in their attempts to settle the guests.

The great double drawing room of crimson and silver tones, and just now beautifully-decorated with choice flowers, was filling rapidly, and Kane joined the throng unobserved by anyone he knew. He determined to hold aloof for a time.

Just at present Abigail was chatting gaily in French with M. Sayer, a famous violinist whom she had met in Paris. He was a tall, ponderous man with a smooth face and straight black hair that fell over his ears in somewhat saintly fashion. There was nothing saintly about the real individual, however, for the story of his romantic escapades, one of which had been with a world-renowned prima donna, would have filled a volume.

Kane knew the artist's reputation, and a chill struck his heart as he saw the leer cast upon Abigail's beautiful shoulders and neck. He himself had never seen her in evening dress before, and to have this almost-holy first impression marred was intolerable.

He saw the sensual-faced Atherton greeted like an old friend by the girl; he saw Theodore Edlington, one of the Real-ists' nastiest poets of decadence, engage her in conversation; he saw "Satan" Montgomery, with most horrible of reputations, touch that white and shapely hand. At last came Harry Arm-strong, fresh, honest, and admiring, and Kane was thankful for the little leaven that his presence afforded.

The women were, of course, irreproachable. Abigail was now wise enough to know that whatever the masculine portion of her devotees might lack in the virtues, the feminine contin-gent must counterbalance in order that her own status might be secure.

It was a bright and entertaining crowd, and the event was at once a success. As the evening wore away, the minister, who had been very cordially received by Abigail and made to feel somehow like a guest of honor, could not fail to notice how the sleek Atherton hung upon the girl's words. Others noticed, too, as he learned when young Armstrong approached him with boyish wrath upon his fair face.

Abigail started at the name and breathed heavily for a moment. Her hand sought her heart . . .

"Isn't it disgraceful, the way Atherton looks at the Countess?" he exclaimed impetuously. "He hasn't a bit of respect for any woman, that fellow. I wish I were her brother for a few minutes. I'd—I'd—"

Kane had no real fear for Abigail; he felt indignation, however, that so much moral leprosy should be almost in touch with her. He was much relieved when Dalzell sauntered up to the window, where he was standing, and observed:

"Atherton's at it again, talking shop now to the fair Countess, and, strange to say, she appears to know as much about stocks as he does." And he yawned and wandered away.

Atherton had interested Abigail very deeply. He was a brilliant talker where finance was concerned, and he spread before her mind pictures of the "market" that were vivid and seductive. Here they met on common ground, ground upon which she hoped to erect the fabric of her ambition. He told her in particular of a company in which he was interested and which would repay her if she cared to place her money to good advantage. Her instinct told her that he was sincere, that he was fascinated by her and would put wealth in her way so long as he was favored.

"Some of the best operators on the 'Street' are in it," he had declared, "and its president is that luckiest of plungers, Guy Hamilton. You've heard of him, perhaps."

Abigail started at the name and breathed heavily for a moment. Her hand sought her heart. Her face was tense and drawn. To think that that despised name should come forth at such a time and in such a place! Atherton must certainly have noticed her agitation for he was as keen as a ferret, but a sudden disturbance in the hall attracted his attention.

The protesting tones of a servant uttered in very rapid, broken English rose above the general hum of conversation, followed by a high-pitched, squeaky voice in reply.

"Huh! I tell ye we *will* go in, consarn ye. Parson Kane's in thar, an' it's him we come ter see. An' mebbe our Abby's thar too. Leastwise, we're a-goin' ter find out, ye landlubber."

In another instant there appeared in the broad doorway the strangest trio that ever set foot in a New York drawing room. The tiny figure of Hank Donelson was flanked on one side by the big and ruddy Captain Sykes and on the other by the wizened Artemas. There they stood shoulder to shoulder, like the three guardsmen of deathless fame, but with all their courage of a moment ago utterly wiped out by the brilliancy of the scene before them. Hank began to despise his cherished tight lavender trousers and Artemas had dark suspicions of the immense scarlet necktie he had purchased especially for the trip. A well-bred titter added to their pitiable confusion. They were helpless, speechless, and were just about to turn and flee when—

A tall, beautiful vision in moss-rose satin sprang from somewhere within the gay throng and ran across the room to greet them. The vision wrung each one's hands warmly and kissed each in the simple fashion of childhood. It was Abigail, yes, their dear "Abby" grown so handsome and so grand that she overawed them, yet not too grand to remember old friends. The warm-hearted little Hank could have wept with delight, but he realized that dignified composure was due this splendid young woman.

Abigail turned with a little apology for the interruption and introduced the three mariners to the company.

"They are very dear old friends of my childhood," she added simply, "and comrades of my dead grandfather."

All this was accepted by Abigail's guests as a delightful manifestation of the eccentricity of genius; give a woman a title, and society will applaud if she chooses to turn handsprings in public. So they made much of the sailors as interesting specimens from another world, and before the evening had far spent itself Dalzell had exacted a half-promise from Artemas that he would give him a sitting for a study to be called "The Ancient Mariner."

When the people dispersed, Atherton was among the last to leave, loth to depart from this woman who had so impressed him. After Abigail had bid him good night, she added, "I will call at your office tomorrow, Mr. Atherton, and we can resume our very interesting discussion."

As the financier descended the steps he chuckled and rubbed his hands together with a lingering, caressing motion, characteristic of him when he thought that his plans were maturing satisfactorily. His overweening vanity led him to imagine that Abigail's interest in him was special and personal, and he determined to foster this by every means in his power, good or ill—it mattered very little.

If he had reentered the house, his smile of self-congratulation might have turned to a grimace, for, forgetful of him and even of the Guy Hamilton whose ghost he had raised, Abigail Renier—Countess Fornay—was sitting cross-legged on the floor in her satin gown and before her, charmed, amazed, and a bit bewildered, were the three old sailors of Tuckerman's Wharf.

~❧XXX❧~

For
Higher Stakes

he visitors from the wharf were installed for the night in the most luxurious quarters they had ever known. Hank, Artemas, and Captain Sykes each got as beautiful a bedroom as any society queen. What to do with such magnificence they scarcely knew, but a bed, at least, needs no introduction to tired human beings, and at last they were settled for the night.

At breakfast next morning they were as happy as larks. However, gentlemen at heart, they feared that their ignorance of the amenities of a refined table might shame Abigail in the eyes of her servants. Wonderful men, these servants! Such lordly dignity as encompassed the butler, in particular, had never been seen before. Sykes noted Abigail's movements and imitated all that she did, while Artemas, more independent than either of his friends, fed himself in his own way serenely.

"Sumthin' like ol' times, eh?" asked Captain Sykes jovially, as they ate and chatted and were very happy. Then, seeing the shadow that passed over his hostess's face, he added gently: "'ceptin' one."

"Yes, dear old Grandfather," murmured the girl with glistening eyes. "And the *Harpoon*—has she—has she been broken up?"

No answer came. Artemas looked at Sykes, Sykes looked at him, and both looked at Hank Donelson. Hank looked at the French clock on the mantel with a gaze of intense concentration.

"Yes, Hank, is she broke up?" piped Artemas.

"Oh, no. She ain't broke up—yet," he replied and his ruddy face gradually worked itself into the semblance of a smile.

"I'm glad of that," said the girl simply, and all three of the old sea fossils chuckled. Abigail wondered a little as to what amused her guests so much, but knowing them to be "odd fish," nothing they could do appeared strange to her.

Breakfast over, the trio retired to the library. From that room came, from time to time, the sound of Hank's voice addressing something in a pleading tone to Artemas. Then Sykes's deep bass joined in, and finally all three seemed to be talking at once and rather excitedly. Abigail ventured in to ask what the matter was.

"Why, yer see, Miss Abby," explained the captain, "the boy, here, is pesterin' Artemas to take him down to the bow'ry ter see the sights. Artemas was here once before an' knows the ropes. But we don't know as how the young feller ought to be took to such a place."

"Oh, I think it entirely safe," replied Abigail, as seriously as she was able. "With two such guardians as you, Hank will not be corrupted, I am sure."

Thus encouraged, they sallied forth.

Soon after their departure, Abigail was driven by James Anderson to Wall Street as its rushing flood of business was at its height.

The offices of Atherton were high up in an immense building near the Stock Exchange, and were typical of that luxury in which the kings of gaming delight to surround themselves. Carpets of the richest velvet hushed the hurrying footfalls of employees and customers; fine paintings gave relief to eyes wearied by the ceaseless procession of figures on the "tape"; beautiful and elaborately appointed desks were at the service of speculators, and there was a handsome, glass-enclosed room for women clients, of whom Atherton had a large number. Here Abigail sat for a moment until the broker should appear; she knew he would not delay.

A ticker was spewing forth its endless strip of narrow paper, hammering upon it the fateful figures that so many thousands of eyes were watching at that very moment. Abigail lifted the coil from its tall wicker basket and passed it quickly through her fingers, noting the selling prices of certain stocks. Evidently the gods of chance were well-inclined, for she smiled at what she saw, and reached for one of the little order blanks on a shelf nearby. She was about to write something under the boldly printed "SELL" on the slip, when Atherton entered.

The strongman of finance was most fastidiously dressed and freshly groomed; even his daily orchid had been chosen with lingering care. He greeted his beautiful visitor with so deferential a manner that even the clerks took notice, especially as one of them recognized the Countess from her newspaper portrait. The whisper ran around the room and Abigail was at once the object of keen scrutiny.

"Ah, my dear Countess, I am indeed charmed to see you. I trust you are as well as you look this morning," was Atherton's greeting, to which Abigail replied in a few direct words and with no notice whatever of the broadly implied compliment.

She told the delighted financier that she had been much interested in his conversation of the evening before; that she had often wished to learn something of stock transactions from a master of the subject. She even confessed to having taken a few little "flyers" since her arrival in New York, which had resulted rather well. To the man of the world she seemed almost like a pretty child rejoicing over a new toy.

"The stock market is so much more exciting than Monte Carlo," she exclaimed with enthusiasm. "There you see all the cards, and poof! It's all over in a moment."

"But at Monte Carlo they play fair. Here in Wall Street the cards are marked," he said significantly, leaning toward her with a look in his beady eyes that aroused her distrust and told her that if she were to use him as a pawn in her match with fate she must make her moves skillfully, "but I can teach you to play the game in safety."

She wondered what his price for the instruction might be—she knew that all men of his stamp had a price. But she dismissed the thought as having no immediate bearing on her visit, and turned again to the matter at hand.

"I thank you, Mr. Atherton. But you were talking of mining stocks last night, were you not? What is there in particular that you can recommend?"

"There are several, Countess," he replied, lowering his voice almost to a whisper, "but the best of them all, the kingpin in the money-making line, is, in my opinion, the stock of the United Mines Syndicate."

The broker flushed deeply, and into his little eyes there came a look of greater respect for his caller.

"I do not know it."

"It has only been listed a few days. As a matter of fact, it is not a mining company at all, but a combination of a number of concerns whose stocks are now active, such as Huronide, Gotham and Michigan, Quixote, Norumbega, and others of that sort."

"But not one of those stocks is paying a dividend now, and there are assessments on two of them," said Abigail quietly.

The broker flushed deeply, and into his little eyes there came a look of greater respect for his caller.

"My dear young lady, it is not a question of getting dividend payers, or even of escaping assessments. The simple facts are that we have consolidated those stocks under one management; that many of the stockholders in the smaller companies have handed in their shares for exchange; that there are, however, a great many transactions still unclosed—"

"A large 'short' interest, you mean?"

He looked at her with ever-growing wonderment. "Yes, a large short interest in the various stocks. For some time we have been buying in all these companies through a varied assortment of brokers to avert suspicion, and today we have practically a 'corner' in every one of them. When we get ready to move we shall—"

"'Squeeze' them?"

"Ah, Countess, you are superb! We shall do more—we shall wring them by the neck until there is not a drop of gold left in their wretched bodies. How? Very simple. When the shorts find that they are struggling against a corner of the most unrelenting sort, we shall announce that shares of the United Mines Syndicate will be accepted for delivery in place of Norumbega, Huronide, or whatever the stock may be. Then you will see a rush for United Mines such as Wall Street rarely knows, and we who hold it will profit by hundreds of thousands of dollars. I hold success in my very hand; I cannot fail," he said solemnly.

> . . . When she turned and she saw that it was Guy Hamilton, she commanded herself to compose her face.

"About Mr. Hamilton—you said that was the name of the president, I believe?"

"To tell you the truth," he replied cautiously, although his infatuation was now complete, "Hamilton has not played square with me in this deal, I'm afraid. At any rate, he is carrying a great load just now, and with proper manipulation, he might be forced out of the United."

"Beaten at his own game!" said Abigail, her lips tightening. "Exactly."

Abigail rose to go. "Well, the prospect is alluring," she said. "Perhaps I may invest a little money in the plan."

At that moment she glanced through the glass partition and noted a tall, elegantly dressed man talking with one of the clerks. There was something so familiar in his figure and bearing that she was scarcely surprised when he turned and she saw that it was Guy Hamilton. She commanded herself to compose her face, that the broker standing so close to her should not read the secret of her hate. She turned to him with nonchalance.

"I really must be going," she said. "That mining stock you speak of—how high are the stakes?"

"I think twenty-five thousand would be needed if you wish for large returns."

"So little? Well, you may depend upon me."

As Atherton returned from the escorting of his fascinating visitor to her carriage, his joy was profound. For her money he cared little; it was the prospect of at least friendly relations with her that intoxicated his soul. Perhaps he might even win her love!

Abigail went away feeling that she had embarked on a dangerous voyage, in the course of which she would need her utmost cleverness and self-possession. More money than she now had would also be demanded, but this she had good reason to believe she could obtain; her ventures in the market thus far had been very successful, and she followed the maxims of Mrs. Copeland in every move she made.

Just how she should proceed against Guy Hamilton she did not know, but, since the mention of his name the evening before, her determination that in some way he should feel the blight of her revenge had been intensified. Cost what it might in money, she would bring him to the dust in which he had once prostrated her.

She lunched at Delmonico's, and was then driven back to Twenty-third Street to do some shopping. There, thinking of her three old friends, she dismissed James with the injunction to go home and see if they had returned.

～XXXI～

A Signal
of Distress

On the whole the three friends had a very pleasant after-noon on the Bowery, and had the satisfaction of seeing that they created something of a sensation. They feasted on peanuts and bananas; they were weighed on dial machines; they blew into a lung tester, which Sykes almost ruined with a tremendous puff; they lunched royally at a dime restaurant on baked beans and griddle cakes; they then found a row of comfortable chairs under an awning, into which they climbed to smoke their pipes, only to discover that it was a bootblacking establishment and that they must submit to and pay for a polishing.

Finally they trudged along to find a theater. The Pan-Olympian pleased their fastidious tastes, because its exterior was very red and very yellow, and brilliant posters promised excellent entertainment within. The prices of tickets were ten, twenty, and thirty cents, and as Hank insisted that the best was not a bit too good, they soon found themselves in orchestra seats well toward the stage.

The piece that afternoon was a melodrama of the fine old sort in which villainy runs rampant for four acts, only to be crushed to earth with a tremendous thud in the fifth. To the simple old salts, not one of whom had ever been in a playhouse before, the mimic scenes were intensely real. The harrowing sufferings of the heroine stirred their manly hearts to pity, and they moved uneasily in their seats as woe was piled upon anguish.

At last came one of the most widely advertised scenes in the play; the villain was to seize the heroine by the hair and drag her about the stage, laughing in fiendish glee. The lovely girl was prone upon the floor and the evil gentleman had grasped her tresses, when Sykes, unable to control himself, arose in his seat and shook his huge fist at the actor.

"Let that gal alone, ye consarned sculpin, or I'll—"

The house was in an uproar in a moment. Jeers, whistles, cat-calls and cries of "sit down" and "put him out" made a bedlam of the place. There were shouts of laughter, too, for many thought the interruption a clever trick of the management, and expressed their approval of the captain's "make-up." But he, nothing daunted, his chivalrous soul thinking only of duty to be performed, started down the aisle on the work of rescue.

"Come back, ye gol darned fool," piped Artemas, "don't ye know it's only actin' out?"

Sykes would have climbed upon the stage, but that two burly theater guards seized him. Then Hank and Artemas, rushing to his aid, were also made prisoners, the whole party was dragged to the sidewalk, and a policeman summoned.

"I'm afraid I'll have to run you in, my ancient friends," he declared. And he stepped to a signal box on a lamppost, opened it, and said something into a telephone. In a few minutes a long, covered wagon drawn by a fat and lazy horse and carrying a couple of additional officers heaved in sight. It backed up against the curb for its passengers.

"Now then, you're goin' to have a nice ride at the city's expense," chuckled the policeman. "Get in."

The poor, bewildered mariners were about to obey, when suddenly there broke through the dense crowd of curiosity seekers the figure of James Anderson.

No vessel bearing down upon shipwrecked sailors on a raft was ever a more welcome sight than was the well-known face to the beleaguered men. Anderson quickly became informed of the situation, and he went at once to the proprietor of the theater. That gentleman came forward with apologies and requested the release of the prisoners. A cab was called, and Anderson bundled the old fellows into it.

It so happened that one of the spectators of the rescue of the three was another Old Chetford man of former days, Guy Hamilton, who had been called into the district by his desire to see a certain lawyer of rather shady reputation. Noting the tumult, he had joined the crowd in idle fashion, and had been startled to see James Anderson and the three sailors. All the bitter hatred he bore the man who had once struck him was overmastered by curiosity, and he drew as near as possible without detection.

He heard Hank say something about Abigail's probable displeasure and he caught the number given by Anderson to the driver. There was no doubt about it—she was in New York, and living in an aristocratic quarter. With characteristic reasoning he jumped at the conclusion that she was spending what remained of the Copeland money in a life of gaiety. Further particulars he must have, and he immediately employed the Bowery lawyer, who was not above playing detective, to investigate for him. The old spirit moved within him, and he determined to renew the acquaintance with Abigail if there were any possible way to do so.

The musketeers had had enough of life in the metropolis, and on the following day they took the boat for Fall River. Not one of them could be persuaded to go by train if a boat could be found to take them.

"Them pesky trains are so dangerous," declared Sykes, the hero of more thrilling escapes from perils of the sea than any man in Old Chetford.

~XXXII~

The Skirmish Line

One evening James Anderson came to see Rev. Kane with curious news. Three days before, he said, a lot of workmen had arrived at Abigail's home with wire and some strange-looking machines, which they had taken to the library. Other laborers had performed some mysterious operations on the roof, and since then the library had been kept locked, and his mistress had spent most of her days inside. All he could tell was that a peculiar clicking, "like the sound of a horse champing a bit," could be heard faintly from the hall.

The minister knew from experience that Abigail's evenings were more than ever given up to social gaieties. He rarely mingled in them, although he was invited cordially enough, for he felt that he did not speak the language of the flippant and artificial set by which she was surrounded. Although he still believed in her nobility of nature, he sighed at the difficulty of the problem.

But to Kane the real, the hideous menace to Abigail's happiness was the continued presence of Atherton in her house.

He now knew more about Atherton's disregard for the honor of womankind. To learn that he was a favored visitor, as well as the girl's escort to places of amusement, was as of the bitterness of gall to the minister.

With all his indignation, however, Kane felt that neither he nor the world knew the truth that must be behind Abigail's apparent preference for the financier. It was preposterous to believe that she could feel any sympathy with a man of Atherton's stamp. Nor was it possible to deceive her now, as in the days of Guy Hamilton. But here was the fact of favors bestowed, and it haunted him.

Had Abigail chosen to be Delilah, she could have shorn this financial Samson without a protest on his part.

After considerable self-communion he suddenly grew disgusted with himself and his "moonings," as he termed them. Was he to think and dream and hope forever, and do nothing? Where was his reputation as a practical man? He determined to take the initiative boldly, and try to interest her in other directions—perhaps in some plan of his own. He would go to her at once. And with that decision a bit of sunlight seemed already to cut into the gloom.

Almost at that very moment Abigail was in the midst of a deep discussion with Atherton in her library. His friends who declared that he never mixed business and pleasure did not know their man; they had been right simply because he had never before met a business woman who was also alluringly feminine. The Countess talked of stocks like an intelligent man, and his commercial ear heard her with respect; she breathed adorable womanly charm, and he drank that in with the thirst of the senses. Had Abigail chosen to be Delilah, she could have shorn this financial Samson without a protest on his part.

"So you think the situation in United Mines is favorable to us, do you, Mr. Atherton?" asked Abigail.

"As favorable as I am able to make it," he replied. "But I will be frank with you, and tell you that I have not quite a controlling interest in it. We let more of the stock slip into the market than we intended, and somebody is holding on like grim death. If I only knew for certain what Hamilton holds, I would be better satisfied. Of course he and I could combine and do as we chose with the company; but if he should get offish and unite his big holdings with others, they could—well, they could make it unpleasant for me."

"Then if one could gain the confidence of this—Mr. Hamilton, and find out just what he owns of the United Mines stock—"

"It might make a very great difference to me and to you," he replied. "If he has not got control, we can beat him by buying the outstanding stock at any price, and then vote that exchange with the short I spoke to you about. If he has, we are at his mercy so far as this deal is concerned, because he could then go over to the enemy, compel the company to abandon my plan, and make a barrel of money by going short on the stocks of the combined companies. He would beat the corner, and you and I would fail to get our profits. The great question is how he stands on United Mines."

"Perhaps I can find out."

"You?" he asked wonderingly.

"Yes—that is, I—I think I may be able to ascertain."

"But you don't know Hamilton."

"There are many ways in which one can get information in the market," she returned.

"If we can find out positively how Hamilton is situated in the matter," said Atherton, "all will be clear sailing."

The broker departed a little later on excellent terms with himself. Not only had he apparently became a needful element in this attractive woman's life, but he was in a fair way to have the whiphand over Hamilton.

Coming down the steps he met Kane. He bowed graciously, showing his white teeth with a sinister smile. He had at first feared the "parson," but of late had seen so little of him at the house as to drop him from consideration. He could afford, therefore, to be generous.

Kane was told by a servant that the Countess would see him in the library. There he found her at a desk in a maze of papers, pamphlets, reports, balance sheets, and yellow tissues. A ticker at her right side was tapping out its monotonous song, and a beautiful desk telephone was within easy reach of her left hand. She turned with a bright smile.

"I am glad to see you, Mr. Kane," she said. "You have not been any too sociable of late. Are you, too, busy—as I am?" and she drew his attention to the financial paraphernalia with a comprehensive sweep of her pretty hand.

"Yes, Abigail, very busy. But not, I fancy, in a very profitable way. Your occupation, I suppose, is more to the point in dollars and cents," he said quizzically, tapping the tape-basket as he spoke.

"I told you once that I should get money," she retorted. "Well—I am getting it. Is there any harm in that?"

"No harm in itself, Abigail, perhaps, but do you ever think of the result of continued gambling? Can you play with fire and not be burned? I would rather see you the poorest of the poor than to have you dragged down to spiritual ruin by the weight of gold thus obtained."

The girl flushed, and her eyes glinted with resentment. What right had this man, old friend though he were, to talk to her thus, to assume proprietorship over her affairs, to try to block the course of her righteous resolve?

"I am grateful—I have always been grateful to you, Mr. Kane," she said, "for your kindly interest in me. But now that I am a woman I must help myself. I have a work to do—you know how sacred a work. I am doing it by the only means possible. I have no fear for myself."

"But your happiness, Abigail?"

She looked at him almost scornfully.

"Long ago I said that when I had achieved fortune and social position, I should have too much to do to think of trying to be happy. It has come true."

"Ah, but this exacting life of yours—you look weary."

She laughed, but not with the merriment of old days.

"I never felt better. I need work, and more work, and still more work!"

"Then, Abigail, listen. If you need something more than you get from your society life and your finance—and God knows I believe you ought to have it—why cannot you spare some of your time to me, to the things I am trying to do? I know of some strange cases of suffering just now for which a woman's hand is needed. Can you help?"

All her feminine sympathy came to the surface at his earnest words and the expression on his fine, pleading face. For the first time in years she thought of the past without bitterness, of the old days in the Copeland house before sorrow had withered a single petal of the roses in her spring garden of happiness.

"In years gone by," she said very slowly and tenderly, "you were kind enough to devote a part of two days each week to my education and culture; I will give two afternoons a week to you and your interests."

After Kane had gone, his heart full of thanksgiving, Abigail turned to her ticker and her telephone. Then she began writing hurriedly, and for a long time her pen kept pace with the clack of the ticker. At last she threw it down wearily.

"Heigho," she sighed, "I shall be glad when three o'clock comes. Then I shall be free from the necessity of watching you, you old monster," and she shook her small fist in mock anger at the garrulous machine at her side.

~XXXIII~

A Trap

uy Hamilton was certain, from what his lawyer-detective had gleaned, and from the newspaper accounts of the Countess's victorious passage through the social "forbidden country," that the once-fascinating girl had become a magnet that seemed to draw him ever forward. It was that infatuation of memory which often casts a tinge of glory about its object, strengthened by the half-jealousy that shakes a man of strong passions.

He heard of Atherton's apparent supremacy in the Fifth Avenue house and a bitter hatred filled his heart. That his financial chief—or, at least, one who deemed himself so—should be in the place he ought to occupy at the side of a beautiful girl was an added blow of fate.

But the past! He racked his brain to find something that would make a visit even plausible, but all his ingenuity stopped short, and he cursed his impotence to devise a plan.

Time was when he would have turned from his perplexity to the reassuring spirit of drink, but for three years he had kept his old enemy almost completely at bay. His eyes had opened to one important fact: iron nerves were needed for the successful playing of the great game of Wall Street. It was a question under which king he should serve, Alcohol or Mammon, and he chose the latter.

Though his motives were decidedly unworthy, Hamilton had prospered from the first day of his rehabiliment. As his associate Atherton had said, he had become in less than two years one of the luckiest as well as the most unscrupulous of plungers. He was always up to his ears in heavy obligations which the least breeze of misfortune would have raised above his head. But at every critical point something would occur to his advantage, and he would emerge triumphant and money-laden. As a result he had come to have great faith in his luck.

One night he paced back and forth for a long time opposite Abigail's house. He saw a carriage, with James Anderson on the box beside the driver, draw up to the fine front and discharge a passenger. He hurried away without another look, for he could not yet nerve himself to see the woman of his dreams, even at a distance. He cursed himself for his cowardice, yet seemed to be a toy in the hand of destiny.

But at last the inevitable sight of her came. She stepped from her brougham at Sherry's one afternoon just as he passed on the other side. She did not see him, but he had a full, though fleeting, look at the beautiful, changed face, and it made his infatuation complete.

That night he slept little. It terrified him, almost, to think that the Abigail Renier whom his aunt had befriended in her pretty poverty, and whom he had insulted in his drink-fanned passion, had become this radiant woman, courted for her beauty and admired for her intellect.

Through his excited brain there rolled the pictures of the days when she, a simple child, would hang upon his elaborate stories of what had occurred in "society"—the society of Old Chetford, he thought with a smile—and he would encourage her and tell her that she was worthy to take her place anywhere. What a fulfillment of his prophecy!

Several weeks passed by, and then Guy Hamilton met the Countess Fornay face to face. It was at a reception given by the French consul, a volatile gentleman who added charm and variety to his official life by a considerable dabbling in stocks. He had profited by some of Hamilton's deals, and looked up to him as a veritable giant of the market to whom now, for the first time, he was glad to pay social attention.

Hamilton was talking to his host when he saw Abigail approaching with the consul's wife. He would have fled, but his muscles seemed to defy his will.

"Countess, allow me to present to you one of our Wall Street friends, Mr. Guy Hamilton; Mr. Hamilton, this is the Countess Fornay."

Hamilton stared straight ahead, his eyes fixed stupidly on a marble bust of Pandora at the end of the room. Then her words, clear and beautifully modulated in the well-remembered contralto voice, struck upon his ear like an awakening bell.

"Mr. Hamilton and I have met before, in my early days," she said.

"Ah," returned their hostess, "then you will wish to talk over the old times; I will leave you."

They stood facing one another in silent thought for a moment. He felt that it was incumbent upon him to speak, but knew not what to say. She clenched her fingers with such savagery that the marks in her palms were visible for days. By a supreme effort she steeled herself to play her part.

"Well, Mr. Hamilton, Madame Bouvet will scarcely believe we have met before," she said coldly.

"I—I—didn't expect to see you here," stammered the man.

"Oh, the Bouvets are very dear friends of mine. They were kind to me in Paris, and I could not fail to be present at an affair in which they have so much pride."

She clenched her fingers with such savagery that the marks in her palms were visible for days.

The unreality of the meeting was intensified for Hamilton by the calmly conventional tones of Abigail's speech. Remembering their last words years ago, he wondered what had happened to make this emotionless conversation possible.

"Are not the decorations superb?" she asked. "Let us walk about a bit, and see them."

Like a man in a dream he went by her side through the handsome rooms, noting with a pang the countless salutations she received, the eagerness of many to pay her attention. He wondered if this very change in her life might not furnish the key to her changed attitude toward him; perhaps the new conditions had thrust out the old bitterness from her mind.

He saw Abigail again just before she was leaving, radiant, glowing with comeliness, and proud of her triumphs. Why should others rush in where he dared not tread, he asked himself. He would dare, too.

"Good night, Countess," he said humbly. "May I be permitted to see you—to call upon you? There are some things—"

249

"Certainly; I am at home Thursdays," was all she dared say.

In her carriage she had the first opportunity to reflect upon what she had done. How she hated him. How the mere touch of his hand seemed to contaminate her! And she hated herself scarcely less intensely. Yet she must go on. Some day there would come a great moral cleansing, and she could hang her smirched self-esteem out to dry.

Hamilton's days until the following Thursday were full of uneasiness and apprehension. What if she were waiting to pour out upon him the full vials of her wrath and scorn in the privacy of her own house? He was half-inclined not to see her. But then came the thought of the others, and jealousy gave him strength.

Abigail was alone when he was ushered in. She saw his embarrassment and tried to put him at ease. Their talk was conventional for awhile, till he could no longer steer away from the subject that he knew must arise sooner or later. He spoke with humiliating self-contempt of his forgery, and asked her to believe that it was undertaken only at the direst necessity and with the solemn intent to pay back the money. In proof of this he showed a letter and a dated draft of restitution.

She listed with apparent kindliness, and helped him in the difficult task of excusing himself. Then he went a step further back in both their lives, and attempted to refer to the days in the Copeland house. She only smiled.

"I hoped you had forgotten that youthful folly," she said. "Perhaps I was quite as much to blame as anyone. We are men and women of the world now, and can afford to forget the misunderstandings of the past."

He was surprised and delighted that the obstacles to winning back her favor were so easily removed. He chatted easily and entertainingly of stocks, spurred on by skillful questioning. He was on sure ground now, and Abigail found that his information as to certain market conditions was most useful. Of the status of the United Mines operation, she learned enough to warrant the writing of a note to Atherton as soon as he had gone.

"Faugh!" she exclaimed, as she set to work at her desk, "The price we have to pay for success is heart-sickening sometimes. What if Ralph Kane were right? But even if he were, I shall carry my work through to the end, and when it is finished, we shall see whether Abigail Renier is better or worse for it."

To Forgive
Divine

ane, with the quick intuition of affection, had already begun to see the traces upon Abigail's face of the wearing, grinding life she had chosen so deliberately. Even if he had not learned from his ally, James Anderson, of the visit of Hamilton, he would have known from her appearance that she was under a great mental strain.

She went nowhere, excusing herself on the plea of ill health, and she held no more functions in the fine house. Society wondered, and then ceased to inquire about her. The papers hinted at all sorts of mysteries—that the beautiful Countess was immersed in the writing of a new book that was to set New York altogether by the ears; that she was deeply interested in holy things and might soon take the veil; and, finally, that some unhappy love affair had cast a deep gloom over her hitherto sunny nature. She read these things, smiled, and worked the harder.

So far as Hamilton was concerned the minister felt, as in the case of Atherton, that Abigail was using him as pawn in the development of her game of vengeance.

One afternoon he had another earnest talk with her. He did not reach the house till after three, for he had learned from experience that she rarely left her library or cared to see anyone until the stock market had closed. He found her wearied, full of moody silence which told that this was the moment to strike if he wished to do any good. He implored her by their old friendship, by the memory of Mrs. Copeland, who had planned so zealously for her welfare, to care for herself.

"If this thing continues, Abigail," he said, attempting diplomacy, "you cannot hope to do the work you have set your heart upon. You are playing upon a single string of your emotions; when that breaks, what is to happen? No more harmony, Abigail; a ruined and useless harp. Can you afford to run such risks?"

He could see by the thoughtful look in her eyes that this practical way of putting her case appealed to the girl's mind. Now to arouse her heart.

"You have suffered, it is true," he went on. "But do you know that in this great bedlam of a town there are thousands whose tortures of soul are tenfold greater than any you can even imagine? You said the other day that you would give me two afternoons a week whenever I should call for them. Why not one tomorrow?"

With the mood of pity strong upon her she replied: "I shall be glad to go—to help, if possible. Shall I take—money? I am willing, you know, to do—anything."

"Not tomorrow. I shall show you human beings beyond the reach of conventional charity. Some other time, perhaps—"

When he had gone, Abigail went to her room and took a packet of letters from the little satinwood box her grandfather had made long ago. Her eyes filled with the gentle mist of a revived sorrow. Then another thought came to her heart, perhaps for the first time, as she saw the many envelopes addressed

"Mrs. Sarah Copeland, Hotel Richelieu, Paris, France" in the bold and symmetrical handwriting of Ralph Kane.

"Why did he never write to me?" she asked herself, trembling with a strange emotion that she only half-heartedly tried to subdue. For the first time in many weeks she drew forth the picture of her mother and kissed it as in girlhood days. Then she replaced it with loving care and closed the box. Suddenly she remembered that Atherton was to call on the morrow, and she went to the telephone.

"I shall not be at home tomorrow afternoon," she said, "so if you will call this evening then we can talk over the last necessary steps of our deal—the U.M., you know."

Abigail's carriage was in front of Kane's house early the next afternoon.

"Now," she exclaimed brightly, as the minister opened the brougham door, "I am at your service. Command my driver."

She had expected an immediate pilgrimage to the horrors of the East Side tenement region, and was astonished when they stopped before a splendid apartment house on Madison Avenue. In a handsome suite they found a wealthy widow, whose son lay crippled and speechless on a bed of pain. But the chief sufferer was the mother, through whose lack of caution had occurred the accident that had brought her son low. Her agony of self-blame had finally settled into deep melancholy as it was seen how hopeless was the case of her son.

"Oh, if he could only speak to forgive me, or even to reproach me, I could endure it," she would repeat every day.

It was the minister's mission to try to lighten this morbid grief, to stimulate new interests where the cripple was concerned. It was a hard task, but he had persevered until he had, at least, aroused respect and admiration in the burdened heart.

Upon Abigail, who had been warmly welcomed by the sufferer as an old friend of her counselor, this visit made a profound impression. She saw as never before the compelling charm of Kane, she realized the soothing power of his voice, and, as they rode away from the place, she felt proud that the man beside her was her friend. A warm physical delight in life took possession of her; she was glad to be near this man on this beautiful afternoon. He chatted entertainingly about his various "cases," little dreaming of the very personal form his diversion for Abigail was taking.

Next they visited a writer of books whose beautiful young wife, for the paradise of alcohol, would trample honor, truth, and self-respect in the mud, only to awake to the frightful torture of broken nerves and intense self-loathing. Either before or after one of her outbursts Kane had a peculiarly soothing influence upon the woman, and the literary husband had often called the minister from his bed in the dead of night to come to the work of mercy. Abigail caught a glimpse of the poor creature, and the sight of her bloated face and red eyelids haunted her for many a day.

These things and many more the girl saw, and in all of them there was some peculiar element that showed Kane's originality in the matter of doing good. She was impressed for the time being, but the force that held the citadel of her soul was still too strong to be dislodged, and she returned to her schemes.

Several days after this trip Kane suddenly appeared at the Fifth Avenue house in a cab, and asked Abigail if she could come with him at once. It was not one of his afternoons, she reminded him pleasantly, and she was afraid she could not spare the time.

"I would not trouble you, Abigail," he said, "but a dying woman has asked that you might come to her."

The deep solemnity of his tone and a subtle something in his face had its effect upon her, and she put on the simple attire she was accustomed to wear when on her rounds with him, and they were soon being rapidly driven toward the Lower East Side.

A throng of conflicting emotions surged through the girl's mind as they proceeded on their way. More and more, she told herself, she was obeying the bidding of this strong personality. Would he at last win her from her allegiance to duty as she conceived it? No, that should never be, she thought almost fiercely. He was good and kind, and doubtless believed that he was right; but there were different standards for different natures, and who should say that hers was not as lofty as any?

For some time neither spoke; then it was she who broke the silence.

"Is it the Cartwright woman who is dying?"

"No, Abigail," he replied, in a tone that somehow precluded any further inquiry.

The carriage drew up before a tenement house that Abigail did not remember. It was a shabby building, but with some brave attempts at gentility. Up four flights of stairs they climbed, assailed by the odors of coarse cookery and the cries of fretful children.

A woman in the garb of a nurse opened a door in response to Kane's ring.

"Is she—" he whispered.

"Still alive, but very low," was the reply.

Abigail, vaguely wondering why she should be brought to a deathbed, gazed about the two rooms visible from the hallway.

They were pitifully bare of furniture, but the few remaining pieces showed that the apartments had once boasted better things than could have been expected in such a place.

"Come," said the minister, beckoning to his companion, and as they crossed the threshold he whispered gently, "Remember, she has but a few moments to live."

And there, stretched upon a bed from which she would never rise again in life, Abigail saw Lucy Worth-Courtleigh.

The poor, pallid face, wasted by disease and drawn by mental suffering, had lost all of its loveliness. Only the rich beauty of the hair remained of all the glowing treasures of comeliness that had once been so admired. Yet somehow the countenance had been purified.

No one spoke and no one moved for, it seemed to Abigail, interminable hours. And yet this meeting, totally unexpected as it was, gave no shock to the girl. The solemnity of the scene, the hovering presence of death, robbed the situation of all but its aspect of human suffering.

At last Kane said gently to the frail figure upon the bed, "Abigail is here."

The head on the pillow turned with painful deliberation, and into the dimmed eyes came a transitory gleam of recognition. A thin finger beckoned slowly to Abigail, and she leaned over toward the bloodless lips.

"I sent for you," came the thin and trembling tones, like some ghostly utterance from another world, "to beg your forgiveness. I felt—that with it I could have more hope of the— forgiveness of God in the hereafter. No, don't speak. I did you a terrible wrong, but I was mad—mad with outraged pride, jealousy, infatuation."

The grip of mortal pain throttled her utterance, and she lay for a minute inert and like one dead. Abigail raised her head tenderly and moistened the trembling lips with water.

"I wronged you," the pitiful voice resumed, "and I wronged another. But for me, Guy Hamilton might have been a different man. I have been told, too, by Mr. Kane that my wretched letter was attributed to him."

> But he saw the beautiful face he loved so well looking down on the dying woman with a gaze of divine compassion. It was the victory of an awakening soul.

There was a swift gesture from Abigail at this confession, and Kane turned quickly, fearful as to what might follow. But he saw the beautiful face he loved so well looking down on the dying woman with a gaze of divine compassion. It was the victory of an awakening soul.

"Bitter has been my punishment and bitter my repentance," quavered the dying woman. "If you can find it in your heart to pity, if not forgive, I shall die more easily."

Abigail opened her lips to speak, but the other lifted a warning finger.

"Wait one moment. I have done what I could to make reparation. . . . Mr. Kane, give me the packet."

The minister drew from his pocket a large envelope and gave it to Mrs. Worth-Courtleigh. She in turn placed it in Abigail's hand.

"There," she said faintly, "is my sworn statement of the facts—my confession of the greatest sin, great sinner though I have been, of my life. It will exonerate you, if my own disgrace has not already done so. Think well before you answer. Can you forgive me?"

❦❦❦ ❦❦❦ ❦❦❦

Kane had left the room a little before, for he believed that the scene was too sacred for even his kindly presence. In a few minutes Abigail joined him, pressing her handkerchief to her tear-stained eyes. She pointed to the inner room with a gesture more eloquent than words. He left her, but returned almost immediately.

"All is over," he said quietly to the nurse, "and, thank God, all's well."

Then, with the grandeur of the presence of death still about them, they sought their carriage in the squalid street below.

Tightening the Noose

therton knew himself well, and he felt that in his personality was little to attract a woman of Abigail's qualities. He felt, too, that her hot pursuit of money in the market, her placing herself in dangerous situations, was not for any small object. The key to her secret, he felt sure, was her ambition to become a woman of great fortune, and with that golden lever to pry open the doors of the socially elect of New York. Ah, how he would slave and plan and grasp opportunities in order to be able to gratify her imperious desire; with the elaborate setting that wealth could give, he felt that he could pass muster.

So he had been weaving his web for several weeks, tightening a thread here, breaking another there, but ever sitting in the center. By and by, when the flies, which to him were Hamilton and the public, should be where he wanted them he would strike.

His scheme had changed two or three times in as many weeks. At first it was merely to invest the money Abigail had entrusted to him—some $25,000—together with $40,000 of his own, in the quiet purchase of enough United Mines to give him control. But he found it impossible to get hold of a sufficient quantity in the open market. Hamilton had evidently taken alarm, and was gripping his shares tenaciously. Atherton had found that his associate was holding a great portion of his stock on margin, and that the demand inspired by himself merely sent up the price and made Hamilton's position more secure. He had learned, too, from Abigail that Hamilton had told the truth when he said that he did not control. There was one thing to do, a dangerous, audacious thing—but he would do it.

As the scheme flourished, so did his infatuation with the woman involved in it. Her beauty called loudly to his senses, while her keen wit, her clear financial vision, appealed powerfully to his mind. The unusual combination was irresistible.

But shrewd as he was, he failed to consider that Abigail might be playing her own game in the market quite apart from his tender care, which, in fact, she was doing. Using information from both Atherton and Hamilton, she employed the fluctuations in the smaller stocks that formed the United Mines to her great advantage. She made money rapidly, and, flushed with success, felt herself completely ready for Atherton's promised stroke that was to shake Wall Street and ruin Guy Hamilton.

Her plan would have astonished the rosy-faced broker who adored her, for it involved his own defeat as well as that of his rival. She felt justified in attempting to humble him, for his coarseness had given her frequent offense, and she despised his proposed treachery to his business associate and friend. Once the battle was over, and she a victor, she could teach him his place.

For Hamilton, however, she had no pity. Although the scene at Mrs. Worth-Courtleigh's deathbed had affected her deeply, it had increased rather than lessened her bitterness toward the man, for, in spite of the tormented woman's self-accusation, she held him in great measure responsible for luring a wife from her honor and duty. She would crush him, and by her own hand alone, although she now knew that Atherton would have brought about his ruin had she not existed.

One evening when she was nursing her impatience at the long-continued failure of Atherton to launch his thunderbolt, she received a note which read—

> I shall come to your house tomorrow before the market opens—and stay until it closes, perhaps. In that privacy I can work to better advantage. H. is away on a yachting trip, and the hour to strike is at hand. You will applaud the plan; it is impregnable.
>
> — H.A.

That night sleep was long in coming to the youthful mistress of the great house. The eve of her vengeance was here; the time toward which her every thought had long set its current was winging its way softly toward her. She was not happy, she knew, but there was something higher and stronger than happiness: the feeling that through her own energy and will a wrong was to be righted, a memory avenged, and a defamer brought low.

She saw Kane's grave and handsome face between her and her goal. How noble he looked, how unlike either of the men she was to play one against the other. She knew how he would regard the *coup*, but she stifled the whisperings of conscience by the resolution that after tomorrow she would show him how grateful she was for the past. She would be free, free! She would help him as he had never been helped before; he should see that

Abigail Renier could be Lady Bountiful as well as Countess Fornay. She would—

Then came the gentle touch of sleep, and forgetfulness of all things mortal, for her dreams that night were of her mother.

Atherton arrived early the next morning, smiling and immaculate. He rubbed his hands in joyful anticipation of the day's triumph, and, after a few of his customary compliments, he unfolded to Abigail his plan of campaign. She listened with every faculty alert.

"Now, my dear Countess," he began, "the situation at this moment is plain: we are not in control of United Mines, nor is Hamilton. We have not been able to acquire the stock in the market—nor has Hamilton. We must get control today, if ever, for Hamilton, as I wrote you, is out of town. How shall this be done?"

Abigail shook her head slowly. Even had she known, she would not have suggested at this time. But she hung upon his words as she had never listened to a human being before. On her correct comprehension of what he should say rested immense possibilities.

"It shall be done by a stroke that will make Wall Street talk for many a month. We shall sell United Mines."

"But I thought—"

"Exactly. We shall sell—but we shall buy."

"Ah!"

The audacity of the move fascinated her. It was as clear as crystal now.

"They will be 'wash' sales, of course. My brokers have orders to pick up the stuff that my other brokers let out. After an hour or two we'll put a raft of United on the market and smash the price to smithereens. The bottom will drop out, and as

Hamilton holds thousands of shares, mostly on margin, he will be wiped out, and we will pick up what his brokers are forced to sell. When three o'clock comes, we shall be joint masters of United Mines. Your money I shall use in buying on the break."

During this elated recital Abigail's brain had been busy with the problem she had set herself to solve. How should she outwit this man of iron nerves and unscrupulous will, and at the same time be empowered to wield the lash over Hamilton's cowering frame? By one of those sudden mental illuminations, the solution came when she least expected it. The preliminary buzzing of the ticker as it ground out its repeated "ABCD" for the morning test warned her that now, if ever, time was golden.

Under pretense of examining her memorandum books, she sat down at her desk and wrote something on a small slip of paper. Then she went to the door, opened it quickly, and looked into the hall. The slip of paper went into a big flowerpot standing just outside the room, and there in a quite remarkably short time it was found by James Anderson, who read it and hurried away to another part of the house.

"I thought I heard one of the servants prowling about the door," she said as she returned. "One can never be too careful in such matters, you know."

The broker nodded approval and picked up the tape that was now being belched forth with a regularity that denoted the opening of the market. For many minutes he sat in silence, his eyes glued to the battalion of figures as they followed one another in single file from out the glass case. At last he muttered his satisfaction.

"Here's the first sale of United," he said. "A hundred shares at ninety-one. Good. It closed yesterday at ninety-two and a quarter. The game begins well, my dear lady."

For an hour or more the stock was offered in moderate quantities, and practically held its own in price, as the ticker told the two anxious watchers. As the noontide hour approached Atherton pulled out his watch.

"In a few minutes," he said grimly, "the slaughter will begin. It's the greatest joke of the season. Everybody will see my stock going to smash and will pity poor Atherton. . . . Ah, see this, five hundred United at ninety—three hundred at eighty-nine and seven-eighths—four hundred at eighty-nine. Bravo, Countess! It won't take much of this sort of thing to hamstring our friend Hamilton. . . . Eh; what's this? Four hundred United at ninety-one—five hundred at ninety-one and three-quarters—a thousand at ninety-two. My God, what's going on?"

Atherton quickly dialed his office number.

"Hello, Jones?" he said in a low voice that was tremulous with excitement. "Have I seen the booming United Mines? Certainly. No, I don't know what it means but order everybody to pour out all I've got of it. Flood the market, d'ye hear? Flood it!"

Then back to the ticker again, where the story of misfortune was accentuated every moment. Huge blocks of the United Mines were coming out, only to be snapped up with a readiness that sent the price soaring. Great beads of perspiration stood out on Atherton's forehead as he surveyed the terrible miscarriage of his plans. Then the telephone rang. He answered the call.

"Eh? So it will, by heavens. Order 'em all to stop selling my holdings at once."

He turned to Abigail to tell her what he had learned.

"My man says that there is some tremendous force supporting United, nobody knows what. My brokers, who were not ordered to protect the stock, but to depress it, have been outbidden on the floor by the brokers of this other power. Who it can be the devil himself only knows. Hamilton is away, and I can conceive of nobody else who could possibly want the stock. Ah, that suggests something."

He pulled the long strip of paper from its basket and, beginning at the opening of the market, made a swift mental calculation of the number of shares of United Mines that had been sold. As he brought into the total the latest transaction in the stock, he groaned with dismay.

"Countess," he said humbly, "I have to ask your pardon for bungling one of the most promising deals I ever undertook. It is morally certain that we have lost control of the company by my stupidity in not instructing my brokers to buy in my stock at any price if they saw any special outside demand for it. I am sorry and ashamed."

"Don't let yourself be troubled overmuch about it, Mr. Atherton," said Abigail sweetly. "Perhaps you were not so much to blame, after all."

"I fear I was. And it is too late now to recoup ourselves; we evidently cannot buy back the stock at any price from the combination that has got possession of it. If I had only put your money into Huronide and the others, you would have made a handsome thing of it. See how they're booming with United."

"But I own five thousand of Huronide and the others, as you call them, already."

He looked at her with admiring wonderment.

"I congratulate you, Countess," he said dryly. "You have made a neat thing by today's work. Perhaps if I had let you engineer the big deal, it might have resulted differently."

Confessing himself baffled by the result of the *coup*, he went downtown to see if any light could be obtained in the "Street," leaving Abigail to her jubilant thoughts. She felt certain that her instructions to her brokers to buy all the United Mines thrown upon the market, at any price, had been obeyed to the letter. She was the power that had so mystified Atherton; she controlled the stock. The knowledge that vengeance was within her grasp, that on the morrow she had but to give the signal and Hamilton would be ruined, filled her with supreme content.

In the middle of the afternoon a note was brought to her by a servant. It had been delivered by a messenger, he said, and an answer was expected. It was from Guy Hamilton, asking if she would receive him that evening. With a thrill of triumph she wrote at the bottom of the note the single word "yes."

~XXXVI~

The Mask
Thrown Off

n the early afternoon of the day of Atherton's financial disaster, the steam yacht *Buccaneer* drew up to her dock on the East River side of the city. The *Buccaneer* had not been expected until the following day, but a slight accident to her machinery made it advisable to return to port. So she limped in, and brought with her Guy Hamilton.

That gentleman was in high feather, for during the trip he had secured the promise of several financial princes that they would cooperate with him in his projected "scoop" of United Mines stock. A fortune and a great reputation were within his grasp. In a week he would be able to lord it over Atherton, and then—well, then he hoped for a more desirable conquest than the winning of mere dollars.

Emboldened by what seemed a foregone conclusion of success, he joined with the other guests of his millionaire host in the consumption of heroic quantities of champagne. Under the inspiration of the choice wine, life for Hamilton had absolutely no obstacles to the winning of whatever prize he cared to take.

And so his thoughts turned to Abigail with a boldness they had not known since that night at the French consul's. Today, great was his joy when his messenger brought back his note with the eloquent "yes" in Abigail's handwriting.

The Countess received him in the library with a graciousness that put to flight any lingering embarrassment he might have felt. She was a vision of beauty in her gown of black lace and jet, and he would have given half his anticipated fortune to fold her at once in his arms. He came in like a conqueror, and she noticed the change in his demeanor before he had walked halfway across the room.

"Did you think it strange that I should have written for permission to call tonight?" he asked sentimentally.

"Why, no," she replied gaily, "of course not. It's quite customary, isn't it?"

"But not between old friends," he replied with an air of assurance that roused her spirit immediately. Was it possible that he, of all men, had lost his memory?

"I knew you would take an interest in what I have done today," he continued.

"I have been with the kings of Wall Street. I have won them to my side completely. They listened to me, Abigail—think of it, to me—as if I were one of them. I shall be soon, for everything is fighting for me. All I need is inspiration."

She smiled in supreme contempt at his meaning, which was clear enough to her woman's wit. Blinded by passion and the excesses of the day, he mistook the smile for something else.

"Ah, you see my meaning," he went on rapidly. "You will let the past rest in its forgotten grave? The present is for us two together. We can conquer the world, I of finance and you of society. I love you, Abigail, I have always loved you. I want you to be my wife. I am at your feet; trample me, if you will, but keep me near you."

The girl turned her head to hide for the moment the triumph that glowed richly in her face. It was the act of modesty, hesitation, yielding, he thought. He seized her hands and clasped them warmly.

"I love you, Abigail, I have always loved you. I want you to be my wife. I am at your feet; trample me, if you will, but keep me near you."

"Ah, Abigail, dear," he cried wildly, "surely you will not keep me in suspense. Tell me—"

"Tell you," she echoed, tearing her hands from his grasp and facing him in a sort of fury. "You offer me yourself and your fortune. You yourself have claims, of course, for you have said it! But your fortune—what of that?"

In bewilderment he began a disconnected recital of his present position and his hopes for the future. She cut him short with scornful words.

"But the price? You are to buy, and I am to sell. I must know the terms. How much do you bid? What is your cash offer for my hand?"

Scarcely believing his ears, absolutely unable to judge whether this were the height of bitter sarcasm or a cold-blooded proposition from an ambitious woman of the world, Hamilton blundered on.

"I am on the verge of a great *coup* in stocks," he said at last.

"A *coup*?" exclaimed the girl contemptuously. "One has been made today while you were wining and dining. Look there!"

She threw aside a magnificent Japanese screen with a swift movement and there, silent but with its mass of paper still clinging to its maw, stood the ticker of the New York Stock Exchange. He looked at it dully for a moment, and then into her face. Something he saw there chilled his easy confidence into dread.

"I—I haven't seen the tape for two days," he said vaguely. "What is it you mean? And what's that ticker doing here?"

"See for yourself," she replied coldly, pointing to the tape. He whirled the writhing mass out of the basket, and began at the opening quotations. He frowned angrily at the innocent figures.

"A break in United Mines, eh? Worse; a slump, a pounding. Who on earth has been at us? If I had only been here! And what the deuce is the meaning of it? The market is strong enough. It's a raid on me. Can Atherton?—no, he's too thick-headed, too businesslike."

He pulled the long strip swiftly through his fingers, noting with adept eye the prices of his specialty as they glided by. Then exultation took the place of anxiety.

"Ah, she strengthens! They didn't have it their own way—that's it, up it goes. Somebody is fighting for us, as I should have done. Magnificent! It closes at ninety-five. I see—Atherton was to the rescue, and routed the bears. Tomorrow we shall win the fight."

"Tomorrow you will be a ruined man," said Abigail solemnly.

"Nonsense! I tell you they can't beat me. Doesn't today's battle show it?"

"Nevertheless, you are on the brink of a great catastrophe," she insisted gravely.

271

He tried to gain some light from her face, but its impassiveness baffled him. Then the significance of the paraphernalia of the market in this room began to dawn upon him.

This, then, was the end—to be a plaything in the hands of a woman, to have to cringe to one he once treated with such cavalier loftiness.

"What do you mean?" he cried hoarsely. "What do you know?" He seized her roughly by the wrist, and again demanded: "What do you know?"

"I know that every dollar you have is locked up in United Mines and the smaller companies forming it. I know, too, that you are holding these shares on margin. Well, you will never see a penny of your money again."

"You talk like an insane woman," he said sulkily, "and I'm half inclined to believe you are. Didn't you see how Atherton supported the stock today?"

"You quite misapprehend the situation, Mr. Hamilton. Atherton did not save you. He did not, he could not, buy those stocks."

"But someone—"

"Yes, someone, of course. That someone was myself. The stocks are mine, mine. Do you understand, or must I repeat it? *Mine!*"

"You—bought—them?" he stammered, completely overwhelmed by the astonishing revelation. This, then, was the end—to be a plaything in the hands of a woman, to have to cringe to one he once treated with such cavalier loftiness. It was too monstrous to believe, and incredulity began to show itself on his face.

Abigail hurriedly reviewed the steps of the campaign that was to have ruined him in any event. Her thorough understanding of the scheme, her complete knowledge of his own most secret plans, made her appear to his distorted imagination like some handsome witch who could read his own thoughts. He was terrified now, and disposed to plead.

"For God's sake, Abigail," he whimpered, "what—what made you do this?"

"Because I hated you," she said bitterly, "because I have hated you for five years. I hated you when you insulted me beneath your aunt's roof. I hated you more intensely when my grandfather went to his death, the victim of a slander caused by you. My hate grew daily, hourly, in the years in Paris. When I gazed at the picture of my dear mother, instead of peace her features brought storm, for they recalled the insults that, because of your unmanliness, were heaped upon her grave by your scandalizing set."

"I—I surely had no share in that," he pleaded, but she went on without heed.

"Your theft from one who had befriended and loved you, till you proved too base for respect, increased my hatred. But I despised you most when you came in the day of my prosperity and fawned upon me, and cringed to me from the depths of your degradation, for then you proved yourself a fool as well as a knave."

He shrank, as one would shrink from the lash of a whip, under her lacerating contempt.

"Now you are on the verge of ruin, and I have done it. I control your boasted company. I can depose you from its presidency, and make your margin-held shares your undoing if I choose. Tomorrow the whole world shall know that your attempt to make of yourself a king, you who are not fit for a king's fool, was balked by a woman!"

There was no appeal, he knew, as he looked at the stern determination on her countenance. Baffled, beaten, humiliated, he walked slowly toward the door. Then he turned with a sudden blaze of wrath.

"This is not your work," he exclaimed, "you couldn't do it. That sniveling Kane put you up to it. I'll—I'll wring his neck."

"As you did the night he would have punished your insult to me, had not a humbler man saved him from physical contamination by use of a horsewhip," she retorted.

Hamilton's wine-flushed face became purple with anger, and his fists clenched as if he would have annihilated her, woman though she was.

"Take care," he shouted, "neither one is here to defend you now." And he rushed toward her as she stood with her back to the wall in an attitude of splendid defiance. Her very beauty, heightened by the excitement, exasperated and maddened him.

"Be careful," she said icily, "you are observed. Well, Pierre?"

Immediately a servant appeared. "Mad'moiselle rang?" he asked impassively, although he had witnessed a portion of the surprising scene.

"Yes, Pierre. This—gentleman has seen fit to insult your mistress. Show him the door."

The tall and powerful Frenchman placed a hand on Hamilton's shoulder and gripped it as with a clasp of iron. The furious Hamilton attempted to shake the servant off, but to no avail, and he was forced from the room and into the hall. Then the one-time favorite of Old Chetford's aristocracy, the would-be monarch of finance, was thrust into the street like some vile intruder.

No sooner had the shutting of the outer door announced Hamilton's expulsion than the strength of bitterness that had sustained Abigail deserted her, and a violent reaction set in. Trembling in limb and faint at heart, she hurried to her chamber. She took from her satinwood box the miniature of her mother and pressed it to her lips. Falling upon her knees by the bedside, she held the picture in her outstretched hands and gazed at the sweet and childlike face as if she would call it back to life.

"Have I done right? Are you satisfied with your child?" she asked.

～XXXVII～

A New Dawn

Abigail sighed wearily. Oh, for rest, for peace, for oblivion! Were all victories in the world bought at such terrible price? Did the fruit of triumph always turn to ashes on the lips? Then why struggle on, to be buffeted by fate, even in one's hour of exultation? She felt that sleep might, perhaps, be persuaded to spread its gentle wing over her, and she asked her maid to get her ready for bed, early as it was.

"But, Mad'moiselle," said the little servant, "I came all on ze purposs to tell you zat a caller is for you downstairs."

"A caller, Jeanette? Who?"

"It is ze curé, ze—what you call meenestaire, Monsieur Kane."

In some magical way—she did not then understand how—all of Abigail's weariness and despondency vanished at the sound of that name. In their place came a throbbing of the heart that filled her with nervous energy. She dispatched her maid to make excuses for her delay, and began to tear off her beautiful gown as if every second were of priceless value. She chose from her wardrobe a simple dress, reddish in tone, and took the diamond ornaments from her hair.

Kane had come to the house in response to an urgent telephone message from James Anderson. And the minister rejoiced, even in his foreboding, for he felt that the time had come when he could take a positive position and stake his all on one final cast of the die. His heart swelled with thanksgiving as he saw from the faces and bearing of the servants that no outward harm, at least, had come to his beloved.

And when she appeared before him at last, clad with a beautiful simplicity he had not seen since the old days on the Hill, when he was teacher and she his pupil, his intuition told him of some spiritual change for the better. By a queer turn of memory the color of her dress recalled that day in the mill yard at Old Chetford, when he had seen her pinning up the rent in her scarlet skirt, an enticing vision of young girlhood.

Was he any more certain now what would become of her? From the depths of his most secret consciousness came the glad "yes," so full and strong that it almost took form upon his lips. She was to be saved from that most relentless of enemies—self. His old prophetic feeling, the Hebraic spirit that three or four times in his life had filled his soul with conviction, was again upon him.

"I am glad to see you, Mr. Kane."

He started as from a revery, and took the hand so cordially extended. He noticed a little trembling of the fingers that lingered in his own a moment longer than might have been absolutely necessary. And the eyes, around which he had so often noted dark circles of late, bore signs of tears. James Anderson had grasped the situation; he *was* needed.

"I am very glad to be here, Abigail," he said.

The familiar name struck upon her ears like a chord of beautiful music. Of late he had not used it; indeed—the thought all at once came to her—Kane had omitted all manner of naming her in direct conversation, except that once he had called her "Countess," which had in a certain sense wounded her, although she could not tell why. Now the old name, fraught with cherished memories, was most pleasant.

As part and parcel of her softer mood came a strange sense of weakness, a hunger for human sympathy. Oh, for an hour of Mrs. Copeland or her grandfather! How easily she could become a girl again under their loving shelter. Yet here—and she thrilled with the swift realization—was their legitimate successor, the true and faithful link between her present and past. Had Kane known the tenderness of her musings, he would not have interrupted them, even for the words of sympathy that he delicately expressed.

"I fear you are not quite yourself, Abigail"—again that dear name—"you look weary, and, if I may be pardoned, ill."

"I am ill," she replied passionately, "ill at heart, sick of the cruelties of the world, the world's wrongs. So sick, and so tired."

Tears flooded her eyes, tears that were more womanly than she had shed since the loss of her benefactress.

Kane would gladly have soothed the girl with the caress that his whole being cried out, "give, give," but before his own impulses he put a practical desire for her welfare. First must the body and the brain be restored to health, and the heart—ah, if ever the time came for him to minister to that, he would know what to do.

"Abigail," he said with gentle insistence, "the time has come for you to break from the stifling influences of the life you lead in this house, if you wish to really live. Go out into the country.

Breathe God's fresh air, with His green carpet beneath your feet and His blue sky over your head. Try that beautiful life for a while, and your cheek will glow and your heart warm with nature's own humanity."

The fervor of his words fitted her mood, the charm of the picture appealed to her fancy.

"Yes, when I have done my work. Tomorrow sees the beginning of the end," she exclaimed, starting up suddenly and pacing the room with nervous tread. "Tomorrow he will be crushed, crushed under the weight of my revenge."

Kane did not ask who was thus to be punished; he knew too well whom she meant.

"He was here tonight."

"Here?" exclaimed Kane, his instinct telling him that the man's presence was intimately connected with Abigail's great mental upheaval. He loathed the fellow now; in fact, he dared not think that he did not hate him.

"Yes, and I warned him what tomorrow would bring forth; that he would be ruined, discredited, and that I alone was responsible."

"*You* would ruin *him*? How?" he asked in surprise.

Walking up and down before him, her clasped hands swaying curiously in rhythm with her step, and her dark eyes glowing with the ardor of a wild thing spying out its prey, she told him in somewhat incoherent fashion the story of her financial victory and the situation into which she had forced Hamilton.

"And what of your conscience?" he ventured, as she finished her remarkable story. "Does it approve?"

"Perfectly. What claim has that man for consideration? For the second time in his life he tried to force his so-called love

279

upon me. This time I was not defense-
less, and I had him kicked out of the
house by a servant."

All the man within the minister's body rose up in a great
thrill of joy at this. Then there
had never been any affection for
Hamilton! The thought was a
subtle intoxication.

> "I admit your great wrongs. I frame no excuse for this man's brutality. It is for you I plead."

She stopped her measured
walk, and faced him as if in defiance.
"You speak of conscience," she
cried. "Would it be worthy of the name
if it did not approve what I am doing? His
sins against me I could forgive, perhaps, but his sins against the
dead are pardonless. You are an honest man; tell me, does he
not merit a far greater punishment than I can inflict?"

"His evil has been great; the punishment is trivial. It is not
of him that I am thinking, but of you."

"Of me? Am I worth considering at such a crisis, when the
memory of those he made wretched cries for vengeance?"

"Ah, Abigail, but does it? Mrs. Copeland, your grandfather,
your mother—would they wish it? Would they wish to see the
girl they loved transformed by hate into a vindictive woman?
Would they be happy to see your nature hardening under the
stress of a revenge cherished for years, and feeding upon your
better self? Would they approve of injuring the innocent—the
minor holders of this stock that is your weapon—to punish
the guilty?"

"I do not know. I only know that I cannot forget, I cannot
forgive."

"I admit your great wrongs. I frame no excuse for this man's brutality. It is for you I plead. Forgiveness is the greatest of the virtues, for it is the most difficult to practice. It is the most noble, for it is the most ennobling."

"My wrongs—their wrongs. You forget them!" she cried with an intensity that touched him deeply.

"No," he replied gently, "nor did He whose forgiveness is the beacon to us all forget. He remembered, but He forgave."

"He was not mortal," she whispered. Then she looked him full in the eyes and added: "You yourself could not forgive."

"Couldn't I?" he asked with a sad smile. "I *have* forgiven. It was a great burden that sorely tried me, but I forgave him years ago."

"Hamilton?"

"Yes."

"What had *you* to forgive?" she queried, her eyes filled with questioning.

"The greatest thing he could have done to injure me," he answered gravely.

"To injure you? How could he injure *you?*"

"By injuring you," he said gently.

"By injuring *me?* I—I don't understand."

"Yes, Abigail, by injuring you." He spoke rapidly now. "Yes, for I love you, loved you then as I—as I love you now."

"*You—love—me?*"

She stood before him in adorable wonderment, her head bent forward toward his own, her lips parted, and her eyes filled with a soft radiance.

His long-repressed ardor burst forth in a torrent of tender words, a storm of passionate phrases that would not be denied. Never had he pleaded for a soul more eloquently than for the

281

cause of his own manly heart, nor ever had he a more entranced listener. And yet—

"Why have you not—told me this before? Why did you not tell me—then?"

"I did not speak then," he answered gently, "because you were in distress and scarcely more than a child. I could not try to force myself into your heart, for—pardon me, dear, I did not know everything then as since—I feared that the heart Guy Hamilton wounded so deeply held some tenderness for him."

"And yet you would have thrashed him that night at the club," said Abigail, the sunlight dancing into her eyes through the mist of recent tears.

Whose was the face that Kane saw with surprise before him? It was strange, yet familiar. The years had rolled backward; there was no more a Countess Fornay; the Abigail Renier of old stood there in masquerade in another's brilliant drawing room. And, most wondrous of all, the hard lines had vanished from her face and the benison of peace seemed to have descended upon her.

"You knew that?"

"Your good ally, James Anderson, told me all about it in Paris. The fragments of the whip he used are among my dearest treasures. Often as I looked at them I have thought of the strong arms—your arms—that were ready to protect me then—"

"And ever have been, dear, and are now and always shall be, if—"

"There are no 'ifs,'" she broke in impetuously, "at least," she added, blushing divinely, "none that I can offer."

"My darling, do you know what that means?"

"Why should I not when I—oh, Ralph, my dear, must I say it aloud?"

"No, sweetheart; there is another way—"

And that other way she chose—the way of loving womankind since the world began, the way of the heart's silent eloquence, of fire and dew, of fulfillment and promise. Clasped in his strong and loyal arms the burden of her earthly struggles slipped away, and the glorified portals of a new life were opened wide for her willing feet.

❧ ❧ ❧

With Abigail's love came new faith, and she wrote to her various brokers, countermanding her orders of the afternoon.

It was not that her scheme of vengeance had yielded to her newfound happiness; that would have been merely the exchange of one passion for another. No, she knew that there had been a new dawn, and that her love was but one of its radiant beams. Her soul, long buried in the ashes of morbid retrospection, had been awakened to redemption, life, and beauty. For when she granted forgiveness to Hamilton, she could finally receive God's gift of forgiveness for herself.

A Debt
Is Paid

ane went directly from the scene of his life's pro-
foundest joy to the Realists' Club, there to arrange for
the forwarding of the notes of instruction to Abigail's
brokers as soon as their places of business should be open in the
morning.

The happiness in his heart must have found expression on
his face, for some of his club acquaintances noted and com-
mented on his appearance. "Satan" Montgomery sauntered up
to the desk where the minister had seated himself to write, and
attempted to rally him upon his altered looks.

"I say, Kane," he began jovially, rolling a cigarette of
Egyptian tobacco, for which accomplishment he had a great
reputation, "you look radiant, positively. Quite a change, in fact,
from the down-in-the-mouth face you've been wearing around
the club lately. Have you at last knocked the devil out for good
and all in your prize fight with sin?"

The minister was too full of his new delight to take offense
at this flippant familiarity.

"Well, not exactly. But I may have exorcised one evil spirit, and that's a good deal, isn't it?"

"Bah! Let's have a whack at the billiard balls, old man. I want revenge."

"Not tonight, Montgomery. I have other things to think about."

And, in fact, he had. For him there was the overwhelming knowledge of Abigail's love, for which his being had hungered these many years.

He knew that the desire of the high-minded girl for the exoneration of her mother and herself in Old Chetford was pure and worthy, and he rejoiced that it could be realized without any of the spectacular effects she had planned. As his wife—"his wife!" how the words thrilled him—her fine gifts and finer nature would soon win for her the loyal affection and respect of all.

He would not have felt it unwarranted had he choked a public confession of his deceit and dishonor from Hamilton, but that, he realized, would only set new tongues wagging. No! Over the obliterated grave of the dead scandal his wife should erect a new temple of truth that would do her honor evermore.

But what should be the man's punishment? He could not conjecture, but he felt a great certainty that in some way life would exact a reparation. He had no patience with the doctrine that the wicked flourish upon earth more than do the good, nor did he care to leave to the hereafter the complete condemnation of the scoundrel.

The ending of the stock transaction, which relieved Abigail from the sullying presence of Hamilton forever, suggested that something was to be done to save the innocent persons who would be involved by any sudden turning of United Mines upon the market. He determined that from the plans of hatred and revenge God could spring great good. So he wrote to a broker of his acquaintance, a man he knew to be honest, asking him for an appointment on the following day when the control of the stocks should be handed over to him for such disposition as his well-regulated conservatism should think best.

He had sealed his letter to the broker and was addressing it, when the sound of loud voices attracted his attention. He saw a little knot of men just outside the library, standing near the marble stairs that led to the floor below. Prominent among the men was the tall frame of Hamilton, and, as the crowd parted a little, he could make out the admirably dressed figure of Horatio Atherton.

Undoubtedly there was violent talk between the two, but Kane could not at first distinguish their words. Could the double-dealing in stocks be known to Hamilton, he wondered. In that case there was a possibility that Abigail's name might be dragged into the quarrel. He arose hastily, armed with a new feeling of responsibility, and walked toward the group of excited men.

"I tell you, Hamilton, you're drunk," Atherton was saying with his utmost suavity. "I hate a drunken man, and I won't dispute with you."

"Well, you've got to hear what I've got to say. I tell you, you tried to cheat me."

The minister's teeth set hard, and his limbs stiffened instinctively. He dreaded but was ready for the next word.

"Hamilton, you're a fool. Go to bed, and you'll apologize in the morning," said Atherton coolly, lighting one of his black cigars. "Easy, now, easy," he remarked, with a blandness that maddened Hamilton, as the latter started forward, his fists clenched and his lips babbling unintelligible threats.

The drink-crazed man was seized and pinioned by some of the clubmen as he lunged viciously at Atherton, who merely laughed and blew a cloud of smoke into Hamilton's face.

"Let me go," shrieked the struggling Hamilton. "I tell you he took that third ace out of his discards. I saw him do it."

A great weight lifted itself from Kane's soul. The disgraceful row had no stronger basis than a quarrel over a gambling game. He prepared to go home, giving a servant instructions as to the sending of the letters early in the morning.

"Good night, gentlemen," said Atherton amiably, and stepped down the marble stairs.

At this vanishing sight of the object of his wrath, Hamilton, by a tremendous effort, broke away from his captors and started for the stairs, reeling as he went.

"Look out for him, or he'll fall," cried Kane sharply, and several of the men sprang forward in alarm. Hamilton turned, half facing them, with a leer of drunken self-confidence.

"Don't you worry 'bout me, you fellers," he hiccoughed with a foolish smile. "I'm all right; I'm always all—"

The boastful words were silenced on his lips, as he wavered wildly on the top step, swinging his arms frantically about in the vain attempt to clutch something for support. Then he fell headlong down the stairs to the marble floor below, just brushing the descending figure of Atherton as he went.

A cry of dismay came from some of Hamilton's friends, but above all was the high-pitched, sarcastic voice of "Satan" Montgomery trying to reassure everybody.

"Drunken men and fools never get hurt, fellows," he said. "He's all right, I dare say."

But when they went down and lifted the inert and unconscious mass, they knew well that the old adage had failed terribly.

With white faces they bore him to one of the chambers, and placed him dressed as he was on one of the club's immaculate beds. Spasmodic moans and an occasional heaving of the chest were all that spoke of life within him. His fair hair was streaked with blood, and his handsome face was the color of death.

A medical member of the club, who had dropped in after a late emergency call, applied restoratives and tried to make the sufferer comfortable. Then he spent a long time in careful examination of the injuries.

"Well, Doctor?" asked Kane, as the physician came from the room at last. The answer burned into his brain indelibly.

"No bones are broken. The shock was great, but the inertness of the fall prevented fracture. He will live, but the injury to his spine is permanent. He will never speak or have the power of motion again. God knows, it would be better if he were not able to think, as well."

Kane left the club with a strange conviction of the unreality of everything. He was like a man under the influence of some powerful drug that takes all substance from the surrounding world.

⁂

Abigail heard of the terrible visitation upon Hamilton with a horror in which, Kane was thankful to see, was also pity. The retribution that had overtaken him was so terrible in comparison with her own puny scheme of revenge that, as in the case of Mrs. Worth-Courtleigh, she felt how weak were human plans of vengeance by the side of the awful decrees of fate.

In a short time the disposal of all of Abigail's stock ventures was arranged. A new and conservative element was put in control of United Mines, and the corner in the smaller companies, so cleverly planned by Atherton, was never accomplished. That wily financier, learning how she had outwitted him in the deal, admired the Countess more than ever. But, on coming up to the brownstone house to express that admiration and incidentally ask for her hand, he had received a curt dismissal and the assurance that their business relations were at an end.

This he accepted with his usual stolidity, although he was bitterly disappointed. Those who knew him well found him nervously irritable for a few days. Then it was over; he had simply lost another *coup*.

No slave ever released from bondage was more glad than was Abigail in handing over to Kane the complete management of her business affairs. She was tired of struggling, happy to have someone to act for her. So he arranged that all her holdings should be sold gradually and profitably. A large sum of money was realized, but she did not wish to touch a penny of it. After much pleasant planning, they decided to use it for the endowment of a hospital where curious and extreme cases of suffering could be treated.

Kane knew that the need for hospitals is never fully met, and he decided that the institution that he proposed should minister to those poor sufferers whose misfortunes were likely to take them from hospital to almshouse.

In due time the Sarah Copeland Hospital was built upon the beautiful banks of the Hudson above the city. The first ambulance to enter its gateway, after the building was in readiness for the reception of patients, brought to the home of mercy the nerveless body of Guy Hamilton.

❧XXXIX❧

Into
Safe Harbor

he glow of a fair June sunset was fading into the shadows of night as a little group of men and women paced slowly up and down the platform of the Old Chetford railroad station, awaiting the arrival of the evening train. One of their number, a sturdy, well-made man was distinguished from the rest by a faster tread and a more nervous manner. He consulted his watch frequently, and at last walked to the little grated window behind which sat the telegraph operator.

"Is the train on time, Harkins?" he asked of the thin-faced young man who was busily writing an incoming message.

"To a dot, Mr. Kane. She ought to be here in thirty-five seconds. There she whistles now."

Kane looked toward the north. Far up the track was the faint gleam of the locomotive headlight, like a pale star of evening. To him it was a star, a star of hope and love and happiness, for behind it was his dearest possession, the sweetest thing the world held. What if she should not come! His heart chilled at the

290

mere anticipation of that most depressing of all experiences—to await the arrival of a loved one who does not appear.

But now the train was at his side, and in a moment down stepped Abigail to greet him, smiling, happy, and beautiful. As he clasped both her hands passionately in his, he was sure that no such queen of women had ever come to Old Chetford before. And come to him! He could have cried aloud for joy. He wondered why all the others in the station did not insist on knowing his right to this vision of loveliness who was so glad to see him.

As a matter of fact, the rest were too busy welcoming their own special arrivals to pay much attention to him and his. Only a few noticed the pretty woman whose hands the minister seemed unwilling to relinquish, and not one of them dreamed of connecting her with Abigail Renier.

"Is everything settled in the old house, dear?" she asked.

"Perfectly. Mrs. Brown is a treasure, as I had reason to know years ago. And best of all, Worth-Courtleigh bid in a great deal of the Copeland furniture and I have got it back again. And you? Did your breaking up go smoothly?"

"Oh, yes. I transferred the lease without a hitch, and salved the pain of the servants with good, round gratuities. They went away almost happy, all except Pierre; do you know, Ralph, I actually think I caught him crying."

"Don't blame him, sweetheart. I should do the same if I had to part with you."

"Silly fellow! As if I'd ever let you."

As they rode along southward, Abigail was too happy and too preoccupied to note the direction of their journey. It was not until the driver stopped and opened the creaking carriage door that she realized that the Hill had not been their destination. She caught the faint fragrance of the salt air as she stepped out upon planking that had a familiar ring, and, looking through the gathering gloom, she perceived the outline of a wharf. There, at its left, lay the dark hulk of a ship.

"The *Harpoon*," she cried gaily, clapping her hands with delight. "Then it's not broken up!" And she gave her lover's arm a squeeze that he thought would have been full payment for five times five years of anxiety.

"So you brought me to see it," said Abigail tenderly, "and couldn't even wait till daylight. The dear old *Harpoon*. Poor grandfather!"

But sorrow could not linger at such a time, and her voice rang forth again with an infectious heartiness that warmed Kane's heart. "But what are those lights?" She raised her veil. "And who are those people?"

"Come and see."

Kane drew her arm through his, and they quickly walked down the wharf. Suddenly a cheer sounded on the soft night air.

"Why, it's Captain Sykes and Artemas and Hank and—and—"

As they neared the staunch old *Harpoon's* side, the cheering from the deck was redoubled, and hats were swung into the air. Abigail now made out James Anderson and Tilly Donelson and a dark-eyed, curly-haired girl whose face suggested remembrance but not present recognition. Then there were some of her old-time mill friends, and—could it be? Yes, it surely was Nelly Nevins with a big, broad-shouldered young man who seemed to take a peculiarly affectionate interest in her, and smiled whenever she did. For Nelly Nevins was "Nevins" no longer, but

Abigail's excitement was so great that she ran ahead of him. A moment later, he saw her eyes were filled with tears of memory and of happy home-coming. And for that tender mist he loved her more than ever.

a matron of nearly a year's experience who deemed herself thoroughly fitted to bestow advice on the alluring subject of matrimony.

"Oh dear," sighed Abigail happily, with a gentle pressure of Kane's arm, "isn't it delightful to be welcomed by hearts that really love you?"

For answer there was another resounding cheer, with shouts of "Hooroar for Miss Abby," after which the Three Musketeers of Tuckerman's Wharf stepped from the ranks by virtue of seniority and hurried forward to embrace the lovely woman who was, and ever would be, to them a beloved child. With smiles and tears she returned in kind the greeting of these loyal souls.

"An' now, Miss Abby," bellowed Sykes, evidently on the point of bursting with some tremendous secret, "do ye see anythin' unusual, an', ye might say, extra-ord'nary around here? Do ye, or don't ye? Come now."

"Why, yes, of course, Captain. All this crowd, the lights—"

"The lights! Ho, ho, ho," shouted Sykes, his rotund figure shaken with laughter, "that's just a fact, the lights. But what's the lights around, Miss Abby? I asks yer that."

Then Abigail, at Kane's prompting, looked up at the blaze of lanterns that surrounded a framework over the gangplank of the ship. And there, within the gaily illuminated rectangle, she read, in bright gilt letters—

STEWART MUSEUM OF THE SEA

"O-o-oh!" gasped Abigail delightedly, "How splendid! But who—what—I don't quite understand."

"Your wedding gift to the people you love, dear," whispered Kane.

"But I thought the *Harpoon* was sold when—"

"It undoubtedly was, and I bought it. I have kept it all these years, and, with the help of some good people, I have made of it what you see."

"'Hank Donelson, Custodian,' at your werry best sarvice, Miss Abby," said the little sailor who owned the name, and who now rejoiced in a marvelous suit of blue broadcloth trimmed with gold braid, as well as a jaunty cap bearing the title of his exalted office. "Hours from ten to four but don't ye mind that, 'cause ye knows as how ye're welcome at whatsomever time ye wants ter light up the ol' ship with yer lov'ly face."

"Thank you, Hank," returned Abigail with a laugh. "I assure you that I appreciate the special privilege. I shall not abuse it."

Then Kane and Abigail went aboard, and Abigail kissed Nelly, who had been "Nevins," and shook hands cordially with all the others who were good to her in the old days. Abigail's excitement was so great that she ran ahead of him. A moment later, he saw that her eyes were filled with tears of memory and of happy home-coming. And for that tender mist he loved her more than ever. Among the last to approach was the dark-eyed girl whose face had seemed familiar.

"How do you do, ma'am?" she said somewhat timidly. "I don't believe you know me, do you?"

Abigail looked at the pale, pretty face, and something stirred in her memory; but still recognition refused to come.

"No, you don't," continued the girl, "how should you? But do you remember the 'little mite'—that's what you called me—who got in your way in the St. Agnes vestry one evening long ago?"

"Ah, yes, and she wanted to give me her toys, the warm-hearted little thing. Your name is—"

"Susy; Susy Brent."

"And are you still in the mill?"

"Oh dear, no, ma'am. I've been to school almost ever since, and now I'm a typewriter in the counting room. Ma says I'm too nice for her anymore, and I guess I am, 'cause she drinks pretty bad nowadays. *I'm* going to *be* somebody."

"I'm sure you are, Susy," returned Abigail kindly, "and you may count on me to help you."

Then they made their triumphal progress down the companionway to the cabin, where another surprise was in readiness. The bunks had been removed, and in their place were handsome cases filled with shells, corals, marine plants, and a thousand rare and beautiful treasures of the ocean. In the center, where around the long table the old salts had once made merry, was a great aquarium in which swam many curious fishes and amphibians.

The old place was brilliant with new lights and handsome with appropriate decorations. And there in the rear was Abigail's little cabin, looking just as it did when she had left it years ago for a grander but not a happier abiding-place. Only, over the door, worked out in lustrous little sea shells, was the legend "MISS PETTICOATS."

The rushing in of old emotions, old memories, unsteadied the girl for the moment. The vision of the gentle sailor who had loved her as the core of his own heart filled her with tender melancholy. The ship whispered of his dear presence, and she could almost feel his blessing descending in this hour of her supreme happiness. For she was happy; the dreamy tinge of sadness, the half-suggested ache of regret, only intensified her present peace and joy.

In that hallowed spot they were married. To Abigail it seemed neither a strange nor an unusual thing when Kane brought forward a self-evident clergyman, whom he introduced as a college classmate who had come from a faraway city to perform their marriage ceremony. Indeed, she would not have had it otherwise, for here every association was of purity and honor and truth, and those who surrounded her and wished her every joy in life were of the tested metal that makes humanity's armor strong.

Captain Sykes, resplendent in a new "frock-suit," gave Abigail away with an impressive air that excited the envy of his two associates. But they, in turn, had their revenge by being the first to kiss the bride. Then, when the storm of hearty congratulations was over, and good-nights said, they all united in throwing such immense quantities of rice and so many pairs of formidable boots after the carriage that the fat driver whipped up his sleepy horses to escape the storm. Thus the wedded pair rode away into their new world.

After the guests had gone, Hank went slowly around the ship putting out the lights and tidying up. There was no sound save the gentle lapping of the water against the *Harpoon*'s sides. At last he found himself before the door of the spotless little cabin that was once Abigail Renier's. He looked long and lovingly at an old-time photograph of the girl that he had fastened upon the wall. Then his odd little smile illumined his face.

"Good night, and God love ye, dear little gal," he said. "Ye've had a stormy v'yge an' come nigh ter shipwreck, but thanks be ter the great Pilot ye're in a safe harbor at last."

T<small>HE</small> E<small>ND</small>

Victorian Bookshelf Series